monsoonbooks

NOT A VIRGIN

Nuril Basri was born in a village in Tangerang in western Java, now in the province of Banten, in 1985. A graduate of the Islamic State University in Jakarta (Universitas Islam Negeri - Jakarta), Nuril has worked in a variety of positions over the years: internet café manager, secretary to a police attaché, private language tutor, mini-market cashier, and waiter on a cruise ship. His previously published works include: *Halo, Aku Dalam Novel* (Jakarta: GagasMedia, 2009); *Romantis* (Kuala Lumpur: Buku Fixi, 2015) which was published in Indonesia under the title *My Favorite Goodbye* (Jakarta: GagasMedia, 2015); *Enak* (Kuala Lumpur: Buku Fixi, 2016); and an earlier version of *Not a Virgin*, published under the title *Dosa* (Kuala Lumpur: Buku Fixi, 2012). Additionally, Nuril has authored three short comedic works – *Bagai Jablay Kena Kamtib* (2007), *Banci Kalap* (2008), *Masuka Masukin Aja* (2008) – and one horror tale, *Terowongan Rumah Sakit* (2008), all published by GagasMedia of Jakarta.

Not a Virgin

Nuril Basri

Translated by
John H. McGlynn

monsoon

monsoonbooks

Published in 2019
by Monsoon Books Ltd
www.monsoonbooks.co.uk

No.1 Duke of Windsor Suite, Burrough Court,
Burrough on the Hill, Leics. LE14 2QS, UK.

ISBN (paperback): 978-1-912049-46-2
ISBN (ebook): 978-1-912049-47-9

The Indonesian-language edition of this novel, titled *Bukan Perjaka*,
was first published by Peculiar Books (Jakarta) in 2016. An earlier
version of this novel was published under the title *Dosa* by Buku
Fixi (Kuala Lumpur) in 2012. English language copyright in this
translation©2017 John H. McGlynn.

Cover design by Sukutangan.

A Cataloguing-in-Publication data record is available from the British
Library.

MIX
Paper from
responsible sources
FSC® C018072

Printed and bound in Great Britain by Clays Ltd, Elcograf S.p.A.
21 20 19   1 2 3 4 5

Contents

Spoilt

I begin this story with my brother, Rohim, whose decision to get married was what first set it in motion. Rohim worked as a lackey in one of those mom-and-pop stores that sell basic necessities, the so-called *sembako* or nine staples of the Indonesian home: salt, sugar, fish, cooking oil, kerosene, laundry soap, rough textiles, batik cloth and body soap. His was an ethnic-Chinese owned shop located in the old market in Legok, a part of the city of Tangerang, where he did the job of hoisting sacks of rice and measuring out litres of oil for customers. I sometimes called him a 'Chinese lackey'. That sounds racist, I know, but I called him that because I disliked *him*, not the Chinese shopkeeper, and one reason for that is because he was responsible for me losing my virginity, which happened when he got me kicked out of my own home – even if only indirectly. I'll tell you eventually how *that* came about, but you'll have to be patient with me. It's a long story.

It was in late August 2007, as I recall, when I was in my room and I overheard my parents talking in the kitchen. 'We'll have to put Ricky in a *pesantren*, so that Rohim can use his room,' my old man was saying. They didn't know I was listening; they didn't know I was already home from school. But let me introduce myself: my name is Ricky, Ricky Satria. Actually, my first name is spelled Riki, but I like to write it Ricky because it seems more modern and maybe a bit Western too.

'But where?' This was my mother speaking.

'I don't know, but what are we going to do with Rohim and Erni otherwise? Have them sleep in the rafters with the mice?' my father asked rhetorically.

'But Ricky's so young,' my mother said after a pause. 'How is he going to get on at a pesantren?'

'He can do it; he's just spoilt is all,' my father said dismissively.

It was at that precise moment I decided to enrol in a pesantren, an Islamic boarding school, myself. And not because I took pity on my brother's fiancée – if she had to sleep in the rafters, I couldn't care less – but more as a means of challenging my parents' perception of me. That was an insult, calling me spoilt. Sure, I might have been a bit lazy, but I wasn't spoilt, and I wanted them to know that.

I was almost eighteen and a senior at Karya Bakti Vocational High School, where I'd chosen mechanical engineering as my vocational path, with the aspiration of one day being able to work at a plant or in a factory as some kind of technician. (I knew I wasn't cut out for construction work or that kind of thing.) Originally, I'd thought about electrical engineering, but in the end the idea of taking things apart and putting them back together seemed a lot more appealing than rigor mortis as a result of electrocution.

There wasn't anything special about my school. It wasn't a school for geniuses or anything like that. And I wasn't the religious type who prayed five times a day or spent my spare time reciting the Quran. No, I was just a normal teenager, and the thought of enrolling at a pesantren came as a big challenge for my life.

The day after I learned that my parents intended to kick me out of the house, I took my bike and started peddling around Tangerang (or at least Bojong Nangka, the area of the city near my school) looking for information on pesantren that were accepting boarders. I wanted to pre-empt my parents' eviction notice in order to deprive them of the impression that they had the right to tell me what to do. I didn't like being ordered around. In short, I thought it better for me to leave of my own volition without being ordered to go.

So, anyway, I was on a bicycle I had borrowed from a friend, peddling here and there, stopping at one mosque after another, expecting to find pious teenagers in prayer caps who could give me some free advice. But I didn't find any guys my age at the mosques; most were much older and boring-looking, the kind of people who were full of themselves, more apt to lecture than to listen, the kind I had no wish to deal with.

Not owning a motorcycle, I was forced to pedal that damned bicycle the entire day, until my underpants were soaked through with sweat – not that I wore any special brand of underwear at the time, but that's another story I'll come to – and I was so exhausted I had to rest. I plopped myself down next to a guardhouse where a delinquent-looking group of guys had gathered, the kind with B.O. and cigarettes hanging from their mouths who beat on guitars and slurp coffee at roadside stalls. I didn't fall into that category, but I saw nothing wrong in hanging with them. One of them offered me a cigarette, but I turned it down. I didn't pick up that habit until later.

Sitting there with those guys, I noticed that most passers-by when seeing the group would immediately clench their lips and pick up their pace. Some older people raised their eyebrows and gave us a haughty look, their opinion apparent on their faces.

But then I noticed a young guy about my age coming our way. Because he was wearing a sarong and had a *peci* on his head, I guessed that he must be coming from a mosque. I jumped up to greet him, causing the group to turn their attention to me.

'Hi! Are you a *santri*?' I asked him straight away. Santri are pious Muslims who are strict in adhering to religious strictures, unlike *abangan*, the more nominal-like Muslims who are relaxed in matters of faith.

'Nope,' the guy said, shaking his head.

I was surprised. 'But you just came from prayers at the mosque, didn't you?'

He shrugged.'Yeah, well, my old man ordered me to go.'

That's fucked, I thought. If a person is going to pray, it should come from a personal desire to do so. Immediately, I concluded that it would be a waste of my time to ask him more questions and so, saying no more, I rejoined the group, leaving my prospective informant with a look of surprise on his face.

As I sat down, one of the guys in the group, one with really bad teeth, patted me on the shoulder.

'What was that about?' he asked, with a putrid smell emanating from his mouth.

'Nothing,' I said, trying to hold my breath. 'I'm looking for a pesantren, is all.'

'Aha,' he said, in a tone of mock understanding. 'What? You want to be an *ustadz* or something?'

Me, a religious teacher? I had to smile at that. 'No,' I said. 'Just asking is all.'

He said nothing, I said nothing, and suddenly, as if remembering something, he called out to one of the other guys, 'Hey, Obet!'

'What?' said the guy whom Bad Teeth had addressed – Obet, apparently.

'Obet here used to go to school at a pesantren,' Bad-Teeth-and-Foul-Breath explained.

A guardhouse was not the place I expected to find information about pesantren, but that's exactly where I found it, in the form of this guy named Obet, who proved to be a rich source of information. Unfortunately, he had this really big mole on his nose and even as he told me about his experiences at various pesantren, I couldn't stop staring at it. My eyes were glued to him like on some edge-of-the-seat episode on television. At any rate, at the end of his revelatory speech I made a date to meet him the following day.

The next day I did meet up with Obet and he took me to see a few of the pesantren that were located in Curug and Legok, adjacent wards of the city. They were places where he had once boarded, but judging from his appearance – faded and grubby blue jeans, tattered T-shirt, dreadlocks and no peci, much less a turban, on his head, I seriously doubted that he had ever been a true santri.

'Can't always tell a book by its cover,' he remarked, as if he knew what I was thinking when he revealed that he had spent two full years at one of the pesantren we visited.

'Did your parents force you?' I asked, just guessing.

He laughed, confirming my suspicion. 'Yeah, they thought it would straighten me out.'

I listened as he told me how parents would force their unruly kids to board at pesantren in the hope that they would turn over a new leaf, as if the devil in them, feeling the heat of hell fire in the pesantren environment, would flee their bodies, and their sons would then return home all santri- and pious-like, praying all the time, reciting the Quran, doing good deeds, and acting in every way most admirably. From what Obet told me, I got the impression that pesantren were little more than detention centres for delinquent or troubled youths, and that he was a prime example of that failed if noble goal. That said, and even though that had been my impression, one that was often reinforced, when I finally did board at a pesantren I found that many of the residents were there of their own volition and were truly serious in their desire to increase their knowledge of Islam. I came to see that if one has an open mind, preconceived notions can change with experience and greater knowledge. All this is to say, don't simply accept what people say before you've had a chance to look into the matter yourself.

I never saw Obet again after that. After a look at the final pesantren for the day, I bought a litre of gas for his motorcycle because that's all I could afford at the time. If ever I do meet him again, I'll buy him a full tank.

Arriving home that evening, I sat myself down at the dinner table and lifted the cover off the food my mother had prepared to find beneath it only a small and lonely pile of salted fish in the middle of a saucer. I lost my appetite immediately; the sight alone was proof of my family's poverty. I wondered at that moment if my mother had intentionally cooked something she knew I wouldn't like just to make me feel the urge to move. I looked around at the rest of the house, a small place with just a front room and two tiny bedrooms, one where I slept and the other which my sister, Yanti, occupied. The walls of the front room and the two bedrooms were made of exposed red brick – Dad either never had the money or simply hadn't gotten around to having them plastered – and the floor of rough titles was covered with a room-size linoleum mat with a ceramic motif. The semi-detached kitchen-cum-dining room and the laundry room-cum-bathroom at the back of the house had earthen floors and walls of plaited bamboo slats.

My parents slept on the floor in the living room in front of the television. My brother Rohim slept at the old market in Legok, his 'bedroom' being nothing more than a mat on the floor of the shop where he worked, next to the bags of rice his boss sold.

I'm the youngest in a family of four children. The eldest is Rohim, the lackey, who was engaged to be married. He came home only when he felt himself coming down with something and wanted to have his back coin-scraped. The second child is my sister, Yati, who, after graduating from high school, immediately went to work at a sports shoe factory. She's a hard worker and has a good body to show for it – but that might also be due to the fact that at the factory she's surrounded by lots of young men who are not her brothers. My brother Edi, the third child, I called 'the thief' because the only reason he ever came home seemed to be to pilfer from our mother's purse or to filch our sister's gold jewellery. He'd left home a few years before, when I was still in junior high, and he should have been a sophomore in senior high. I say 'should have' because, the thing is, he never got that far; it took him six years just to get through junior high! And he didn't graduate because he suddenly became smart or anything but because he got to be too old and the school was forced to let him go. The rest of us didn't know where he lived and, with never a word from him, whether he was dead or alive. Even so, when he did show his nose, the knowledge of his continued existence didn't make the rest of us feel happy or glad, because whenever he took off again something always went missing from the house. Stealing from your own family is about as low as you can get.

My father, who has a gimp leg caused by a fall from a coconut tree, works as a watchman at a small snack-food factory not far from our home. My mother is just a normal middle-aged woman, not unlike other women of her background and social class, who spends much of her time looking after the chickens she raises in a coop behind the house and trading gossip with neighbours.

We almost never gathered as a family and only rarely sat down to eat together at the dining table. In fact, I almost never really talked to them – my parents, that is – but that was fine with me. I didn't like discussing things with my parents.

I can't say I ever really got along with my father. I don't think he thought much of me either. I think he saw me as a threat and a burden. It was like he was jealous because my mother seemed to care more about me than him. So it was that when I heard him talking to my mother about the need of a bedroom for Rohim, it popped into my mind that he was actually just looking for a reason to get rid of me; that my brother needed a room to share with his wife was merely an excuse.

Why was the lackey moving back home? Why couldn't he live at his parents-in-law's home? Or rent a place? Why did he have to take my room? I was mad and annoyed for having been called spoilt. I can't say I searched seriously for the answers to my questions. I just wanted to show my parents that I was not the person they thought me to be. Maybe I didn't like salted fish for dinner, or washing my clothes, or mopping the floors, but that didn't mean I was spoilt. A bit lazy, maybe – aren't guys that age supposed to be lazy? – but I wasn't spoilt, the proof being that I would be the one to choose the pesantren where I boarded. As I said before, we didn't have a separate dining room: the kitchen and dining area were the same space and my mother, who was wiping dishes at the time, seemed to notice my lack of interest in eating. She looked at me as if to ask what was wrong.

'I'm moving to a pesantren,' were the words that suddenly came out of my mouth, almost unintended.

I certainly succeeded in capturing Mother's attention; she almost dropped the dish that was in her hand.

'What's this now? Why out of the blue like this?' she asked, attempting to maintain a normal tone of voice.

'It's not all of a sudden. I've been thinking about it for a while now,' I told her. 'I've even found a place, one close to my school.'

Mother seemed unable to speak and, for a while, just looked at me. 'Tell your father,' she then said.

'Tell him yourself,' I snapped at her, then went to my bedroom to get away from that miserable pile of fish still lying on the plate, begging to be devoured. I felt a little guilty for having upset my mother but also thought I had made my point. I wasn't going to give my parents a chance to throw me out of the house. Period.

In my three-square-metre bedroom I looked around me, absorbing its atmosphere for maybe the last time: the pallet-like riser – not even a bed frame really – with a thin, worn-out mattress on top of it and a bedspread and pillowcases that were almost never changed. Then, too, the creaky-looking head-high cupboard leaning against the wall and tilting dangerously to the right because its rear right leg was broken. On its door was a half-length mirror so foggy it showed almost no reflection. That's all that was in there, just that and the room's musty smell – no doubt from not being cleaned enough and the window being kept closed. I always locked the door to my room. I liked my privacy and didn't like other people coming into my room – 'invading my space' – even if it was only to mop or sweep the floor. The room was mine and I was the only one with the right to clean it. Its dust was my dust. But now, here I was, stupidly ceding my right to it because of wounded pride.

I removed my clothes from the wobbly armoire and made a pile on the edge of the bed – not that there were many items to stack. About the only time I ever bought new clothes was once a year, around Idul Fitri. I took everything out, from my too-short pants to socks that were hole-ridden from age. After that I lay down, bewildered.

At around 10 pm I heard a knock on my door, but made no move to answer it. Hearing a familiar scraping of feet, I guessed it was my father. Then came another knock, this one hesitant as well. I snorted through my nose, resolving to ignore him. If he wanted to talk to me, he'd have to gather the nerve to speak up. But he was a man who always tried to avoid confrontation. And I didn't want to talk to him anyway, because I knew just how the conversation would go: my parents and I would sit down together in the living room and they would ask me this and that, like 'Why do you want to move to a pesantren?' even though there would be a gleam in their eyes because I was moving out before they were forced to ask me to leave. I had no interest in chitchat. Such a charade! Family dramas were something I tried to avoid. They were a useless waste of time.

The next morning I went to school as usual, but when I came home I found a cardboard box emblazoned with the Indomie logo on my bed. I looked inside to find all my clothes neatly folded (though some of the more raggedy ones seemed to be missing), half a dozen packets of instant noodles, a tube of toothpaste, a new toothbrush and a bar of soap. Fuck. Maybe I did intend to move, but I didn't think I'd be run off so quickly. For a moment, my mind went blank from sheer vexation, and I wanted to kick the box across the room.

Just then my mother appeared in the doorway. 'I couldn't find a large enough suitcase, so I used that box instead,' she hastened to explain, completely misinterpreting the anger on my face. I immediately began to tie up the box with the raffia cord that was on the bed beside the box.

'What time do you want to go?' Mother asked.

'Now!' I sputtered, the veins in my forehead ready to burst. 'Wait for your father to come home. He'll take you.'

'I can go alone,' I growled.

My mother came closer. 'Don't be that way. Your father wants to meet the *kiai* in order to entrust you to his care. You're not some orphan to be taken in out of pity. You still have parents, you know ...'

My father arrived home before magrib, carrying a new sarong and a long-sleeved, cream-coloured collarless shirt appropriate for wearing to mosque. If I'd known he was going to buy me some clothes I would have asked for black, like the ones that the pop-singer Pasha Ungu wore when singing religious songs in the fasting month. My father told me to change into the clothes he'd bought so that I'd look neat in appearance when meeting the kiai. Even though I didn't want to, I did what he said. The very smell of my just-purchased-and-ready-to-wear clothes was a statement that stressed my position as a poor kid from the *kampung*, the village.

Before leaving my room, I snagged a peci from the nail on the wall where it was hanging and put it on. Old-fashioned in style, the round prayer cap was made of stiff black felt and sat high on my head, the kind typically worn by guys who didn't pray much and rarely needed to wear a peci. Looking in the cloudy mirror I saw that my appearance as a poor but earnest young man was now complete.

My mother slipped a fifty-thousand rupiah note into my hand. 'If you run out of money, you can always come home,' she whispered as she squeezed my hand. Wow, I thought. Mother had never given me such a large sum of money before. At most five thousand rupiah, enough to buy a snack during the day.

I was still feeling perturbed when my father and I finally left on his motorcycle. We didn't say much on the way; for my part, just directions on where to turn. For a half hour or so, we made our way past empty plots of land, down avenues, through side streets and kampung housing blocks until we finally came to Al Husna Pesantren, where I had chosen to board.

The pesantren was located on the edge of the lower-class residential area of Legok, in fact just off the main road, where cars, buses and trucks full of sand sped by, but I had intentionally led my father there on a circuitous route, through the area's maze-like system of lanes and alleys, just to make him confused. Maybe he'd get lost when going home! The plot of land on which the complex stood was a large horizontal rectangle, about 500 square metres in size, with a low, sparse hedge marking its outer border and barely separating it from the residential district behind and beside it. A footpath running from the main road to the kampung behind the pesantren split the complex into northern and southern sections and further diminished any kind of demarcation between the school and the *kampong* around it.

On the southern side of the path was a large, brightly lit gazebo. This, I learned, was what the boarders called the *majelis*, a highfalutin Arabic word for 'meeting chamber', where classes were held and instructions given. Directly to the east of the gazebo was a bath house and latrine, beside which was a well for drawing water and beyond it, abutting the eastern boundary, a large, rectangular hollowed-out stone, which the boarders filled with water for ritual ablutions.

The two main buildings in the complex, the home of the kiai who had founded Al Husna and the actual pesantren, the dormitory where boarders lived, were located on the northern half of the complex. By the standards of the area, the kiai's home was fairly imposing with its stone walls, large verandah, stained glass windows, and even a car port, but the pesantren was a much more humble affair. The building or the 'lodge', as the boarders called it consisted of two barrack-like units, one on the east, the other on the west, which were divided into bedrooms for the boarders and separated by a walkway between them. The two buildings were joined by a peaked roof that straddled the two buildings and bridged the walkway. The walls of the pesantren were made from woven bamboo, and the two structures that formed it were raised about a metre off the ground by wooden supports, creating a crawl space which was used as a storage area. Visible inside were stacks of lumber, broken-down portable ovens, sacks bulging with unknown stuff, and other cast-off junk. The impression was one of benign dereliction, but of all the pesantren that Obet had taken me to, this is the one that I had chosen. Maybe it was the leafy guava trees scattered throughout the complex, which gave it a welcoming look.

Neither large nor grand-looking, the pesantren had relatively few boarders, thirty to thirty-five at most, and it could not be described as modern at all. Obet told me that Al Husna was a Salafi pesantren, traditional both in terms of its teachings and regulations, using only the so called *kitab kuning* or 'yellow books' for instruction. These books, written in unadorned Arabic script, were primers that covered subjects ranging from legal maxims, mysticism and traditional sayings to theological exegesis and sociology. An indispensable part of pesantren life, the books got their sobriquet from the cheap yellow paper on which they were printed. Al Husna was also traditional in the sense that school rules were somewhat lax, unlike the stricter, Wahabi-run schools today. Plus, the place was said to be quite 'tolerant' and 'free' when compared to others, at least in quotation marks. Finally, Al

Husna was the pesantren closest to my high school, no more than a kilometre or so away. So, even though the place was somewhat ramshackle, I didn't care.

Driving down the path between the two sections of the complex, my father parked his motorcycle next to the lodge, at the rear. The place was quiet.

'Where does the kiai live?' he whispered.

Not knowing at the time that the big house next to the lodge was his residence, I shrugged. I had just assumed that the kiai lived in the lodge itself.

At that point we heard the sound of a man speaking in a loud voice. Looking to the south and back towards the front of the complex, we noticed the gazebo, whose ceramic floor tiles gleamed beneath the bright neon lights overhead.

Inside were a number of santri, each one bent over a yellow-papered book in his lap. There, I located the source of the voice as well: a portly man who was seated in front of the santri, apparently guiding their lesson.

'Is that the kiai?' my father asked. Again, I shrugged my shoulders.

We waited where we were until the recitation was over, squatting silently as we were attacked by thousands of mosquitoes, until around 9 pm when the santri were dismissed and began to make their way towards the lodge. As they approached, several gave my father and me a look of curiosity, quickly followed by a gleam of comprehension.

'Go get Bang Ali,' said an older santri to a much younger student. 'Tell him we have guests.' The younger santri immediately turned and strode back in the direction of the gazebo.

'*Assalamualaikum*,' my father said to the clutch of santri as he rose to his feet.

'*Waalaikumsalam*,' they answered in unison.

I remained in squatting position, reluctant to stand.

Soon after, Brother Ali approached with hurried steps. To this day, I still remember his smile with pronounced canine teeth and the friendly but somewhat mischievous expression on his face. On his head was a fez, which only partially covered a thick mat of curly, shoulder-length hair. He sported a wispy beard and moustache as well. I guessed him to be in his twenties. He wasn't a large man; in fact, he was rather small, but he looked very fit.

My father expressed his greetings again, this time with raised hands clasped together. 'If possible, we'd like to see the kiai ...' my father said, pointing his head down towards me. He knocked my head with his calf, an order for me to stand.

Ali bowed slightly, raised his closed right hand and extended his right thumb, signalling a request for us to follow. 'Please come along. I'll take you to meet him.'

That's when we discovered that the teacher's home was there, just beside the lodge, almost indistinguishable from the houses behind it. After silent observation, it was then I noticed that there were no fences separating the pesantren from its environs.

At the teacher's house, Ali ushered us into the front waiting room and invited us to sit down on an expensive-looking sofa. The floor tiles appeared to be marble and reflected the dim light of the fake crystal chandelier hanging from the ceiling. Once we had taken our seats, Ali bowed and wordlessly took his leave.

Seated on an ornately carved chair before us and resembling as much a bloated frog as a king on his throne, was the teacher, the portly man we'd seen in the gazebo previously. He wore only a sarong and singlet, as if overheated from the lessons he had administered earlier. He looked at me with a smile while nodding his head.

'I'm afraid he's not much good at anything,' my father suddenly blurted out in reference to me. 'He's always been a bit spoilt, you see.'

Damn it, my father's comment really got my back up. It would have been OK if he had described me as unruly or difficult to control, but it stuck in my craw to be called spoilt, especially when seeing the expression on the teacher's face which seemed to confirm this view. As if all this time my father had had such a hard time raising me. What a load of crap. I wanted to gag and throw up.

Suddenly the teacher rose from his chair and disappeared inside the house for a short while. He returned with a large glass of water in his hand, though a servant had already served us cups of hot sweetened tea.

'Drink this,' he said, handing the glass to me. 'It will make you feel comfortable here.'

I looked at him uncertainly until my father nudged me with his elbow. I then drank from the glass hesitantly, half-expecting something miraculous to happen, sure that I'd been given some kind of magic potion. The taste, a bit mossy, like well water, nonplussed me. I managed to drink only a quarter of the glass.

My father spoke with the kiai for quite some time. I remained close-mouthed and spent those minutes studying my nails and peering at a large wooden book case in the adjoining room, lined with thick books whose titles were all in Arabic.

When their conversation finally ended, my father clasped the teacher's hand and gave him an envelope.

My father and I walked back to the pesantren, where Ali emerged from one of the rooms and gave us a brief tour. Each of the two units of the pesantren was divided into five small rooms, facing another row of rooms across the open-air walkway between them. All the rooms were exactly the same size, just three metres square, with a single window for ventilation on their outer wall. The windows were closed. The place resembled a chicken coop to me.

'For the time being, you'll stay in my room,' Ali said.

My father said he had to leave. I didn't *salam* or even say goodbye. I just watched as he went to his motorcycle and then putted away.

When I went into the room I was to share with Ali, I found that my Indomie cardboard box was open and a few packets of the instant noodles were missing.

Brawls

High school. Let's start there. In high school, I was an ordinary student: not super bright, not stupid either. I could be described as typical, a little different from the others, a student whose absence would not be missed unless there were a roll call. Karya Bakti Vocational High School, located on the outskirts of Legok, was pretty much like other schools outside the city centre. The building was a nondescript two-storey structure, and the students wore uniforms. But the guys at my school had a special way of wearing trousers: they'd make them look tapered or cone-shaped by binding the ends of the pants' legs with rubber bands. I don't know why they did this, but combined with their lank, unwashed hair, stocking hats and assorted piercings, I suppose they were trying to look cool or punkish or some other style I didn't understand. By and large, most of them smelled like buffaloes.

As to my style of dress, I didn't follow the crowd, not because I didn't like to dress up but because I saw no reason for doing so. After all, almost the entire student body was male with the exception of a few girls who didn't really count, because they dressed and acted like boys. There was no reason to spend time trying to attract their attention. Plus, they probably wouldn't have been interested anyway. But that was actually one of the good things about the school: there was no wasting time dressing up or looking after our appearance for the purpose of attracting the opposite sex.

One inescapable aspect of high-school life was the brawls between rival schools in the area, mine included. I can't say I liked them, but my story and how it developed is very much linked to this phenomenon. Frankly speaking, unless you're an anarchist given to wanton destruction or a sadomasochist who gets a thrill from being clubbed or stoned, brawls are, for the most part, just a way for teenage guys with raging hormones and strong libidos to vent their emotions.

What I remember most about the brawls is their distinctive war cry – a shrill sound like 'Wooii-Woooiii-Woiooiiii!' – and the acrid smell of sweat, clouds of dust in the air, the heat of the sun burning down, and the pounding of one's heart. Yeah, trust me, there is definitely a link between young males' hormonal urges and their emotional state. I know, I've seen it myself. Once, when a gang of students from another school faced off with students from mine, all of a sudden they pulled their dicks from their pants and began to shake them at us.

'Eat my dick!' they screamed as they twirled their cocks and groped their crotches. I'm not kidding.

One morning in the first week of September, a week after I'd moved to the pesantren, I was at a food stall near my school having some *nasi uduk* for breakfast when I overheard some other students talking about a surprise attack they planned to stage on a rival school. The school bell had rung ten minutes before, but we were still taking our time, waiting for the teacher on guard duty to find us and tell us to get a move on.

By lunchtime that day the rumour of the pending attack had spread through the school. For reasons of solidarity, a fair number of guys had already agreed to join in the attack. I didn't intend to participate because my stomach wasn't feeling well –

maybe it was the rice in coconut milk I'd eaten for breakfast – but when another student asked if I was going to join the attack, I nodded and pretended to agree. In fact, I planned to hightail it out of there. Another time, maybe. Though I rarely joined in these melees – I wasn't one for throwing or taking punches – I was usually there on the sidelines to voice my support or throw rocks at the rival school gang. It was a minor role, which added to my school's show of force; but, truthfully speaking, my presence was not particularly important. I've told you already that I was nobody special, not a leading player at all.

Usually, when there was going to be an attack, you'd hear about it at least one day in advance. Brawls weren't spontaneous affairs; they were something one had to prepare for. In that sense, there was little difference between them and war. On the day of a brawl we'd come to school with slingshots – leather belts with heavy metal ends – and sometimes rusty knives as well, which we'd alternately conceal and proudly display, but the most prized weapon to have was a long sword. We didn't bring these weapons into the school building, of course. Even though raids were infrequent, that would have been looking for punishment. Usually, we'd hide larger weapons in a clump of bushes near the school or at a food stall whose owner was willing to look the other way. We never used bombs or guns, and we wouldn't have known where to get them, anyway.

That afternoon, when my fellow students gathered to prepare for the brawl, I retreated to the latrine and waited there, trying not to gag from the smell of piss, until, suddenly, I heard a knock on the door.

'Are you in there, Rick? Are you coming or not?'

That was the voice of Heri, the gang's 'treasurer', whose job it was to collect dues from non-participants. Not all the students joined in these brawls; probably only about twenty percent. But as a sign of solidarity, the rest would usually make a 'voluntary' contribution when Heri came to them looking for money. But, hey, better to hand over two thousand rupiah for our soldiers' needs, or so the reasoning went, than to find yourself at the end of a knife. As I never had money, I usually went along to the battlefield rather than pay.

'Hey, I'm sorry,' I moaned, 'I'm not feeling well in here.'

'Shit. Some of the others guys have backed out too,' he complained with a sigh.

'I'm really sorry,' I said again. Damn, I swore to myself. Here I was hiding, and Heri still managed to track me down.

He said nothing more to me, but as he left the latrine I heard him grumble, 'What a bunch of chicken shits we got here.'

It was just my bad luck that when I finally stepped out of the bathroom, I ran into one of the teachers.

'Where's the attack going to be?' he asked me straight away.

I shrugged my shoulders and said, 'I don't know.' The fact is, I didn't know.

Speaking of teachers, don't think they didn't know about the brawls. They did, but they closed their eyes and ears and acted as if nothing was happening until a student got hurt or a parent filed a report. That was rare, however; parents seldom got involved, and students who got hurt usually chose to stay in seclusion until they were better again.

'Come with me to the office,' the teacher said, as if he didn't believe me.

At his office, I was ready to be interrogated, but he didn't ask me a thing. Instead, he led me to a stack of sealed cardboard boxes and told me, 'Take these to the library.'

I wanted to refuse but had no choice. The boxes were heavy

and full of government-issued textbooks. It took me close to an hour to finish the chore, because I also had to take the books out of their boxes and arrange them on shelves. As a result, I left school much later than usual, at around 3:30 pm. The food stalls near the school were empty and there was no one at the bus stop – which is where students would usually gather to stop open-back trucks that passed and jump onto them to hitch a ride. The area was so quiet it seemed abnormal.

As I said, I'd only just moved to the pesantren the week before. For that reason I still wasn't sure of the fastest or easiest path between the pesantren and my school. The warren of houses between my school and the pesantren was criss-crossed with lanes and alleys, whose every intersection was a hub of activity. The day was hot and cloudless, and the bright sun burned my neck and brow. Feeling another wave of indigestion, I stopped momentarily and squeezed my eyes shut, but when I opened them again, I saw standing directly in front of me two guys who looked as sturdy as concrete pillars. Both were sweating profusely from running, I guessed, and had a wild look in their eyes.

'You're from Karya Bakti, aren't you?' one of them asked.

My heart shrank as I tried to suss out the situation. My school's gang must have gotten trounced and were now being run down by rival gang members whose superior strength would permit the gang to track their victims into a neighbourhood not their own. Even though I hadn't taken part in the brawl, it looked certain to me that I was going to become one of its victims.

Not waiting for my answer, one of them looked at the badge on my shirt where the name and number of my school stood out in bold letters. Only an idiot would not have been able to read it. I might not be a fighter, but I did know some tricks for self-preservation. With the two of them probably thinking that

I would turn and run away, but what I did instead was to rush forward towards the space between them, hitting them as hard as I could with the full strength of my body. I caught them off-guard and made them unsteady on their feet, and I sprinted straight ahead without looking back.

It took the two guys a moment before they were able to steady themselves and come after me, but that small amount of time gave me an opportunity to gain a safe distance from them. I tell you, though, I kept seeing in my mind the PVC pipe that one of the guys was holding sailing through the air in my direction and knocking me dead mid-stride.

I ran until the back of my jaws felt numb from the straining of the muscles in my neck. My chest ached from the blood pumping inside. Because I wasn't feeling well, I couldn't run as fast as usual. That's when I made my first mistake. When I turned my head back to check the situation, I saw that the duo were pretty far behind me but then, not watching my step, I tripped on a cobblestone and fell. I managed to break my fall with my knees and hands but they stung with pain. With fear now controlling the rest of my brain, I hurriedly rose and tried to ignore the burning sensation.

I knew the two guys were getting closer, but my energy was nearly spent from having run so far. I also knew that when they caught me, bystanders could not be counted on to do anything when the two guys beat me to a pulp. Not my business, they'd be thinking.

At the next corner I came to, I turned my head and quickly scanned the narrow street. On the other side was a row of shophouses, with the closest one to me containing a small restaurant offering Padang-style food. Hoping to find refuge there, I ran inside. The few customers looked at me as if seeing a wild bull. Unable to spot a safe place to hide, I scampered towards the kitchen at the back and slipped inside. There, a woman was cooking and she jumped with fright when she saw me and began rubbing her chest with one hand from the shock.

'Help me, Ma'am. I need a place to hide,' I pleaded with panic.

'Thief! Thief!' she cried instead, and started jabbing at me with the long, hot metal spatula she was holding. Shit, I thought, here I needed help and this woman was going to turn me into curry. Unable to flee back through the front door, because the customers were bound to block my exit if I tried to escape and were unlikely to patiently wait for me to explain the situation, I ran around the cook and exited the place through the back door. The banging of the aluminium pans that I smashed into on my way followed me outside.

At the back of the row of shophouses was an empty field. Nothing there. No place to hide at all. A surge of panic overcame me, but I wasn't about to let myself be trapped out there or to submerge myself in the waste-filled drainage ditch that ran behind the shophouses. I looked again and saw that the back door of one of the shophouses was propped open. I crouched and ran toward it, and quickly slunk inside.

In the back room of the shophouse were what appeared to be two large wash basins with chairs in front of them. Beside the doorway that divided the back room of the shophouse from the front was a large cupboard with glass windows, behind which were numerous kinds of bottles. I placed myself in the corner between the back of the door and the cupboard and prepared to clamp my hand over the mouth of anyone who came into the back room and tried to scream.

Not long later, I heard the sound of footsteps coming towards me from the direction of the front room. I had just two choices:

gag the person or try to explain my way out of the situation – which, based on my experience at the restaurant earlier, was likely to fail. I hoped the person would be a woman, but when the person appeared and found me hiding there, both of us were surprised out of our minds.

All I could see was long blond hair, tied at the back, sharply pencilled eyebrows, and extraordinarily full lips that suddenly opened wide in horror.

So surprised was I by coming face to face with a man who looked like a woman, I found myself unable to do anything: neither gag him nor explain.

'*Thair B inu pinersen hineer! Inu ginie!*' he screamed, in a weird tongue completely alien to me, wildly gesticulating with his hands. I found myself unable to move. Two seconds passed and the doorway filled with faces.

'*Hinue Helga B? Winat Helga B dueen hineer?*' asked one of them, also greatly surprised.

'*Helga B ina looker thoe! Inu nugit!*' said another while giving me a look I could not decipher. And then the person who will play the lead role in the story I'm telling appeared, in a nicely pressed white and grey outfit, with wet hair clinging to his scalp. Maybe it was because of that damned school badge on my shirt or maybe because he knew me (which I didn't think was the case), he recognized me straight away.

'*Staap! Helga B Ieriss F!*' he screamed.

Pesantren

That was my first real meeting with Muhammad Farisyi – who preferred to be called 'Paris', perhaps thinking himself to be a kind of Paris Hilton. We went to the same high school and though I knew of him, I didn't actually know him. Why? Because we had no common interests and nothing else that obliged us to communicate with each other. As with most of the other students in my school, I had my own life and Paris had his. I preferred to remain off the radar but Paris was another story altogether; he was like a celebrity at my school.

What I knew about Farisyi or Paris is only what I'd heard: that he was the only child of an upper-class family whose life was a complete mystery. No one I knew had ever been to his home but we knew for sure his family was wealthy. This could be seen in his clothing, his manners, and his pampered attitude. But there was something special about him as well. Most rich kids, guys and girls alike, are pampered or spoilt, but Paris was a *banci*, a woman in a man's body. I didn't have another word for him at the time; that was the only way we had to describe him. Seemingly unconscious of his own behaviour, he'd sulk and fret, plead for attention, play with his hair, rearrange his limbs, and purse his lips in different expressions. He truly did seem to be a woman in a man's body.

Whatever the case, and though a banci he may have been, he saved my life that day at the salon by having me hide beneath one of the basins for washing hair. After the two thugs who had been chasing me burst into the salon, he convinced them to leave the place with no more than a cursory inspection in remarkably short order. Not only that, after my pursuers left, Paris saved me from the clutches of the jaded cross-dressing hair-dressers who owned the place and were wont to dine on young blood like mine.

When I was trying to hide in the back of the salon that day and he had screamed *'Staap! Helga B Ieriss F!'* he was actually saying 'Stop! He's my friend!' One day, I, too, would come to understand that secret language – never with complete fluency but at least enough to understand what people were saying – but that day I knew not a single word. Paris, however, was a master of the tongue, and able to speak it fluently anytime and anywhere he chose. *'Yoelandu minust talken D leengoe.* You must be able to speak the language,' he later advised me. 'Mastery of a language allows you to control the situation,' he stressed.

'You're Ricky, in C-class, aren't you?' Paris asked me that day, just like that, dropping my name.

I was stunned. Here he was of a completely different social class, yet he actually knew my name. 'Yes,' was all I could answer. 'I'm Farisyi, but call me Paris,' he said, extending his hand. 'Since you're here, would you like to have a cream bath? Or maybe a facial?' he asked. 'Better that than brawling don't you think?'

But by that time, after that very long and trial-filled day, I was so tired that my lids had begun to droop, and I knew that I had to say goodbye and leave right away. I couldn't imagine what would become of me if I were to fall asleep in the salon.

After that incident, it wasn't like Paris and I became close friends right away. Not like that at all. Sure, we'd say hello to each other at school but that was being polite, little more than small talk. He was he and I was I. He had his position as the reigning celebrity in school ... while I ... Well, I just ... continued my very ordinary life both at school and at the pesantren.

On the evening of my second Friday at the pesantren, after the boarders had recited the Yasin chapter of the Quran in the majelis, Ali and I went back to his cell. Removing our sandals, we left them on the ground outside, and then went inside where I sat leaning against the wall of the cell. Bang Ali had covered holes in the wall, where the woven bamboo had come loose, with newspaper, a kind of makeshift wallpaper to keep out the night wind. Although the floor of the room was uneven, the wood itself was old teak, impermeable to termites. Part of the floor was covered with a roll mat of woven pandanus leaves. This is where Ali slept. I slept on my prayer rug because I hadn't thought to bring a mat from home.

Bang Ali handed me a book. 'The title of this book is *Safiinatunnaja,*' he said. 'It's about *fiqih* or legal precepts but touches on the concept of *tauhid,* the oneness of God as well.'

The book was thin and printed on flimsy paper, like a cheap notebook, and the text was in Arabic, but at least it included phonetic markings for vowel sounds, which enabled me to pronounce the words. That was true of the Quran as well: I could read it but not understand it. Even though piety wasn't high on my list of attributes, as a boy I had practiced reciting the Quran at the home of an *ustadz,* a religious teacher who lived near my home. Of course, I didn't go there because I wanted to learn about religion; I just wanted to hang out with other guys my age. That, in the end, I was able to recite the Quran was merely an added benefit. The important thing was that I knew by heart the prayers a Muslim is supposed to know and could recite the Quran and perform the requisite rituals, as well. That was enough for me.

After I came to stay in Ali's cell, I took to exploring his possessions – mostly the dozens of books he owned, many of which were quite thick and several in multiple-volume sets. Most of them were printed on yellow-tinted paper. I picked up one of them and opened it. It was in Arabic but without phonetic markers, so I couldn't read it. There did arise in me a slight urge to know how to pronounce the text and to understand what the writer was saying, but that, I knew, would require time, and I wasn't at the pesantren because I wanted to study religion. I was there because I'd been chased out of my home.

'If you want to read those books, you're going to have to study Arabic,' Ali once remarked, when he found me leafing through one of his books.

OK, maybe someday I would study Arabic and find out whether words were 'masculine' or 'feminine'. Yeah, maybe someday, but for now I didn't intend to spend much time on the subject. Arabic was difficult, and anyway I didn't really want to study those yellow books, which I was sure were all about Islamic religious laws. I had no desire to become a teacher of religious recitation.

Despite my reservations, I did over time become familiar with other books: *Akhlakul Baniin*, for instance, a kind of primer on how to behave: how to show respect for your teachers, your elders, and so on; *Ta'lim Muta'alim*, which also has to do with manners and respect; and *Fath Al Mu'in* which I found more interesting, because it had to do with advanced legal precepts. Then there was a collection of old tales titled *Durratun Nasihin*, most of them having to do with sayings and deeds of the Prophet, and another, titled *Jalalain*, a kind of interpretation of the Quran.

Obviously, I couldn't afford to buy such books; I had no budget for that. When I was practicing religious recitations, I was forced to read over the shoulders of fellow boarders, watching as they inserted phonetic marks in the plain unmarked texts in order to remember how to pronounce the words – whether a series of consonants was pronounced 'fatah' or 'kasrah' or whether the letters 'm' and 'n' stood for '*man*' or '*min*', meaning 'person' or 'from'. They'd also write comments in the margins of the books whenever there was something they didn't understand – and there was plenty we didn't understand! It made me dizzy thinking about it, if you want to know the truth. And we had to do this five times a day, after each of the obligatory prayers. To put it short: that part of life at the pesantren was no fun at all.

At first, I found it hard to get used to the life there, and I wasn't sure if I could put up with staying there for long. I found no sense of comfort. It's just lucky that I shared a cell with Ali. By the way, 'cell' is what the boarders called our bedrooms: Cell One, Cell Two, and so on. Ali and I were in Cell Ten, which was also known as the 'Chief's Cell' – 'chief' referring to Ali because he was like the chief of our little village; in a regular school, I suppose he would have been called a prefect or student leader. Whatever the case, Bang Ali was our chief and had been chosen for that position based on his knowledge, experience and leadership skills. There was also a secretary-treasurer who took care of things like collecting money from the residents for their share of the electric bill, but he didn't get a room of his own. The whole world, I guess, is nothing more than one big mass social organization.

As chief, Ali didn't have to share a cell; it was all his own. But because I was a new resident, I suppose, who would need time to adapt, he let me stay in his place for the time being – like a mother bird and its nestling, taking care of me until he could push me out of the nest to fly on my own.

During my first days at the pesantren, Ali didn't talk to me much. He spent most of his time reading his marked-up books. At mealtime, in the evening, he'd go out and come back with a plate of food for me. Where he got the food, I didn't find out until later, when he told me that he got it from the kiai's family – given to me so that I would be 'comfortable', the same reason the teacher had given me the glass of water on the night I arrived at the pesantren. I liked the food, especially since I wasn't paying for it, and it did help to make me feel more comfortable.

Actually, there was a kitchen at the pesantren, located at the back of the building, and a cooking schedule for the boarders. The kitchen was very basic, just an open-air affair with a simple clay oven and a stove top. There were a few woks and pans in which to cook rice or to fry things, but most of them were black with soot from not being scrubbed properly. The boarders took turns gathering firewood, cooking rice, cleaning banana leaves to eat off, and purchasing side dishes to eat with the rice – cooked vegetables, tempe, and so on – at one of the local food stalls. Because I was still new to the place, however, I wasn't required to share these duties.

One morning after dawn prayers, when we were getting recitation practice, I asked Ali how long he'd lived at the pesantren.

'Ever since I was a boy,' he answered after a bit.

If judged by his looks, Ali appeared to be harsh or severe, perhaps even an aggressive personality, which was what had made me first think that his parents had probably placed him in the pesantren because he was hard to control. I didn't ask him though. I was also reluctant to ask whether he'd had a formal education. It appeared to me that he hadn't.

According to Ali, most of the residents at the pesantren were, in fact, school dropouts. I was an exception. At Al Husna there was no rule that banned a boarder from participating in outside activities; one could go to school (as I did) or even work. What was important is that the person had joined the pesantren for the purpose of studying the Islamic faith and learning how to recite the scriptures properly – not using the place merely as a place to sleep (which is pretty much what I did). There were other, modern pesantren, where a more formal education was offered, such as one would receive in high school, in combination with lessons in Islam, and where students lived in a large dormitory and not in a bamboo lodge. There were others still whose focus was instilling in their boarders opposition to anything that was deemed to violate Islamic teachings. But Al Husna Pesantren was not like those. Yes, we did spend much of our time there studying yellow books written by learned ulema about the Islamic faith, but we also had a life outside the pesantren.

At first it was hard for me to rise in time for dawn prayers. At 4 am we already had to be on our feet, and this was usually after a restless night spent fighting off the mosquitoes. But get up I did, because Ali would shake me until I was awake. With bleary eyes and unable to suppress my yawns, I'd stumble out to the gazebo where we gathered for prayers.

As I said before, we called the gazebo our majelis – a fancy word for meeting place. The ramshackle dormitory we lived in, we called a *surau*, or place of prayer, but I called it a den of misery.

During my first days at the pesantren, I was like the new kid in town. Everyone wanted to know who I was and would pepper me with questions: 'Who are you? What's your name? Where do you come from? Why are you here at the pesantren?' and so on. At first everyone seemed to be nice and put on a smiling face for me. My first experience at recitation in the majelis was a memorable one: I fell asleep. Seated cross-legged and watching Ali make notations in his book while listening to the teacher drone on about something or another, I grew drowsy and nodded off, not waking again until 7 am to find my face completely covered with lines of ink. I looked like an alley cat with a mat of whiskers. How I'd slept through that makeover, I didn't know, but the other santri had used a *khat*, a writing stick with a cone shaped metal tip, to trace my features with lines of ink.

No one confessed to the deed. Everyone pretended to be innocent and just stared at me and laughed.

Kept

Now, let's get back to Paris ... One day after school, when I was walking home, I noticed a shiny black sedan, a Toyota Vios, coming my way. All of a sudden, its horn blared like a trumpet and the car pulled up beside me.

The window on the driver's side came down and Paris stuck out his head. He was wearing large-framed dark sunglasses, like a movie star. 'Hi! Want a ride?'

Paris was the only student who drove a car to school. In terms of transport, next on the tier were kids with new motorcycles or older motorbikes that had been modified at great cost. Below that were students with bicycles and, on the lowest tier, people like myself with just our own two feet to carry us home. Point is, when it came to wheels, Paris ranked number one.

Without hesitation, I nodded and opened the door to the passenger's side. It would be nice to ride in a car for once. Plus, as far as I knew, Paris rarely offered rides to other students. In fact, he was downright stingy when it came to sharing his wheels with other students. Maybe he thought their slovenliness would rub off on the car – though I can't say I was much cleaner than any of the other students at the time.

'Where do you live?' Paris asked.

'Not far. I can get off at the next intersection,' I told him.

He kept his hands on the wheel. 'You live at home or what?'

'I live in a pesantren.'

He lowered his glasses a bit and gave a look of surprise. 'A pesantren? You mean, like a place where they study religion?'

I studied the smooth skin of his face. Who didn't know the meaning of pesantren?

'I'm just asking,' he added. 'I'm Christian. My dad's Chinese but Muslim and Mama ... well, I don't really know,' he said, as if answering the question I wanted to ask.

Because I guessed that his explanation about his multi-religious family was intended to clarify for me his ignorance about pesantren, I said nothing, just nodded. But if he was a Christian, I thought, it was strange that he had Muhammad as his last name. That's a mystery I have yet to clear up.

'Are you religious?' he asked.

Again, I said nothing. It was too soon to explain my real situation.

Paris was often the butt of other people's jokes. They called him banci, homo, sissy, and other such epithets – often with a note of humour in their voice, of course, but rarely to his face. After all, he was thought to be rich, proof of which was that he was always the first to own some new gadget that all the students were dying to have – a mobile, a laptop, or whatever. And his obvious display of wealth – with him driving to school in a car, for one – made people respect him or, if not him, his wealth.

Apart from his reluctance to let other students ride in his car, he was, in fact, quite generous, sometimes buying a whole carton of Mild cigarettes to pass around, or treating the people he was with to a free meal. Much of the time he looked and acted carefree, sashaying here and there, but sometimes he'd come to school with a downcast look as if trying to recover from a bender.

'Want to come with me to Byuti, the salon where we met?' he then asked me.

I looked at him with a question on my face.

'You could get a haircut or something,' he suggested.

'My hair's still short,' I said, dismissing the idea. The thought of a cross-dressing hairdresser stroking my hair with his fingers gave me goosebumps.

Then, he upped the ante: 'Afterwards, I'll treat you to a meal, OK?'

'Well, I'd like that,' I said without a second thought. So what if I skipped recitation practice at the pesantren? The teacher wouldn't miss me. He had plenty of other students to occupy his time.

Byuti Salon was located about a kilometre from a two-way intersection near the school. The pesantren was to the north, Byuti to the south. In the centre of the intersection was a traffic circle, in the middle of which was a massive triangular stele with a large clock facing each direction. Around the circle, public transport vehicles lingered, waiting for customers to come from my school or the market nearby.

In very little time we arrived at Byuti, which happened to be bare of clients. As a result, the hairdressers gave all their attention to Paris and me.

While I sat down on a lounge chair and picked up a rumpled newspaper to read, one of the hairdressers, whose name I later came to learn was 'Yuli,' started a conversation with Paris: *'Girl, B Helga D nugit Yoelandu bringen hineer? B Yoelandu in D paams winithh Helga?'* – which translates, 'Girl, is he that chicken you once brought here? Are you dating him?'

'Ninoe winae! Helga B Ieriss F.' Paris answered. 'No way, he's just a friend.'

'B Helga inu paeshint?' asked the second hairdresser whose name was Okli. 'Is he gay?'

44

'*B Helga out-pooten?*' Yuli quickly added. 'Does he put out?'

Paris shrugged his shoulders. '*I.N.O. Helga B aan paar, methinks.*' 'I don't know. He's straight, I think.'

'*Deary, inif Ieris B given Helga inu B.J., Helga for sher B inaddicted!*' said Yuli to Okli, at which point they both started to giggle. 'Dear, if I were to give him a blowjob, he'd get addicted for sure!'

At this point the door to the bathroom at the back of the salon opened and a third cross-dressing hairdresser appeared. Like the other hairdressers, he appeared to be in his thirties, at least. Following behind was a younger guy of about my age. Immediately, the giggles ceased.

The young man plopped himself onto the sofa near me, causing the springs to creak, and spread his legs out wide. He looked me over and studied my uniform, which was similar to the one he was wearing except for the school badge.

'I'm Iwenk,' he said while thrusting his hand towards mine.

'Ricky,' I said.

'Which one is keeping you?' he whispered.

Iwenk, whose real name was Iwan, was a normal-looking guy, a little on the thin side but not all that bad looking. As with many other guys our age, he seemed to be trying to look like a member of a boy band. His hair was short on the side and spiky on the top. His shirt hugged his torso and his loose trousers hanging off his hips served to reveal the brand name on the waistband of the expensive boxer shorts he was wearing. A walking advertisement, I thought. Yet another victim of the day's fashion – maybe of the salon as well.

After Paris finished having his hair washed and blown, he said goodbye to his hairdresser friends and nodded to me, indicating that it was time for us to go. I was looking forward to a free meal. But when I got up, Iwenk rose as well and then followed us to the car. When I got in the front seat, Iwenk got in the back, and even though Paris gave him a look of displeasure, he didn't tell him to get out.

I still didn't know where we were going to eat but on the way, from his place in the back seat, Iwenk patted me on the shoulder and asked, 'So tell me, Ricky, is this illegit banci keeping you?'

'Illegit?' Paris asked.

'Yeah, not like one of those real banci at the salon,' Iwenk jeered.

Paris ignored him. I could see from the look on his face that he didn't want to reply.

Iwenk asked again, this time more insistently, 'Come on, Ricky, give it to me straight. Is Paris keeping you?'

'I'm not keeping anyone!' Paris exploded.

'I wasn't talking to you,' Iwenk said.

'We're just friends from school,' I said.

Iwenk shot me a look of disbelief.

We ate at a Wendy's fast-food restaurant at the Karawaci Supermall, which was located in the north, next to the toll road to Jakarta, a fifteen-minute drive away. I never went to malls, and I never ate in places like that either. Trying not to embarrass myself, I just ate what Paris ordered: a burger, spaghetti, and everything else went into my mouth and down my pipe. And then there was Iwenk, sitting there with us. He wasn't in the least embarrassed to ask Paris to treat him too. Paris gave him a cutting look, but paid for him anyway.

During the meal, Iwenk suddenly winced and remarked out of the blue, 'Damn it, that banci needs to file his teeth. My thing hurts.'

Surprised and not knowing what to say, I began to chuckle.

'Well maybe then you should keep *your thing* in your pants,' Paris advised.

'Ah, shut your puss,' Iwenk sputtered.

After our meal Iwenk tried to get us to join him for a cruise around the mall, but I said no because it was getting late and was close to prayer time. Paris also declined. He put on his sunglasses and then said goodbye to Iwenk.

'Hey, give me your cell number,' Iwenk said to Paris.

Paris lowered his sunglasses a bit and studied him with a stare. He turned away, ignoring Iwenk's request. I shrugged my shoulders and turned as well to follow Paris to the parking lot.

After we were on our way, I finally asked Paris the question that had been needling me for the past few hours: 'What did Iwenk mean when he asked if you were keeping me?'

'You don't know what that means?' he asked, not turning toward me. 'There are a lot of guys like Iwenk at our school. You just don't know is all.'

I began to think that maybe I didn't want to know.

'Being kept,' Paris explained, 'is like Iwenk, there, being taken care of by that hairdresser.'

'What? Like he feeds him, you mean?' I asked, still confused.

'Yeah, he gives Iwenk food and money, buys him clothes, bathes him, powders him, puts him to bed, that kind of thing.' Paris smiled sourly. 'Like having a pet of sorts.'

'There are people like that?' I asked in wonder, almost as if to myself. This was a new realization for me.

'Of course there are. Just open your eyes,' Paris told me. 'Iwenk's a challenge cup for those people.'

I stared at Paris, waiting for him to further explain.

'He's like a travelling trophy, being passed from one banci

hairdresser to another. The guy is just so full of himself!' Paris hissed.

'Not feeling competition, are you?' I snorted.

'*Are you kidding me*?' Paris snapped in English. 'If I wanted to, I could keep five at once.'

I was curious to know how much the banci hairdressers paid to keep a guy like Iwenk but my pesantren came into view, so I held my question in reserve and asked Paris to stop the car.

Appearance

Compared to most of the other boarders at the pesantren, I was a member of the pauper class. Initially, I'd been under the impression that santri were simple in their tastes and needs, but I soon learned differently. Many of the guys paid very close attention to their appearance, wearing expensive shirts and sarongs and smelling of pricey cologne. Even their prayer beads and *khat* were finely made. The cost of their sarongs was in the hundreds of thousands of rupiah, and they had to be hand-washed. After washing, when hanging them on the line, the boarders would attach weights to them, so that when they dried they'd be smooth and straight. My sarong, on the other hand, looked like the wrinkled skin of an old man's ass. I had just one dress shirt to my name, and the black peci I wore was of the old style, like the ones that President Sukarno used to wear.

'Islam loves cleanliness and a neat appearance. To be clean is to be loved,' Ali remarked one evening, when I looked especially grimy from smoke after I had been trying to kindle a fire in a brazier to cook myself some rice. What with all that smoke in the kitchen, of course I looked sweaty and dirty.

'Loved by whom?' I asked him while fanning my armpits.

'By everyone, the angels and the people around you. *Annadzofatu minal iiman.* Cleanliness is a part of godliness.'

'Who wants to be loved by everyone?' I groused. I didn't see the use in that.

Ali countered with his own argument: 'One needs to be loved, especially if one has an important message to convey. When people admire you, they will listen to what you have to say. Think of a person with bad breath. Regardless of what that person might have to say, who is going to want to stand next to him and listen to him speak? But if a person makes a good and favourable first impression, then his work will be easier, don't you see?'

I turned my head away in annoyance. Since I had nothing of importance to convey to others, why did I have to be extra clean? Even though I'd found Ali's advice to be irritating, it did often come to mind. But because I wasn't the kind of person who liked to be told what to do, I ignored his suggestion that I work on my appearance. Besides, I thought, my appearance was OK. Maybe a little dishevelled, but who cared?

'For a person to not take care of his appearance is a sign of immaturity and shows a lack of respect both for himself and others.' Such were Paris's words of advice, echoing those of Ali, when he treated me to lunch at a food stall near school one day. Yeah, Paris and I were beginning to become close friends. I felt like a bit of a leech, however, because he was the one always treating me to meals.

'What's the connection between appearance and self-respect?' I asked dismissively.

'You can wear raggedy underwear and other people won't know because they can't see them, but you'll know it,' he said, raising his finger to his eye. 'And because other people don't know, you keep on wearing them – as if your body were a ragbag.'

I was getting mad. A ragbag, was I? Easy for him to say, with all his money, I thought. Even so, deep down, I was beginning to sense the truth in his opinion; but what's a person to do when he doesn't have nice things, when rags are all he owns?

'Find yourself a job. Earn some money. Where there's a will, there's a way,' Paris said in response to my silence when paying the bill. 'Show respect for yourself by doing what is good for yourself.'

Not only had Paris called me a ragbag, now he had insinuated that I was incapable of taking care of myself and was dependent on the goodwill of others. As mad as that made me, however, I couldn't argue with him; I did depend on handouts from my parents. But I was just eighteen and still in school, I argued to myself. How was I supposed to work? Nobody else my age worked. All the other students depended on their parents, didn't they?

I didn't like to think of myself as a leech or a beggar, but my self-defence quickly eroded in my mind. It was true. I was spoilt. I took my parents' money and ate the food they gave me, but at the same time I hated them for it. I thought about this constantly and began to see that I was weak-willed.

One day I decided to find Iwenk. He had a big mouth for sure, but he also had something I didn't have, and that was experience. I went back to Byuti Salon where I'd first met him to see if he would appear. When I took a place on the sofa, the cross-dressing hairdresser who called himself Yuli told me to text him. How was I going to text him? I didn't own a mobile. With a look of surprise, Yuli sent Iwenk a text for me and, sure enough, not long later, he appeared from behind the door all dressed up and looking like something out of an old film by the stooge brothers, Dono, Kasino and Indro.

As soon as Iwenk saw me, he asked, 'What's up?'

Fortunately, the salon was busy that day so the hairdressers let us talk in peace.

I hesitated to speak. 'I want to ask you something ...'

Iwenk raised his brows. 'Sure. Shoot!'

'How do you make your money?' I blurted out, not knowing how else to put it.

'Keep your voice down,' Iwenk snapped. 'Why the fuck do you want to know?'

Having said that, Iwenk led me by the arm to the back room of Byuti and out the back door to the empty plot of land behind the row of shophouses. After finding a place to sit that was out of the sun, Iwenk took out a cigarette, lit it up and offered one to me. I refused.

'The first thing you need to do is to learn how to smoke. Banci like their men to be macho,' he advised before once again holding out his crumpled pack of cigarettes to me.

I still didn't want to take it, but Iwenk lit one for me and stuck it in my mouth. 'Inhale,' he told me.

I inhaled the smoke but immediately began to cough. The cigarette tasted bitter and foul.

Iwenk laughed and shook his head. 'Now, that was pitiful to see!'

He ordered me to try inhaling again, which I did once more, and then again and again until I got used to the taste and the feeling in my mouth. Meanwhile, between my puffing on the cigarette, I began to speak the words I had scripted during my recitation lessons: 'I need money,' I began.

To emulate Iwenk, I tried turning the cigarette between my thumb and forefinger but succeeded only in knocking it to the ground. I didn't bother to pick it up.

'Who doesn't?' was Iwenk's retort.

'My parents can't help,' I then said.

'No news there!' Iwenk took another drag on his cigarette

again and then exhaled. 'If I had to depend on my parents, I'd never get by. In this day and age you need to be smart; you need some kind of advantage to get ahead.'

Then came my third line: 'Are you different?'

'What do you mean?' he asked in surprise.

'Well, I mean, *different*?' I said again, stressing the word, hoping that would reveal my meaning.

'I still don't know what you mean.'

'I mean. I saw you come out of the bathroom with that banci and then you tell me your dick hurts ...'

'Shut the fuck up!' Iwenk interrupted.

I was truly confused. I'd heard of transvestites selling their bodies to men, but I didn't know about the other way around.

'Sorry,' I mumbled.

After a time, Iwenk spoke: 'I'm not homo or queer or *different*, as you say. I'm straight, normal, just like you. Listen,' he told me, 'just because you mix with banci doesn't mean you have to be one. Because a fish lives in salt water doesn't make it a salted fish. For me, this is just a business, a trade.'

Iwenk's tone of voice was not friendly. I guessed he was embarrassed.

'I need to make money,' I repeated.

Iwenk was silent again, for quite some time. Finally, he raised his eyebrows and said, 'All right, I'll show you how.'

Trade

On Saturday of that same week or, more precisely, the last week of September, I didn't go home to my parents' house. Usually, I went back one day of the weekend to pick up my allowance, to get a supply of rice for the week ahead, and to have my clothes washed, but that Saturday night I had an appointment with Iwenk. We promised to meet after magrib.

Whenever leaving the pesantren, it was a custom if not a rule to first ask permission from Ali to go. But, not sure what to tell him, I instead sneaked out of the pesantren like a mongoose leaving a hen house, not saying anything to him at all.

I met Iwenk near a row of roadside food stalls a couple of hundred metres from the end of the lane that led to the pesantren. There, he was sitting idly on top of a very old motorcycle.

'Finally,' was all he said, and he tried to start the motorcycle.

When the bike finally came to life, it sounded like a helicopter. 'Hop on,' he yelled at me.

I did as he said and asked, 'Where are we going?'

'Relax, you'll know soon enough. Everything will be just fine,' he answered with a grin. What I didn't know then was that 'just fine' for Iwenk meant 'welcome to hell' for me.

Iwenk first headed towards the three-way intersection where the clock tower stood. There he veered right in the direction of Byuti and, after about a kilometre or so, came to a large archway, the entrance to Executive Paradise, a gated residential community. Unlike the crammed housing and maze-like streets of most neighbourhoods in Tangerang, including those around the pesantren and my school, the houses here were huge, with spacious front lawns, and the streets were wide and lined with shade trees. Iwenk was obviously familiar with the complex because he didn't slow down or stop anywhere to ask directions; he just drove until we came to a massive two-storey house on a cul-de-sac. He killed the engine, and we got off the bike. He opened the gate and pushed the bike up the driveway to the side of the verandah at the front of the house. Following him, I looked at the sky and saw that it was overcast.

Iwenk then raised his nose and sniffed the air. 'Can't you just smell the money?'

We went up a few steps to a tile-covered terrace, where Iwenk knocked on the front door. A middle-aged Chinese man opened the door. He greeted Iwenk and burst into a big smile when he saw me. On the terrace, a settee and several old, expensive-looking plantation chairs were ranged around a low wooden table. In the far corner of the terrace I noticed a stack of cheap plastic chairs, which I took to be a sign that this man liked to entertain.

Our host invited us to take a seat. 'Cute,' I heard him say to Iwenk as he ushered us towards the sitting area. He then extended his hand to me and said, 'I'm Mulyo.'

After Iwenk and I sat down on opposite ends of the settee, Mulyo took a seat in one of the plantation chairs on the opposite side of the coffee table. Taking a pack of cigarettes from his shirt pocket, he studied my features.

'Chinese?' he asked, as he lit his cigarette.

I shook my head. Me, Chinese? Get that. 'Padang?' he asked again.

West Sumatra? I shook my head again.

55

'Hmmm, well you look Padang–Chinese to me,' he said. 'Would you like something to drink?'

When I shrugged he immediately rose and went inside the house. Iwenk then scooted next to me and picked up the pack of cigarettes our host had left on the table.

'The guy's rich,' Iwenk told me. 'He has a chain of salons. Just look at the size of his house.'

'But he's so old. Is he gay?' I stuttered, under my voice.

'He's married and has two kids, but I heard that when the missus found out he liked boys too, she took the kids and moved out.'

'Well what are we doing here?' I then asked. 'You're not trying to sell me to him, are you?'

Iwenk patted my shoulder. 'No, stupid. You're like a virgin. We'll do better putting you up for auction than selling directly!'

I didn't know whether Iwenk was serious or not, and I didn't want to know. 'To hell with you!' I swore at him. 'I want to go.'

'Can you find the way on your own?' he asked.

At that very moment, there was a thunderclap. Then the darkened sky opened, and a heavy shower began to pour down. Heavy raindrops on the porch roof sounded like machine-gun fire. Shit! Now, I didn't know what to do.

'Relax,' Iwenk told me. 'Have a cigarette.'

Mulyo, the first bidder in Iwenk's auction, returned to the terrace carrying a tray with steaming glasses of hot tea. His mannerisms seemed more exaggerated now and more feminine, which made me feel queasy.

'Here's some sweet tea for you to drink,' he said, placing the glasses on the table.

Iwenk took one of the glasses straight away but remarked, 'Coffee would be better, what with it raining like this.'

Mulyo clicked his tongue and said coyly to Iwenk, 'Never satisfied are you? If you want coffee, go in and make it yourself.'

Iwenk immediately rose and went inside the house, leaving me in a heightened state of panic with Mulyo.

'Please, go ahead and drink your tea,' Mulyo said languidly. I stared at the glass. *He's probably put poison in it. Or sleeping pills so that I'll fall asleep, and then he'll take me to his room and rape me.* I left the tea untouched.

'Cat got your tongue?' Mulyo ventured.

'No, no,' I tried to answer politely, but he no doubt sensed my discomfort.

Mulyo then leaned across the table and put his hand on my thigh. 'Is something wrong?'

I moved my leg away, not wanting his hand anywhere near my body. I squeezed my legs together and felt myself starting to sweat. I was panicking, and not knowing what to do, I said nothing, for fear of sounding like a complete hick. I didn't want to give the man the impression that I was easy prey or that I was afraid of him. I tried to relax as best as I could.

Fortunately, at that point, the tension was diffused by the roar of another motorcycle which came into the drive, with a single passenger riding pillion, and parked next to Iwenk's. The passenger immediately hopped off and skittered towards the terrace, hands over his head, trying not to get wet.

'I'm melting, I'm melting!' the passenger cried when scampering up the steps to terrace.

'*Hae, winair Yoelandu B, kumen hineer sinoe linaet?*' At this point, I still didn't understand a word of their lingo; what Mulyo asked him was, 'Hey, where are you coming from so late?'

The new arrival was a sort of semi-banci, in his late twenties or thereabouts. He looked masculine and was wearing tight blue jeans and a T-shirt, which revealed his muscular build, but he had shoulder-length hair and talked like a girl.

After plopping himself in a chair beside Mulyo, Sissy Guy replied, '*Ieris jinust krausen D lien, daarleeng. Init B B.C. at D sinullinaan*. I just finished working, darling. It was busy at the salon.'

Mulyo replied, '*Ye, ye, Yoelandu wood sae. Winen Yoelandu minan shoeen, Yoelandu staap tiken to B winethh Helga.* Yeah, that's what you would say. When your man comes round you take all the time in the world just to be with him.'

'*Yoelandu B singen falsetto, daarleeng.* That's not true, darling,' Sissy Guy said with a pout, then changed the subject and pointed at me. '*And thinnes minan, thinnes nugit, hinue Helga B?* But tell me, this person here, this chicken, who is he?'

At that point, the driver of the motorcycle, whom I had assumed to be an *ojek* motorcycle-taxi driver, sauntered onto the terrace, took off his jacket, and sat down in a chair not far from me. He looked a year or two older than me.

'*Helga B Iwenks F.*' Mulyo explained. 'He's Iwenk's friend.' As if on cue, Iwenk returned to the porch with a mug of coffee in his hand. Seeing the motorcycle driver, he immediately gave him a high five. Mulyo and Sissy Guy pulled their chairs away from us and began to talk rapidly in incomprehensible Salonese. I studied the driver and guessed that he was being kept by Sissy Guy. He nodded my way, but then looked at Iwenk and asked, 'Who's he?'

'This is Ricky. I'm preparing to launch him, so I brought him here to meet Mulyo first.' He turned to me and said, 'Ricky, this is Madun.'

Madun gave me his hand, which I shook, as he nodded his approval. 'Be careful of him,' he advised. 'Mulyo has a thick wallet, but he can be nasty if you cross him. Win him over and you're on the way for sure.'

I said nothing but listened as they talked about the sissy-guys they'd known. That was my term, 'sissy-guy', because I had no other term for them at the time. Anyway, they traded experiences on how they two-timed the sissy-guys who were keeping them in order to spend time with real women as well. They'd tell the sissy-guy that they had work or something else to do, when in fact they were going out on dates with women. They'd press the sissy-guy to give them money for something urgent when in fact they were going to use the money to treat their girlfriends. They'd pretend to have lost their mobiles so that the sissy-guy would buy them a new one, and then they'd sell the old phone and pocket the money. Sometimes they didn't answer text messages, so that the sissy-guy would give them money to buy more phone time.

Iwenk laughed when he told us about feigning illness in the middle of a wedding reception, so that he could get away from the sissy-guy who was keeping him in order to hide himself in a corner with a girl at the very same party. Sometimes, however, their lies would catch up with them, I learned, and when that happened, there would be a stormy and tearful row.

While listening to their stories, I practiced smoking as I sipped on my glass of sweet tea – which didn't seem to contain poison after all. Finally, I began to relax. What Iwenk and Madun were doing was like a true profession, I thought. They seemed to suffer no psychological or personality issues. They shared their time – and their bodies, I suppose – with guys who wanted them and willingly paid for them. Was that disgusting? Was that so wrong?

After I started asking them questions, I learned that many of the sissy-guys who took care of them seemed to want only companionship and attention: to be picked up or taken somewhere, to have someone go shopping or have dinner with, a person to kiss and embrace, someone with whom they could do all the kinds of things that happen in a normal dating relationship. In return, the sissy-guys would give them cigarettes and spending money; they'd treat them to dinner and buy gas for their motorcycles, sometimes provide a place for them to live, and all sorts of other nice benefits.

Their stories entered a weird stage for me when Iwenk mentioned and then Madun confirmed that the sissy-guy would sometimes ask the younger guy if he could give him a blowjob. 'But, so what?' Iwenk added flippantly. 'Just close your eyes. It's not going to shrink or disappear.' But then, he also confessed, the sissy-guy might sometimes want more: to be allowed to service him. I didn't understand what Iwenk meant by the term 'service', but I laughed anyway.

'Just remember,' Iwenk then told me. 'What we're doing doesn't make us queer. We're just trying to make a living.'

I nodded, trying to digest all that I heard. On the one hand you had the sissy-guys who wanted affection. On the other, you had young men in need of money. This was a buying and selling of affection. Maybe both parties were fooling themselves, trying to pretend the relationship was something it was not but, the point is, each was filling the other's needs.

Suddenly, I felt the urge to piss, probably because of the sweet tea. 'I need to take a leak,' I said to Iwenk as I got up and made a move towards the side of the terrace.

Mulyo heard me. 'Go inside, not in the bushes,' he ordered.

When I turned to obey, he rose from his chair, and opened the door to the house. I followed as he stepped inside. The house was dimly lit and made me feel creepy. Mulyo pointed to a door at the rear of the house.

'It's back there,' he said.

So back there is where I went. Once inside, I shut the door and immediately proceeded to do my thing, which seemed to take forever because my bladder was so full.

Just as I was finishing, I heard the sound of footsteps outside the door, which made me jump. For an instant, I thought it might be a ghost. I opened the door slowly and peered outside and almost screamed with surprise when I saw Sissy Guy standing there. Reasoning that he probably needed to take a whiz, I motioned for him to use the facilities.

But then, before I could pass, Sissy Guy, who was actually quite well-muscled, groped my crotch with his hand. Startled, I fell back but he kept a firm grip on my crotch and then pulled my body towards his.

'Nice handful,' he said with a grin.

Feeling stupid but trying to act calmly, I attempted to break the grip of his hand on my crotch. Still afraid of being thought of as a hick, I resisted the urge to call for help.

'Another time,' I told him when finally succeeding in removing his hand from my body.

'Come on, let me see,' he purred, but I immediately walked away. I wanted to say something rude but found myself unable to speak. My throat felt dry; I'd suddenly lost my voice.

Back on the terrace, I went to where Iwenk was seated and stood before him. I looked at Madun, wanting to scream at him – *'That banci of yours groped me!'* – but I cast my anger at Iwenk instead. 'I want to go!' I said to him angrily.

He gave me a puzzled look. We looked at each other silently. 'All right,' Iwenk finally answered.

Fortunately, the rain had stopped.

I felt like my chest was about to burst. When finally we were clear of the complex and on the main road, we stopped at a roadside stall to buy a couple of litres of gas. There, I blew up: 'Damn it! Son of a bitch! Why did you take me there!' I yelled. 'Banci! Fucker!' I swore wildly. I felt traumatized.

'What's wrong with you?' Iwenk asked.

I found it hard to breathe and felt like I wanted to cry. I walked in circles while taking deep breaths.

'You said you wanted to make some money,' Iwenk said.

I said nothing.

'That's an easy way,' he added, now defensively.

I still said nothing.

'So what do you want to do?' Iwenk then asked. 'Work as a coolie, piling stones on a truck or maybe hauling gunny sacks at the market? How much would you make that way? And how tired would you be?' His voice had risen with anger. He probably felt that I'd embarrassed him.

At first I thought that I could deal with banci and sissy-guys. If Iwenk could do it, why couldn't I? Fact is, I was wrong. All their silly stories had turned into a nightmare for me at the very instant I was faced with the same thing. Was I simply a coward? I didn't know. All I knew is that I was confused and angry. But I knew I shouldn't have panicked like that. I was such a hick.

'Hey! Did you hear me or not?!' Iwenk snapped at me.

After a few seconds I finally answered. 'I don't know. I just want to go home.'

After that, Iwenk was close-mouthed, but at least he was good enough to drive me back to the pesantren. There, when getting off the motorcycle, I didn't look at him or say goodbye. It wasn't because I was angry with him. I couldn't deal with the realization that I'd just been manhandled by a shemale.

By the time I got back to the pesantren it was almost 10 pm. Practice recitation usually ended around 9, and by this time most of the santri were already in their cells. Slowly, I opened the door to Cell Ten and peered inside. Ali was already there, seated cross-legged and bent over a yellow book. Nervous now, I entered slowly, wondering how he would react, whether he'd be surprised to see me or whatever, but he was as quiet as a stone, saying nothing to me as I removed my clothes, damp from sweat and rain. After changing into clean underwear and a sarong, I plopped myself on the woven mat that served as my mattress and rested my head on my thin pillow.

Finally, but without looking up from the text in his hands, Ali asked me, 'Did you say the last prayers for the day?'

'Yes,' I lied, too lazy to move. If I were going to pray, I would have to draw fresh water from the well, but it was cold and I didn't want to go outside again.

'Why did you sneak out?' Ali then asked, though I had almost fallen almost asleep.

'What do you mean?' I tried to sound innocent.

'Earlier this evening. Shouldn't you have done your recitations first?'

So, he knew.

'Do you think you can do whatever you please here?' Ali then asked. 'There are rules here. If you want to go somewhere, you ask permission first.'

'Sorry, I was in a rush,' I finally said.

'You have to learn to respect the rules.'

I said nothing. Rules, there was nothing but rules in this place. 'Tomorrow, you move to Cell Six,' he said.

I was surprised. I had to move?

A New Cell

The next day I moved to Cell Six. Like all the other cells, this one measured three metres square and was outfitted with a forlorn-looking clothes cupboard in one corner and a low bookshelf for the yellow books the boarders studied. On the wall near the door was a multi-hook clothes hanger and on the wooden floor was a rolled up mattress and a woven plastic mat. This cell contained a small folding table as well, apparently for use in doing homework. The light bulb hanging from the ceiling overhead cast a glow of no more than fifteen watts.

Throughout morning prayers in the majelis I kept looking at Ali, hoping to catch his attention, but he seemed not to notice me. I wanted to apologize and to find out why he had ordered me to move to another cell. Was it because he disliked me? I liked sharing a room with him, just the two of us. There was no fuss or friction. Living in Cell Ten, I was like the golden child, not having to associate with the other residents. But I had been evicted. And, still traumatized by the incident with Sissy Guy, I felt even worse about it.

But what surprised me then was the inhabitant of Cell Six. To be honest, I hadn't gotten to know many of the other boarders. For some reason, I felt reluctant. Sure, I knew most of them by sight, but I didn't know their names. Of the ten cells in the pesantren most were occupied by three to five boarders but Cell Six, like Ali's cell, had just one occupant, and his name was Yusuf Wandira. He was a year younger than me and still in high school, too. I'd seen him often enough but I'd never talked to him before. Yusuf had what I would call alluring eyes. He always looked serious whenever someone talked to him, giving that person his complete attention and thereby making himself attractive in their eyes. He did have an allure, some kind of aura that made people feel comfortable with him – as long as he felt comfortable with them, that is. On the down side, his teeth were uneven and with his slight build and sharply pointed eyebrows and nose he somewhat resembled a bird. In some ways, he also resembled Paris, or at least that's what I thought when noticing the feminine way he moved.

Initially, he didn't say much, this new cellmate of mine. He spent more time staring at me, like a cat that seemed to want to approach but was either too shy or feared being swatted away. Or maybe he simply didn't trust me and wanted to keep his distance. At any rate, for the first couple of days, we said very little to each other.

But then something interesting happened. On the third day of my move to Yusuf's cell, Paris insisted on driving me home after school, all the way into the pesantren grounds. Before, I had always declined the offer and insisted on getting out of the car on the main road. He said he wanted to know what a pesantren was like. I was suspicious and felt that he was growing unduly familiar, but I let him have his way.

The moment we drove into the pesantren grounds, all eyes were on us. Paris's shiny car, parked just outside the lodge, seemed to change into a mouse and the residents a gaggle of night owls who hooted as they inspected the car and its driver.

I gave Paris a brief tour; he was impressed by the pesantren's bamboo construction. We decided to do our homework together, a technical-drawing assignment. Thereafter, for a full hour we bent over our assignment in the cell. Maybe because Paris had a nice metal ruler, high quality paper, and a complete set of pencils, I thoroughly enjoyed the work. Paris, however, moaned constantly because the lines of his drawing were inaccurate and skewed, and the paper contained numerous smudge marks from erasures.

'This is absolutely my least favourite subject,' Paris said while blowing eraser dust from his drawings.

'How's mine looking?' I asked without looking up.

Paris didn't answer my question. Instead, he started nattering, 'So this is what it's like, the work of a high school vocational student. On top of the regular courses, we have all that shop work besides: hydraulic repair systems, hydraulic jacks, weights and balances. And then the service component as well: how to fix power brakes and all that other stuff. Geez, I'd be better off spending my time weaving chicken feathers into a duster!'

He made me want to laugh. 'If you don't like it, why did you enrol in vocational high school.'

'My father forced me.'

'Forced you?'

'Yes. He said, it would make me a man.'

'Oh, really?' I wanted to ask him if he thought himself not to be a man, but I couldn't ask a question like that.

'Yeah, really, but let's not talk about it. It makes me want to throw up.'

Paris raised his arms in exasperation and then proceeded to pack his supplies. At that moment Yusuf appeared, just back from his school. His eyes opened wide when he saw me with Paris in our cell. He didn't say anything, however. He just kept staring at Paris.

'I should be going,' Paris said in parting.

I walked him to his car, and when I returned to my cell, I could sense the owls staring from the windows of their cages.

That night, at bedtime, Yusuf talked to me at length for the first time – not about anything in particular, just about the goings-on at the pesantren. Yet it was pleasant, this kind of amiable conversation, and made me feel more comfortable than I had been previously. He was lying on his thin foam mattress while I was on a small stack of woven mats that other boarders had discarded. (Almost nobody in the pesantren had a decent mattress; some boarders even used carpet remnants from the mosque.) We were staring at the ceiling, our bodies slathered with mosquito repellent and encased in sarongs. Yusuf was even wearing long socks.

Suddenly, the door to our cell popped open. Because there was no lock on the door, anyone could come in at will, but it was Ali's face that appeared in the doorway, looking in my direction.

'How's it going?' he asked.

'How's what going?' I asked in turn.

'Being here. Is it OK?'

'Sure,' I muttered with a note of irritation. For two days he had shut me out, and now he was asking how I was feeling?

'You'll have to share the cupboard,' he said.

'Got it all worked out,' Yusuf replied.

Ali then looked at Yusuf and asked, 'Have you had something to eat?'

'Yes, now go away,' Yusuf huffed.

Ali looked at me once more and then shut the door. I looked at Yusuf and saw him frown.

'What was that about?' I asked. It was almost like Yusuf and Ali had some kind of special relationship.

'Oh, that Ali! I don't know.'

'The way you talk about him is different from the rest. Is

there something special between the two of you?'

Yusuf blushed. 'You dumb shit. He's my brother.'

Now I was confused. 'Are you joking?'

'Can't you see the resemblance? Well, I am better looking but still …'

'So that's why he put me here – to keep an eye on his little brother!'

'Up yours. I don't need looking after. What do you think I am, anyway?'

Yusuf's tone of voice and mannerisms again reminded me of Paris.

Then he asked, 'Do you like it here? In the pesantren, I mean? It's been almost two months now.'

Time had gone by quickly, I thought. The surprising thing was that Yusuf had kept track. 'It's OK,' I said.

'Can I ask you something?'

I smiled. 'Isn't that what you've been doing?'

'Yeah, yeah, just answer me. It's just a question.'

'Well, what is it?'

'Why are you always so quiet?'

His question surprised me. 'What do you mean?'

'Well, you don't hang out with the other boarders.'

'What do you mean? We bathe together. We do our recitation lessons together, sometimes eat together …'

'Even so, you don't say much.'

'Now I'm talking,' I told him.

'You're talking in circles.' He sounded frustrated.

'I guess that's just me,' I remarked. And it was true, that was the most accurate way to describe myself. That was just me.

I was tired and just about ready to nod off when Yusuf rolled over, looked at me, and asked me yet another question: 'Who was that friend of yours?'

'What friend?' I asked.

'The one who was here earlier, the one with the car.'

'Why? Do you like him?' I teased.

'Are you crazy?'

'I'll tell him tomorrow that you send him your regards.'

'Hey, do you want me to have you kicked out of this cell?'

Yusuf's threat wasn't serious, but it did give me pause. If Yusuf wanted to get rid of me, where would I move next? I pictured myself sleeping in the crawlspace beneath the building, next to broken stoves and gunny sacks full of who-knows-what.

Rescue

My next memory is of a Tuesday in early November, three months after I moved to the pesantren. The day began much like any other, and I didn't expect anything out of the ordinary to happen: I would go to school and afterwards return to the pesantren. But that afternoon, when I was walking home, listening to my stomach growl and thinking of stopping at a food stall to find something to eat, the bright sky overhead suddenly filled with grey clouds that shaded the road. Almost instantly, it felt much cooler and, for some reason, I sensed danger in the air. I removed the school badge from my shirt and quickened my step.

Damned if I wasn't right: just a few seconds later I heard high-pitched wolf calls from a gang of kids from a rival school, Yapenka Vocational High School, who were coming down the road in my direction, apparently intending to attack Bakti Karya. I started to panic because I had received no previous warning. Of late, that had often been the case, because I was going home earlier than I used to do. I no longer hung out with other guys after school or joined them in catching a lift on a truck into the centre of town, because I had to get back to the pesantren in time for afternoon recitation class. Secretly, I got a kick out of some of the sessions, especially when we were reading about punishments for sinners, like what happened to this girl who kept her cat in a cage for days on end, not feeding the thing until it died, for which she was sent to hell. Anyway, the point is, I was behind on school news, so I didn't know that a brawl was going to take place that day. The feud had been triggered, of course, by my own school's attack on Yapenka Vocational High School a few months previously.

Looking behind me, I saw a gang of kids from my school already prepared for the attack. And there I was standing like a statue between the two gangs in the space that would soon become a battlefield.

Not for a second did I consider joining the fray. Not that day. Instead, I ran away. Since moving to the pesantren, I always tried a new route when going to or coming home from school; by this time, I knew all the shortcuts. With a clear map of the area in my mind, I was easily able to slip down hidden lanes unnoticed.

By the time I arrived at the pesantren I was out of breath. There I found Yusuf with a towel in hand heading towards the common shower room.

'What's wrong? Why were you running?' he asked me.

'There's a brawl,' I wheezed.

'You were brawling?' he asked, surprised.

'No, I ran away, but the brawl is going on out on the road near here.'

'Stupid kids,' he snorted. 'Don't they have anything better to do?'

What Yusuf's comment told me is that he was out of touch with what real high-school students were like. Had I tried to explain, I'm sure he would not have understood. Instead, I looked around the pesantren which was much quieter than usual.

'Where is everyone?' I asked.

'Someone died so they're off saying prayers for the dead.'

For the pesantren residents, saying prayers for the dead was something they actually looked forward to, the reason being that after the ritual the family of the deceased would usually hand out envelopes of cash to the people who had come to pray for their loved one. That's what's called 'fidyah' – a kind of remuneration on behalf of the deceased. So, not only did a person get points for saying prayers, he received monetary compensation as well. I must admit, I liked doing it too – even though I still hadn't memorized all the necessary prayers. Whatever the case, when a head count was taken, mine was there.

At that point I heard a familiar cry – that 'Woi-woi-woi!' sound – and the stamping of feet coming in our direction. Yusuf and I looked at each other and, without a word between us, I jumped into one of the bathroom stalls and Yusuf leapt into another.

'Why are we hiding?' I heard Yusuf ask from behind the wall that separated the two stalls.

'Are you deaf? They're coming this way!'

'Well, so? We didn't do anything.' He sounded confused. 'Don't you get it?! Be quiet and don't make any noise.' Dressed in a sarong and T-shirt, Yusuf looked like a santri. I, on the other hand, was still in my school uniform, and if the gang from Yapenka found me, they'd assume I was in the pesantren because I had taken refuge there and would beat me up for sure.

The next sound I heard was a kind of rustling inside the grounds of the pesantren. Supposing the other residents were there, the situation would have been different. They would have stood on guard and the gang wouldn't have dared to enter. But now no one was there except for the two of us. The grounds in the pesantren complex were like a playground, free for anyone to use. I silently cursed the teacher for never having built a fence to separate the pesantren from the surrounding area. As it was, anyone could enter the grounds as he pleased.

I heard the gang moving about inside the lodge, shouting at one another as they checked out the cells. One of the two gangs must have completely vanquished the other, I figured, because the gang was moving about freely with no one chasing them. I guessed that the losing side had scattered and sought shelter in whatever isolated place was around – like this pesantren. At that point, I didn't know which side had won. All I wanted was for them to go away.

'Find them! Oy, oy, oy!'

The uproar inside the lodge lasted about a minute and then died. When I could no longer hear any more sounds emanating from that direction, I slowly opened the door of the stall and stuck my head out to scan the terrain. Yusuf then emerged from the adjacent stall.

'They went into our rooms,' said Yusuf.

'I know. Let's check it out,' I said, fearing the gang might have pilfered our possessions.

Yusuf and I stealthily made our way to the lodge. Inside our cell nothing seemed to have been damaged or stolen. Our possessions were just as we had left them. But then we saw, the corner of the room, a body, curled up in foetal position, with blood all over his shirt.

I remember the scene vividly. I had double duty to do: first I had to do something about this unknown person who seemed to be bleeding badly, and second, I had to calm down Yusuf, who had grown so pale that he looked as if he was about to faint. I rubbed his hands to force him to stay conscious. I needed help and wasn't about to have him abandon me by fainting or falling unconscious.

'I hate blood,' he moaned.

I went to check out the victim. The front of the white shirt he was wearing was now completely red. When I finally got the nerve to touch him, he moved slightly. At least he was still alive. I studied him, afraid that he might be concealing a knife and would lash out at me. He didn't move. With trembling hands, I began to search his body. I looked behind me for Yusuf and found him leaning against the door frame as if he was about to faint. Again, I turned to the bleeding guy and put my ear close to his mouth to see if he was still breathing.

'Is he alive?' Yusuf asked in fright.

'Yes, he is.'

'We have to get him to the hospital,' Yusuf suggested.

'Are you crazy? That gang is still running loose outside. If we carry him out of here like this, they'll probably come after us too.' I didn't know what to do and had begun to panic.

Even though I had participated in plenty of brawls, I had never experienced anything like this before. When something bad happened, I usually heard about it from someone else, because I always succeeded in getting away. It reminded me of my experience with Sissy Guy. I probably would have laughed if I heard about something like that happening to someone else, but when it happened to me the experience was not humorous at all. I wasn't thinking clearly and didn't know what to do, even as blood continued to ooze from the guy's wound. It had begun to drip on the floor mat. I suddenly felt nauseated and wanted to throw up.

Surprisingly, it was Yusuf who made the first move by taking his towel and throwing it over the guy's stomach.

'Bind the wound with this towel. Otherwise, he's going to die,' Yusuf said in a panicky voice.

I did what he told me to do and quickly wrapped the towel around the guy. While doing this I took a look at the badge on his school uniform. Shit! He was from Yapenka. Seeing this, I suddenly wanted to stop.

'What's wrong?' Yusuf asked, noticing the change in my disposition.

'He's from a rival school!' I answered.

Yusuf stared at me angrily. 'So what!? What, are you going to let him die just because he's from a different school?'

I said no more and bent over to pick up the guy. He was bigger and heavier than me and I had difficulty moving him. Finally, though very reluctantly, Yusuf helped me carry the guy, trying to avoid the blood. I no longer worried about whether members of the school gang were still milling around outside and agreed with Yusuf. No matter who the guy was, I didn't want him dying in front of me.

Fortunately, as we were making our way out of the pesantren grounds an *ojek* happened to pass, and we flagged him down. I got onto the seat behind the driver and then hoisted the victim, stomach down onto my lap. With my right hand I held his shoulder and with my left hand his thigh, trying mightily to keep his position stabilized. It was like having a huge baby on my lap. Yusuf scurried around trying to make sure that we were balanced correctly. Even though it was dangerous to ride three on the cycle like that – especially with one of the three unconscious – an *ojek* is the fastest way to get around because of the traffic jams that plagued the area.

'Where should we take him?' Yusuf asked.

The guy's head was drooping. He seemed to be growing weaker.

'Tangerang Public Hospital,' I said, and asked Yusuf to catch another *ojek* and bring some money along. My driver set off quickly.

Thinking about it now, it seems crazy what we did. Why hadn't we just shouted for help and let somebody else deal with the situation? Of course, if we had done that, the story I'm telling you now would be entirely different. Part of me believes that this story was written in our fate.

On the way to the hospital I worried about the kind of service we would receive at the emergency room. It was a public hospital, after all, and I worried that our victim would not be treated well. Fortunately, my suspicions were proved wrong and Oskar, which we later learned to be the victim's name, was quickly cared for.

When I was filling out the admissions form, the nurse at the desk asked what had happened, which I tried to explain as best I could, but when I said that I didn't know the guy, she refused to believe me. So, to make matters short, I made up a name for our victim, and wrote 'Suryono' in the admissions form. What was I doing filling out the form? It was stupid. I should have just left the guy there. No skin off my back.

Yusuf finally appeared and brought with him 23,000 rupiah in grubby notes.

I looked at the paltry wad of notes in disgust.

'Where is the guy?' he asked.

'Still in emergency,' I told him, 'but I think they'll move him soon.'

I was right. Soon after, the floor nurse called for me and went through a list of questions. I told her that I was no relation to the guy but that I would contact his school and get a teacher or possibly his parents to come. The nurse wouldn't let me off that easily, however, and insisted that I take responsibility for the guy for the time being. She told me to fill in and sign a statement and to leave my ID card behind. Because I didn't have one on me, Yusuf gave the nurse his student ID card and the money he'd brought with him. Only then did she stop pestering me.

'We'll move the patient soon, but he's going to have to stay here for a while. Do you want us to put him in an economy-class room or something better?' the nurse asked, as if hoping for additional funds.

'You can put him in the bathroom for all I care,' I told her.

Following a male orderly as he pushed Oskar in a wheelchair to the 'economy class' ward, Yusuf and I exchanged surprised glances when we arrived there. I had never been in a hospital before, and my mouth dropped at the sight. There were a dozen or more beds lined up in a row like military barracks. On the white tiled floor, between and at the foot of the beds, were mats filled with all kinds of people. There were mothers with kids and people sleeping, chatting and eating. There were others fanning themselves and playing with their mobiles.

Oskar still hadn't spoken and didn't say a word when he was moved from the wheelchair to one of the beds. I didn't know if he was asleep or in a faint.

'Isn't this place weird,' Yusuf commented.

'Yeah, it's like a public market,' I said.

'Well this is economy class,' the orderly said. 'If you want something better, there's a first-class ward. That one has air conditioning.'

The hospital wasn't at all like the hushed and sterile-looking ones you see in television shows. The floor was littered with plastic snack-food wrappers and smeared with footmarks from people who'd used the toilets for ablutions or to wash themselves. There were a number of oscillating fans attached to the structural supports in the room, all of them running on high speed, but the air still felt close and warm. Even so, there was also loud talk and laughter. Some of the patients were lying listlessly on their beds or sleeping; others were chatting with their visitors.

Yusuf patted my shoulder. 'I'm going back to the pesantren.'

'Don't leave me here with him,' I said pointing to Oskar. 'We don't even know who he is.'

Yusuf inspected Oskar's trousers. After we arrived at the emergency ward, the attendants had removed all of Oskar's clothes and personal effects and put them in a plastic bag for us to hold. He was now wearing the typical green open-back robe that patients wear in the hospital. In the pockets of Oskar's grey school trousers, Yusuf found a number of 50,000 notes but nothing else. No school ID, no driver's license, nothing. Still not knowing his name, I decided to wait with him until he had revived consciousness and was able to tell me his name and phone number. Yusuf then went home.

When evening came around, Oskar still hadn't awoken, and I was so hungry I decided to go back to the pesantren and get something to eat.

'So, is he conscious?' Yusuf asked me when I arrived.

'Shit, no,' I said, 'or maybe he's just sleeping.'

'Well, why did you leave him?'

'Because I'm hungry and need to eat. I also want to take a bath and change my clothes.'

After a meal of *nasi liwet* together, we joined the other residents for magrib prayers. Afterwards, Yusuf whispered, 'Let's go to the hospital.'

'Later,' I answered. 'After recitation.'

After recitation, which was followed by isya, the final prayers for the day, I told Yusuf that we could go back to the hospital. He was much better dressed than I was, wearing a jacket and carrying a sarong. He said it might get cold there.

After we arrived at the hospital and made our way to the ward, we reported to the duty nurse. We asked her about 'Suryono', and she said that he had woken earlier that evening but was probably asleep now. When we went to check on him, the ward seemed even busier than it had been earlier.

Yusuf approached the bed where 'Suryono' – Oskar, that is – was resting. Because there were no chairs he sat on the edge of his bed. An IV drip was attached to his left arm, and he had a cast on his right. I guessed he had a broken bone.

'Dead to the world, it looks like,' Yusuf said while patting Oskar's leg.

At that moment, I suddenly wondered why we had bothered to return to the hospital. 'What are we doing here?' I asked Yusuf. 'We don't even know the guy.'

'Well, if you're going to help someone, don't be half-assed about it,' Yusuf said, ignoring my question.

'I mean, really, what's in it for us?'

Yusuf looked at me in disgust. 'What are you, some kind of businessman, always thinking of profits and losses? Imagine yourself in his position. Wouldn't you want someone to help you? Only good can come from helping a person.'

'Well, aren't you holier than thou,' I said huffily.

'Besides, if he had died in our cell, his ghost would haunt us,' Yusuf added.

'Who cares?' I smirked. 'I'd just move to another cell.'

'And that would be just like you.'

At that moment we heard a sigh, a snort in fact, which caused us to look at the patient's face. His eyes were open.

'Shit' was the first word Oskar spoke, with difficulty and a long moan.

'Hi. What's your name?' I asked him.

He said nothing, didn't even look at me. But, I suppose if I reversed the scene and looked at it from his point of view, I would be all foggy and blurred.

'What's your name?' I asked again, this time more insistently.

'Maybe he's got amnesia?' Yusuf suggested when no answer was forthcoming. 'Let me give him a test,' he said and then lowered his face towards Oskar. 'OK, if I am the rising starlet Luna Maya, and you are my boyfriend, what is your name?' He paused, waiting for an answer. 'If you can remember, your name is Nicholas Saputra!'

The patient wrinkled his brow. 'Oskar. My name is Oskar,' he muttered hoarsely.

'Oskar, is it? Well then, it's not amnesia after all! But listen, Oskar, we found you stabbed in our room.'

'What's your telephone number?' I asked. Oskar gave me a sharp and steely-eyed look. 'We need to call your family,' I explained.

He shook his head. I guessed that 'no' is what he was saying.

'Who's going to pay your hospital bill?' Yusuf asked.

'Wallet ...' he mouthed, but I knew what he meant.

'You didn't have a wallet, only some loose bills. Some of it we had to use to buy mosquito repellent and to pay for the cost of bringing you here. We also had to give a down payment for the cost of you staying here. You still need money to pay for the hospital,' I told him.

'Card ...' he mumbled in pain.

'Card? What card?' I asked. 'The only thing on you was some crumpled bills in the bottom of your pocket.'

In the end, we did finally manage to get a telephone number out of Oskar, and with the change we had on us, went to find a pay phone.

The person who answered the phone was a woman, middle-aged, I judged from her voice. She said that she worked at the house and the owners were not at home. I ended up leaving a message for her to tell her employers that if they had a son by the name of Oskar, he was in the economy-class ward at the public hospital. To this, the woman merely said 'Oh, is that all?' I couldn't help but think that it would be no big deal to her if her employers' son were to die. Her lack of concern appalled me, but before I could say anything more she had already hung up.

When we returned to Oskar's cot, we found a nurse beside the bed. 'You need to take your medicine but not until after you've eaten this porridge,' she was saying to Oskar; but then, seeing us there, she turned her attention to us instead. 'You can help here by spoon-feeding him,' she said.

I pulled my head back. 'No way!' I protested. What was I? A nanny or something?

'I can do it,' Yusuf immediately offered. He took the bowl of porridge from the nurse, dipped the spoon into it, and placed the spoon in front of Oskar's tightly close lips.

'Go away,' Oskar growled.

'Yummy, yummy … Now open up wide!' Yusuf twirled the spoon in front of Oskar's lips, but he still refused to open his mouth. His eyes narrowed with annoyance.

Yusuf sounded like a trampy girl in a TV soap opera: 'Come on now, open wide. Oh, you'd think your lips were glued shut!'

Oskar stared at Yusuf. 'I don't want no banci feeding me.'

Yusuf blushed, his face almost purple. Whether because he was embarrassed or angry, he didn't look at the nurse who was still standing there. Instead, he stared at Oskar for a second, handed the bowl to me, and then turned and stamped out of the ward. Again I imagined Yusuf as a soap-opera tramp and saw the whole ward watching as he threw the bowl of porridge in Oskar's face.

Now I was in a dilemma but decided that instead of chasing after the melodramatic Yusuf, I would try to feed Oskar. I took the spoonful of porridge and put it in front of Oskar's lips. When he still refused to open his mouth, I pressed the spoon against his lips. Maybe fearing that I would stick the spoon up his nose if he didn't open his mouth, he finally opened his mouth a crack.

After feeding Oskar and making sure that he took his medicine, I left the ward to look for Yusuf and found him squatting in the parking lot of the hospital beside a flabby old woman who was selling freshly made *serabi* cakes from off a brazier.

Yusuf hadn't seen me approach, and I heard him say to the woman, 'Here, I can help you fan the embers.'

'What are you doing?' I asked, giving Yusuf a shock.

He looked at me in surprise but announced enthusiastically, 'I'm learning to make serabi! Don't you just love these little pancakes! And this woman's syrup with its palm sugar and coconut milk makes my mouth water!'

I saw a gleam in his eyes, one that I had seen before, which always made me wonder. I realized at that moment that Yusuf, unlike me, with my cynical view of the world, was possessed with an indefatigable optimism.

I squatted down beside him. 'Let's go home,' I said but before Yusuf could answer, a motorcycle roared past us. With its helicopter-like sound, I knew it was Iwenk's.

I watched as Iwenk parked the motorcycle not far from where we were squatting. I rose and started walking towards him. 'Wenk!' I called, leaving Yusuf to fight over the fan with the serabi vendor. I wanted to apologize to Iwenk. I felt bad for having yelled at him the last time I'd seen him. It was Sissy Guy and not he who was to blame for my bad behaviour.

His head jerked around and from the look on his face, he seemed to be in a panic.

'What are you doing here?' he asked.

'Visiting a friend,' I said rather than bothering to explain. 'You?'

'To see a doctor,' he answered then began to walk towards the emergency unit entrance.

'What about?' I asked.

Instead of answering, Iwenk began to walk more quickly.

I followed, curious to know why he was going to the emergency entrance when he looked perfectly fine. As he went into the ward, I lingered outside the glass door and watched him as he spoke to the duty nurse. I couldn't hear what was being said but, from Iwenk's gesticulations, he seemed to be arguing with her. Whatever the case, and probably because there were no other people waiting to be admitted, she pointed to a row of seats, and told him to wait there.

I went inside to see what this was about. 'What's wrong?' I asked Iwenk.

'I was poisoned,' he answered with a trembling voice.

At that moment, Iwenk's name was called and he got up to go to the doctor's room. I tagged along without asking, and Iwenk didn't object.

In the doctor's office, he sat down in the chair in front of the doctor's desk. I sat behind him to watch.

The doctor looked tired. 'How can I help you?' he asked. 'Long story, Doc, but I need my butt checked, now!'

Iwenk stood and began to open his belt.

Both the elderly doctor and I were surprised. 'Why?' the

doctor asked.

'I was raped,' Iwenk answered.

At that point the doctor looked at me and told me to wait outside, which I did.

When Iwenk came out of the doctor's room, he had in his hand a prescription slip and he looked even more distraught than before. I said nothing but followed him as he walked in the direction of the hospital pharmacy.

'What's going on?' I finally said. 'First you told me you had been poisoned then you told the doctor that you were raped.'

'I was raped but before that I was drugged – given some kind of sleeping pill. I was raped, Ricky! I was raped!' he cried while pulling his hair.

When Iwenk began to sniffle, I didn't know what to do. 'Who?' I asked quietly.

'I don't know! Probably Mulyo, that fucking fag!' he swore vehemently.

At once, I felt angry and relieved: angry at Mulyo and his banci friends but relieved because it hadn't happened to me. 'What did the doctor say?'

Iwenk shook his head. 'I'm afraid …' he mumbled softly.

'What? That you might be pregnant?' I asked with an attempt at humour.

He looked at me, his eyes red. 'I'm afraid of AIDS, you idiot!' he snapped.

That shut me up. My mind hadn't gone in that direction. Then, to my surprise, Iwenk stopped and turned in the opposite direction from where he'd been going.

'Aren't you going to fill your prescription?'

Iwenk didn't bother to answer and said nothing until we had returned to where his motorcycle was parked. There, he got on his cycle, crumpled the prescription slip in his hand and tossed it on the ground. 'Fuck it,' he said. 'Lots of people have gotten it, and they're still living.'

Iwenk started his motorcycle and zoomed out of the lot. And that's as far as his story went. Meanwhile, Yusuf was still squatting in front of the serabi vendor. Though it was almost the middle of the night, she was still attracting business.

'Want to go home?' I asked him.

'At this time of night, there's no more public transport,' Yusuf answered. 'Was that guy a friend of yours?'

'Yes,' I replied but offered no further explanation.

We decided to stay the night at the hospital and return to the pesantren as soon as buses started rolling again. At first we tried to sleep on Oskar's bed but it was hardly large enough for one person, much less three. We considered sleeping on the floor, but we hadn't brought a mat or anything to sleep on. Finally, we sprawled on a couple of benches in the hall outside the ward. Despite the discomfort, we finally fell asleep. Once or twice during the night, I was awakened by the rattling of a gurney when a new patient was brought in, but I kept my eyes closed. Finally, when I did wake up around dawn, my entire body ached. What surprised me was not the swelling of my limbs, but that no one had yet come to look for Oskar.

A Wedding

Not long after sunrise, we decided to leave. We had to go to school and couldn't wait any longer for Oskar's family to appear. Before leaving the hospital, I asked Oskar for the telephone number of his school so that I could contact the principal, but he wouldn't give it to me. In fact, he rudely told us to leave.

The week passed, and on the following Saturday evening I packed my dirty clothes, intending to have them washed at home. My overalls were especially filthy, little different from one of the grease-stained rags I used to wipe my shop equipment. When I arrived at the house, I was surprised to find no one there. The doors and windows were locked, so I had to wait outside until 10 pm when, finally, a whole troop of people appeared in a van – my parents, my sister, an aunt and other relatives. All of them were neatly dressed. I was famished and out of sorts for having to wait outside so long.

The first person to exit the van was my sister, Yati, who squinted when she saw me out front, my features illuminated by only the fifteen-watt bulb overhead.

'Where have you been?' I asked her.

'We were delivering Rohim's bridal gift,' she explained.

'Where were you?' she asked in an accusatory tone. 'What? Did you forget?'

I said nothing. I just scraped the dirt with my big toe.

Yati's voice rose as she spoke: 'You forgot, didn't you!?

Mother told you long ago that we were going to Erni's parents house this weekend! And where were you last weekend?'

I still said nothing. Obviously, she didn't know that I'd almost been sold as a sex slave the weekend before, and I wasn't going to tell her. How was I supposed to remember about this stupid gift-giving ceremony with Erni's parents? Maybe Rohim's upcoming wedding had slipped my mind.

'We waited for you for more than an hour,' Yati huffed. 'No need for you to be irritated!'

My aunt began to unload large tiffins and trays whose contents had apparently been given to Erni's family and stacked them outside the house. The older women helped, as they nibbled what leftovers remained. My father opened the door to the house, and my mother began arranging food on the dining table and telling people to find a place to sit. The atmosphere was lively and I got the feeling no one cared or even noticed my presence except for my sister.

When Yati went inside, I followed, and suddenly my feeling of hunger instantly vanished as I thought of something: my bedroom. I strode to the room and, just as I had suspected, it was no longer 'my' room. It had been transformed into a bridal chamber. The room was freshly painted; all the furniture looked new, and there was even a canopy over the bed. The only thing missing was a scattering of rose petals on the bedspread.

'Don't put your dirty things on the bed,' Yati called to me from outside. 'And don't lie down! We just finished decorating the place!'

I turned and screamed at her. 'Where's my stuff?'

'We put your things in the hook.'

The hook? That's what we called the storeroom, forming as it did an extension off the dining and kitchen area, like the lower part of an L. My ramshackle clothes cupboard with its faded mirror and the used clothes that were still inside it, comic books I'd borrowed from friends, an old stool and the rickety desk on which I did my homework: All these were my things and they were now in the hook, along with the sacks of rice, a broken bicycle, my mother's brooms and dustpans, my father's machete and tools, and the plastic pails that we used to collect rainwater.

What a wonderful family I have, I thought, as I spat on the floor and made my way to the hook. The storeroom's walls were made of woven bamboo, and the gloomy interior was illuminated by a dim light bulb, which was covered with spider webs.

Peering inside the hook, my clothes cupboard looked miserable and forlorn, like a terminal patient. Even more so when I opened its doors, at which point they seemed to breathe their last. My old clothes and the used books that were piled there were like festering entrails. I could only take a deep breath and sigh. The fact was, I owned nothing of any importance, a realization that made my life seem to be unimportant too.

That night I slept on a chair in the front room in front of the television. I don't know where the others slept.

The next morning I pretended to be asleep even as the rest of the family prepared for the upcoming wedding ceremony. I had no intention of escorting my brother to his wedding ceremony at the mosque near the home of his fiancée.

When Yati tried to wake me, I put on a show of not wanting to be disturbed, like the spoilt younger brother I was. My mother then tried to wake me but finally gave up when I covered my face with a pillow. In the end, not wanting the wedding to be delayed on my account, the rest of the family finally left without me.

As soon as they'd gone, I looked around to make sure that

there was no one else in the house and jumped from my chair and ran to the bathroom, where I pissed and splashed water on my face. On top of the dining table in the kitchen there was still an assortment of foods and though my stomach was screaming for me to stop and eat, I gave the table a sneer and turned away.

I left the house, taking with me the same bag of dirty clothes I had brought home the day before. I knew I was acting impulsively. Whether justified or not, I felt hurt and abandoned, loved and cared for by no one at all. I wanted nothing to do with my family ever again.

By the time I arrived at the pesantren I felt like a fool. Now I was both hungry *and* broke! I was tempted to go back home because there was sure to be lots of food left over from the wedding, but I was too proud. Borrowing money from my fellow boarders didn't seem likely. I'd be embarrassed, plus they'd think I was using them – getting close to them only because I needed something. I was beginning to feel completely hopeless.

I left the pesantren with an empty, growling stomach. I didn't bother participating in the recitations after *zuhur*, the noon prayers. With my sense of self-esteem at its lowest point ever, I walked in the direction of the place this story began: Byuti Salon. My stomach ached from hunger but possibly from fear or trepidation as well. My cheap rubber sandals felt loose and wobbly, maybe from aging in the sun or because my feet had shrunk because I hadn't eaten since the day before. A melodramatic cliché echoed in my brain – 'For a spoonful of rice, I will sell myself' – but when arriving at the salon (the only salon I knew at the time), my heart began to lighten.

'Hi, Paris? What are you up to?' I asked with a smile as I entered the salon.

'I reserve that question for you,' he said in reply.

'Well, I came here looking for you,' I told him straight out.

'Surprise, surprise! But why? Do I owe you something?'

Paris put down the magazine he was reading. He was having a cream bath and the hairdresser was in the middle of slathering an avocado-scented solution on his scalp.

I began hesitantly: 'No, I just wanted to talk about something.' My brain was turning fast. Maybe Paris would take me out and treat me to a meal. He wouldn't object to that, would he? Or maybe I could borrow some money from him. I was sure he had money to spare.

'Is it important?' he asked.

'Yes,' I said almost under my breath.

'Sure, but give me some time, OK? I had lowlights put in earlier, and now I need to have my hair conditioned. Beauty takes time, you know.'

About an hour later, while watching Paris have his hair dried, I struck up a conversation with one of the banci hairdressers who happened to have no customers at the time. Because I couldn't remember his name, I stared at him until he finally stared back at me.

'Where's Iwenk?' I asked, when he finally caught my eye. 'Iwenk? *Helga ninoe B hangen hineer.*'

While I was pleased the hairdresser had answered my question – I would have been embarrassed if he hadn't – I had no idea what he had just said.

'He doesn't hang out here anymore,' Paris translated while looking at my reflection in the mirror.

'How come?' I asked him. Paris shrugged his shoulders.

'*Methinks, Helga B haven ina ninew skweez,*' the hairdresser answered.

I stopped asking questions and turned my attention to Paris

who was combing his hair, which was now a brownish colour.

Paris turned his head toward me and blinked. 'Yuli is saying that Iwenk doesn't hang out here anymore. She thinks he's found a new squeeze. But, more important, what do you think of me as a brunette?'

I gave him a thumbs-up and asked straight away, 'Want to go somewhere?'

Paris gave me a look of surprise – and rightfully so, since I had never been the one to initiate anything.

Shortly thereafter, we left the salon and, without being asked or told to, I got in his car.

'Where do you want to go?' he asked.

'Doesn't matter as long as there's food,' I said boldly, while patting my stomach and looking at him.

'But where?' he asked again.

'Shit, I don't care. A roadside stall will do.'

Paris drove to Karawaci Supermall, where we went directly to the food court. I'd already guessed that never in a million years would Paris deign to eat at a roadside stall. He chose to eat at Wendy's again and told me to order for us. When I asked what to order, he said it was up to me. So I ordered a Fried Chicken Party Pack with five pieces of chicken, a large serving of chilli-cheese French fries, and a large cola to wash the food down. Seeing what I had ordered, Paris shook his head and told me to order a low-fat strawberry-flavour frozen yoghurt for him. As I stuffed my face, Paris slowly nibbled on spoons of frozen yoghurt while nonchalantly playing with his newly coloured brown hair.

After I was full, I finally began to speak.

'Your hair looks nice,' I said as an opener.

'I think so too!' Paris exclaimed. 'Like Rachel Weisz in *The Mummy*.'

'Yeah.' I nodded in agreement, even though I didn't know who or what he was talking about. Searching for something to say, I asked, 'By the way, what's your old man do for a living?'

'Why are you asking about him? I don't want to answer,' he said.

'Your mother?'

'Again, no comment.'

Rather than ask yet another wrong question and annoy him further, I thought it might be better to come straight to the point – that I needed to borrow some money. But then, when I was about to open my mouth, a question passed through my mind: How would I pay him back? Would I be forced to sell myself to a banci hairdresser as Iwenk had done? Would I be forced to go to Mulyo and swallow my pride and anger? Damn! I knew I couldn't do it. So, instead of asking Paris if I could borrow money, and without really thinking of what the fulfilment of my request might entail, I stuttered this question instead: 'Hmm, Paris, would you ... What would you think of keeping me?'

Paris stared at me, eyes opened wide. 'What do you mean?'

'Listen, I'm desperate, and got to do something,' I confessed. 'So I was thinking it would be better to be kept by you than by a banci.'

'Are you comparing me to a banci?' Now Paris was mad.

'That's not what I meant,' I quickly said, while wringing my hands. I didn't want him to be angry.

'Well then, what did you mean?' he asked.

I paused before answering. 'I need money,' I said quietly and felt embarrassed and ashamed to say it. I almost couldn't look Paris in the eye, but I noticed a wry look on his face.

'What for?' Paris was still surprised.

'For food, to live,' I said. I grew increasingly embarrassed as

I explained, 'I had a little problem at home, and I don't think my parents will give me an allowance anymore.'

'OK,' he said.

'OK?' I asked.

'Sure, why not?' he answered lightly, no problem at all.

I didn't know what was on his mind or why he had agreed so quickly to my request after having snapped at me initially. I was both pleased and afraid: pleased to have found a source of much needed income but afraid because I didn't know what would be expected of me in return.

'We can start today,' Paris said as if to himself.

After finishing the last piece of chicken and the final remaining French fry, I was stuffed. But now that I had gotten my energy back, I felt refreshed and optimistic. Unintentionally, I burped loudly.

'Have you had enough to eat?' Paris asked me as his eyes surveyed the destruction on my tray.

I smiled and nodded.

'Well, wipe your mouth; you look a mess,' Paris commented while rising from his chair.

After I'd wiped my lips with a napkin, Paris said that it was time to go and proceeded to walk to the parking garage in the basement of the mall. I followed obediently. Later, I saw this moment as the beginning of my 'marriage' to Paris. In the car, neither of us spoke. I prepared myself to be ready if he put his hand on my thigh or something like that, but he didn't do anything. He acted normal. In fact, he even whistled.

'Now, where would you like to go?' I asked, in a super-friendly and respectful tone of voice.

Paris turned and looked me in the eye, staring at me for a time, assessing, I suppose, whether or not I was good enough to be his kept boy. He then returned his eyes to the road, his hands firmly on the wheel.

'I need to go somewhere,' he said, 'but I'll take you home first.'

That was it? I was curious to know. 'And then?'

'And then what?'

'And then what do you want me to do?'

He released a sigh and said, 'There's no rush.'

When we arrived at the lane leading to my pesantren it was almost magrib. Before I got out of the car, Paris took my hand in his, causing my heart to skip a beat.

'This is for you,' he said while slipping two hundred thousand rupiah into my hand. 'Enough for a week, I hope ...'

Stone faced for a few seconds, I then took the money. I was now a kept boy and there was no need to be embarrassed.

Work

When I returned to the pesantren that evening, Yusuf was ironing his clothes in our cell. He frowned when he saw me standing outside, watching him from the open walkway below. Recently, the cost of electricity at the pesantren had gone up, and many of the boarders were late in paying their share. Just a week before, the kiai had announced that henceforth the use of certain kinds of electrical equipment was banned. Irons and fans, for instance, suddenly became forbidden items.

'Don't say anything, OK?' he told me while continuing to iron.

I said nothing to this as I stepped up and into our cell. Yusuf could do all the ironing he wanted, I didn't care. I lay down on my mat, contentedly full from my meal.

'Where were you?' he asked.

'Karawaci Super Mall. I had dinner there,' I answered while closing my eyes.

'Oh, since when did you start going to malls? Are you suddenly rich or something?'

'No, Paris treated me.'

Yusuf lifted the iron. 'Paris? The guy who came here with the car?'

'One and the same,' I said.

'What, are you his boyfriend or something?' he asked, more like an accusation.

'Wouldn't you like to know?' I asked with a smirk, knowing this would irritate him further.

Yusuf now looked more surprised. 'You're using him, aren't you? Are you taking his money too?'

'If I am, would that be a sin?' I asked rhetorically.

Yusuf said nothing more and continued to iron his clothes.

He pressed down so hard on the iron that I thought he might scorch his shirt. Obviously, he was thinking about something, but I really needed to close my eyes. After that, I heard nothing and felt nothing until Yusuf nudged me with his foot at the time of the call to prayer.

In our cell after isya prayers, I stared at Yusuf as he held the yellow book that he was studying. Ever since our visit to the hospital the week before, Yusuf had been acting strangely, and I couldn't figure the reason why. His moods changed quickly: at times he was high-strung, at other times oblivious. Sometimes he'd be angry, other times light-hearted. Whatever the reason, he made it clear to me that he did not want to go back to the hospital again. I guessed the reason for this was because Oskar had called him a banci. Perhaps influenced by him, I didn't return to the hospital either and began to put the entire incident with Oskar out of my mind. Now my thoughts were focused on myself: my room, my stomach and my new 'profession.'

The next day, with two hundred thousand rupiah in my wallet, I felt that a new life had opened for me. I never felt so free. Sitting in the cell that night after isya prayers, I decided to go get something to eat and invited Yusuf to come along. I wanted to keep him from being annoyed with me all the time.

'Want some fried rice?' I asked him. 'My treat!'

Yusuf, who was idly folding his prayer mat and sarong,

immediately livened up. I was already changing from sarong into jeans.

'You better not be kidding me,' he warned.

When we were both dressed and ready to go, we slipped on our rubber sandals outside the doorway to the cell and made our way down the footpath towards the main road.

'But let's eat out,' Yusuf suggested, 'and not bring the food home. You know how that would go.'

I did know how *that* would go and couldn't but agree. At the pesantren, the boarders were ever ready to share their troubles but rarely their food.

After a walk past the food stalls that lined the main road, at one near the market we decided that the aroma emanating from it – a mixture of chicken and eel in peanut sauce – was far more tempting than the smell of fried rice. Food like that was a luxury for us. We rarely ate either fish or meat and when we did, it was usually a small portion with a scant amount of *sambal*. At the most, every other day or so we might get a chicken egg, but even that we usually had to split.

'I could get used to eating like this,' Yusuf commented as he nibbled on the cartilage of the fried chicken breast he'd just eaten.

'You could get yourself work like me,' I said jokingly.

'I'm not even a senior. What could I do?'

Apparently, Yusuf had taken my question seriously. 'You could find something to do,' I advised, as if I had a sure and constant income.

Out of the corner of my eye, I noticed a familiar face come into the food stall. He sat down on the bench next to Yusuf and, without looking at the two of us, called out for the vendor.

'Wenk ...?' I said.

He turned to see who had spoken to him. I hadn't seen him

since the night at the hospital, and now, remembering the incident, I almost wanted to laugh. 'Well, are you pregnant?' I wanted to ask but bit my tongue instead.

He gave me a big smile, apparently in good mood. 'What a coincidence! I might have some business for you.'

'Meet Yusuf,' I said to him, and the two of them shook hands. 'Wow, soft hands,' Iwenk remarked.

Yusuf immediately withdrew his hand like an eel retreating quickly into its hole.

'What kind of business?' I asked to change the focus of attention, afraid that he might call Yusuf a banci.

'Business, good business,' he said, in an annoyingly boastful tone. But I was grateful his mind was no longer on Yusuf's smooth hands.

'Not with those banci at the salon, is it?' I asked, which caused Yusuf to frown.

'Nah, I'm not doing that kind of work anymore. Changed professions,' Iwenk said. He then ordered eel and an iced orange drink from the vendor, who was waiting patiently at the table.

'Well, OK, but whatever it is, I'm not interested,' I told him. As Paris was now keeping me, it was my job to pay attention to him. I decided to avoid further discussion of the matter with Iwenk.

I nudged Yusuf and stood up to go. 'Let's go. I need to stop at the store to buy a new toothbrush.'

But now it was Yusuf who wanted to stay. 'What kind of business?' he asked Iwenk, ignoring me, which caused me to nudge him again.

'The business I have is this ...' Iwenk started to explain.

I nudged Yusuf a third time but he slapped my hand away. 'Go on,' he told me. 'I'll catch up with you.'

Ungrateful wretch, I thought. Here I had treated him to a meal and now he was glaring at me. I left him there at the *warung*. He could find out for himself what doing business with Iwenk was like.

Meeting

By mid-November, my assignments at school had become increasingly difficult, and because the teacher didn't like to have to repeat instructions, he combined three classes into one. With so many students in the combined class, we had to take turns and do our work in shifts. On the day in question, I was practicing lathing a small sheet of iron and some kind of metal used specifically for making grooves, screw threads and drilling. I was exhausted; my hands were sore, my shoulders hurt and my body was wet with sweat. Meanwhile, my 'boyfriend' Paris, who declined to participate in the training exercise, was sitting by himself in the corner of the room. Even when the teacher yelled at him, he refused to join in.

After shop class that morning, around 10 am, I went to the changing room to change from my overalls into my street clothes. Even though Paris hadn't done anything in shop that morning, he came into the changing room too and sat down on a bench near my locker, apparently waiting for me. When I took off my overalls, he averted his eyes as I wiped the sweat from my body with a towel.

'Why didn't you do any work in shop today?' I asked him.

'Because it's boring, that's why. Besides, it ruins my nails,' he answered coyly with his legs tightly crossed.

'The teacher should have you practice lathing barrettes. Maybe that would get you interested,' I teased.

A light smile crossed his lips. 'Let's go somewhere,' he said invitingly as he played with his mobile.

Not looking at him, I buttoned my shirt and began to put on my grey school trousers. 'Where to?' I asked.

'I don't care. Anywhere!' he said. 'I'm feeling claustrophobic here.'

I wasn't especially keen on skipping the rest of my classes that day, but now that Paris was keeping me I was also reluctant to turn him down.

Because Paris's car was the only four-wheel vehicle in the entire parking lot, it was difficult to sneak out of school without being noticed.

He drove extremely slowly towards the exit. 'We'll be back before next class,' Paris said to the teacher on guard, which was a lie, of course. We were going to the mall to eat and would not be coming back.

Whenever I think of those times it makes me happy. Every time I went out with Paris, there was always a good meal in store. That day was the first time I tried pizza. While I devoured an enormous portion, Paris nibbled on a piece of garlic bread.

Because of a city ordinance forbidding students to frequent malls during school hours, with Paris and I dressed in our grey and white school uniforms, it was hard not to stand out from the crowd. For that reason, we sat in the farthest corner of Pizza Hut so as to not attract questioning stares. Paris opened his bag and removed a laptop. Not particularly interested in what he was doing, I concentrated on my food instead.

For some time he focused his attention on the screen, even as his fingers tapped the keys.

'Do you have a Facebook account?' he asked.

'No.'

Paris pulled his lips back. 'But you have chatted before, haven't you?'

'I don't know how to use the internet,' I explained.

To this, he pursed his lips and shook his head. 'What are you, a cave man? You don't know this, don't know that … Well, anyway, hurry up and finish your meal so that you can come shopping with me.'

I did as Paris requested, gobbling the rest of my meal, then got up and followed him to a clothing store. There he told me that I could pick out a T-shirt for myself, but just when I started to look at a rack of them, he pulled me to another part of the store.

'This is the women's section,' I said.

'I know, I need to pick out something for a cousin of mine,' he explained quickly.

After that, and for an hour at least, we went here and there in the store, looking at everything from mini-skirts to high heels. My own heels were beginning to hurt from standing on my feet for so long, but Paris seemed content and not the least bit tired. Time and again he asked me for my opinion – 'Do you like this? What about this one? How about that?' – to which my only response was 'Fine' or 'OK'. I hadn't developed a taste in clothing. How was I supposed to know about women's clothes?

Young female shoppers in the store stared at Paris as he picked out one thing or another. Sometimes he tried to avoid their looks; other times he asked their opinion, always telling them that the clothes were gifts. I was extremely pleased when Paris finally heaved a sigh and said that he was satisfied. He then told me to choose a shirt for myself.

On our way to the cash register, I saw a black t-shirt I liked and picked it up but then noticed the price tag: Rp. 180,000! I was about to put it back, but Paris took it from me and put it in his shopping basket.

'Stuff that poor-boy act,' he remarked. He paid for everything with a credit card.

Before we left the mall, Paris stopped at a wholesale cosmetics store, where he bought several bags of cosmetic supplies, which he asked me to carry for him.

On the way home, Paris told me that he worked freelance as a supplier of cosmetics and chemical solutions for salons. He'd buy the stuff wholesale and then resell them to salons on a credit basis. Profits weren't bad, he told me. Secretly, I was both astonished and envious of his business acumen. Who would have guessed that he was a wheeler-dealer? It was Paris who introduced me to money and made me see that it could be a source of freedom.

When we were on our way to the pesantren that evening, Paris asked if he could stop by; he said he missed the musty smell of my cell. This time, I ordered him to park on the main road at a fair distance from the lodge so as not to attract attention.

At my cell, I found Yusuf clipping his nails. He looked surprised to see Paris behind me.

'Aren't you going to recitation?' I asked him. I could hear the other residents reciting *Ba'da* Ashar.

'Not interested,' he said indolently.

I introduced Paris to Yusuf but immediately sensed a chill in the air. At first I'd thought that Paris and Yusuf would hit it off, but now I sensed that for Yusuf, Paris was somebody high-class with the airs of a wealthy woman – which only served to emphasize Yusuf's own caste and class.

I didn't know what to do or say; we were suddenly like three people who had nothing in common with one another. But then Paris extracted his laptop from his carry bag and this immediately attracted Yusuf's attention. He looked at it admiringly, not unlike when he saw another boarder in an expensive sarong.

'Do you know how to use the internet?' Yusuf asked Paris softly, suddenly shedding his poor-but-honourable attitude.

'Yes, I do,' Paris replied in his rich yet kind-hearted and also elegant voice. 'As long as you have a dongle modem, you can use the internet anywhere,' he explained, taking a foreign-looking object from his bag.

Thinking it best to give the two some time on their own, I grabbed a towel. 'I'm going to take a bath,' I announced but neither gave me notice or replied. Yusuf, who had been sitting in the corner of our cell on his mattress, moved next to Paris who was seated on the floor, computer on his lap, near the door to our cell with his legs stretched out.

I took my time in the shower and loitered outside as well for close to thirty minutes and, when coming back into the cell, found the two of them huddled together in the corner of the room.

Yusuf nearly jumped when seeing me enter.

'You're looking at porn, aren't you?' I guessed, as I dried my hair with my towel.

'No, I'm not,' he said while writing something down on a piece of paper.

Maybe because he was a student at Public Junior High No. 4, one of the best schools in the district, Yusuf was a fast learner. The students there had a reputation for being super-competitive. In his school, there was a lot of pressure to study hard to keep up with one's classmates and to be up to date on styles and trends.

A little while later, Paris went home, leaving Yusuf looking more restless than usual. He always seemed to get that way when there was something he wanted.

'I'm on Facebook now!' Yusuf whispered excitedly, as we

gathered with the other residents for evening magrib prayers. 'Paris took photos of me on his mobile and uploaded them to my Facebook account!'

'Hmmm ...' What could I say?

'And I learned MIRC!'

'What's that?' I asked.

'An internet relay chat program!'

'And what's a relay chat program?' I asked again.

'It's great is what it is.'

I should have known that something would happen, that a change would take place when Paris and Yusuf met. Paris offered Yusuf a glimpse of a world that previously he could only have fantasized about. Unfortunately, Yusuf, unlike Paris, lacked the wherewithal to acquire almost everything he wanted. But if there was something Yusuf did have, in spades, it was determination.

The Internet

With the hundred thousand rupiah I had left, I could eat well every day for the rest of the week. I still shared cooking chores with the other residents, but after recitation at night I would go out to find something to eat again. Yusuf always tagged along, though he didn't always eat. He was just bored staying in the cell all the time, he said. So it was that on Thursday night of the same week that Paris had come to the pesantren, Yusuf asked if he could borrow five thousand rupiah. When I asked what for, he told me he wanted to try using the internet.

'I want to try chatting,' he told me on the way to a 24-hour internet café. 'Paris taught me how.'

At the internet café, he told the attendant that he wanted to use a computer for two hours, and asked me to give him five thousand. After the attendant gave him a login code, Yusuf looked for an empty booth and chose one at the very back of the room, where no one could see him. He sat there and went to work, typing this and that and clicking on icons whose meanings I did not know. His fingers moved quickly as he opened the MIRC application and typed 'GIM' in a column there.

'That stands for Great Instant Messenger,' Yusuf told me, the smart ass.

A list of code names appeared on the monitor: 'M_19_lkng,' 'bot_now,' 'daddy4boyz,' 'ml_myplace_jkt,' and many more. I could see the names, but I still didn't know how chatting was done.

Yusuf clicked one of the names and began to type using only his two index fingers.

'So this is chatting?' I asked, a light bulb above my head. 'Who with?'

'Don't know,' he answered with a tremulous tone of voice.

'Stats?' asked daddy4boys.

'?' Yusuf typed.

'Age, height, weight,' came the reply.

'16-165-55,' Yusuf then typed.

I had no idea that when you were chatting, you first had to give your age and weight.

'Pic?' the next question appeared.

'C me on FB,' Yusuf typed, 'www.facebook.com/yusufcute.' His chat partner then sent a dot.com address, and Yusuf retyped the address in his Facebook page. Thereafter, the image of a middle-aged man appeared.

'He's old!' was my initial reaction, which I stated with a frown.

'So what? I'm just making friends,' Yusuf said.

To my surprise Yusuf avidly continued his exchange of messages with daddy4boyz. After a time, I began to get bored and patted his shoulder. 'Try a site with pictures. I'm tired of seeing words.'

'Well, stop looking then,' he snapped at me.

Fifteen minutes or so passed, and he still wasn't satisfied. If anything, he was becoming more enthusiastic. He clicked on other names, and when they responded, he began to chat with them as well. In his exchange of pictures via Facebook, I saw only pictures of older men. What's with that, I wondered. But by this point I was going stir-crazy and wanted to leave. When I told him that I was going home, he said nothing, didn't even seem to hear me. In fact, just at that point, he started to giggle.

The next morning, as I watched Yusuf say his prayers, I saw that he was caught in a strange dualism. He seemed both depressed and happy at the same time. A person oppressed but one who still maintained high hopes. I caught sight of Ali looking at him as well and guessed that he, too, was thinking something wasn't quite right with his brother, but I wasn't about to ask. I suspected that Yusuf's dualism had been sparked by the internet. On my way to school, I passed by a *nasi uduk* stall where I saw Paris surrounded by other male students. As always, his shirt was the whitest and the best pressed; his pants were neatly ironed as well, with crisp pleats, and he smelled of cologne. When I approached, I acted as if there was nothing special between us.

Remembering that now, I also remember feeling somewhat confused and powerless, always wondering when the time would come that Paris demanded that I pay my dues. Although I didn't want anything to happen, I expected that it might. Maybe it would begin with a kiss – which, for me, would be my first kiss with a man. The thought was unsettling. Hell, I'd never even kissed a woman before. But that was our unwritten deal, and it was not based on love or mutual attraction.

When the school bell rang, I asked him to walk with me, apart from the other students.

'What did you teach Yusuf?' I asked him.

'What do you mean?' he asked with surprise.

'I mean, with the internet. He's acting strange. You must have showed him something,' I said accusingly.

'I only showed him how to chat and pointed out some sites for him, that's all,' he replied dismissively.

'You shouldn't teach him such stuff. All that chatting with

guys is strange.'

'I simply broadened his perspective,' Paris said firmly. 'And what's wrong with chatting with other guys?'

I seemed to be speaking on behalf of Ali: 'He might turn queer.'

Paris stared at me and said softly, 'Ricky dearest, Yusuf *is* queer. I didn't have to teach him that.'

I stared at Paris, not quite grasping the truth of what he was saying but he offered no further explanation.

'Enough, already. Time for class,' he said with finality, leaving me. 'Bye, honey.'

Throughout the school day, I mulled over what Paris had said of Yusuf. Had he always been gay? I didn't know, and it wasn't my business, but after that conversation, school lost all interest for me. I felt completely bored with the place. Half the class spent their time talking about girls; the other half chuckled as they pored over photocopied porn magazines.

After returning to the pesantren from school that day, I lay down in my cell and soon fell asleep, not waking until after the collective ashar prayers. I had missed recitation lessons.

At magrib I was still in slumber when I felt someone trying to wake me. It was Ali, who'd entered the cell without a bang or boo.

'Where's Yusuf?' he asked.

My soul was still hovering somewhere outside my body. 'Isn't he home?' I asked. Usually Yusuf came home from school not long after I did.

Ali shook his head.

'I don't know,' I answered honestly. Ali was Yusuf's brother; I was just his cellmate. He should know better than I his brother's habits. He left.

After the alternating Quranic reading that followed magrib prayers, I returned to my cell to continue my rest, leaving the other boarders in conversation at the majelis. When the final call to prayer for the day came over the loudspeaker, I made ready to join the other boarders in prayer, but then I heard a familiar sound, that of an old motorcycle. The sound died away, replaced by the slapping of swiftly moving feet. The door to my cell opened, and Yusuf entered. He quickly closed the door behind him.

'Did Ali come looking for me?' he asked immediately, before I had the chance to tell him that his brother had indeed been looking for him. I just nodded in reply.

'What did you tell him?' he pressed.

'That I didn't know where you were.'

'Good,' he said while lying down.

'Where were you?' I asked.

'Looking for work,' he answered.

'With Iwenk?'

He nodded.

'Did he sell you to Mulyo?'

Yusuf turned toward me. 'What do you mean?'

'Did he pawn you to that sissy-guy?' I asked with a grimace. 'No!'

Yusuf seemed completely surprised, as if my question were strange. Now it was my turn to be surprised. 'Then what kind of business were you doing with Iwenk?'

'I can't tell you just yet,' he said. 'Besides, the less you know, the better. Happy are those who know few secrets,' he said with the air of a religious teacher. 'I'm tired and want to rest, so I'm skipping recitation. If Ali asks, tell him I'm not feeling well.'

'What am I, your servant?' I asked before leaving the cell to go to the majelis.

A Destined Meeting

When the next Saturday came around, a week after my brother's wedding, I intentionally forgot to go home. To hell with home; my family didn't care about me anyway. Instead, I got ready to go out with my 'boss'. I imagined we'd go to the mall and buy women's things, but the important thing for me was good food and the next instalment of pocket money.

Around five that evening I left the pesantren dressed in slacks and my new T-shirt. When Ali saw me and asked where I was going, I just told him that I had 'roll call', the term we used for a fixed date with one's special friend. He made no reply.

I waited at the end of the lane where Paris usually dropped me off. It was our first Saturday night together since we entered into our new agreement. Soon after, his car appeared.

'It's Saturday night. Shouldn't you be with your girlfriend?' I asked him jokingly. Guys like Paris were popular with girls. He was well-groomed, smelled of expensive cologne, and he had money besides. Despite the fact that he was rather feminine, I guessed that many girls would like him just as he is.

'But you're my boyfriend, Ricky,' he said in jest.

'What about your other friends?' I asked.

'Ricky, you are my only friend,' he told me.

That was a surprise. I would have thought he had plenty of friends.

'It's true,' he affirmed. 'I don't have friends.'

'What about the banci at the salon?'

He looked at me. 'They are not my friends. Just because I go to the salon often, that doesn't mean they're my friends.' He paused, then added, 'It's hard for me to trust other people.'

I waited for a further explanation, but he offered none. I thought that perhaps he didn't consider the cross-dressers at the salon to be his friends because he was a different class of person. Paris turned the conversation into a comedy. 'Do you think there are banci in Saudi Arabia?' he posed. 'What would they wear there? Can you imagine? With them all dressed in full veil, you couldn't tell the guys from the girls!' Laughing, he then began to teach me some banci vocabulary, words for 'what', 'where', 'when' and 'why', which in the banci language would be *'winut'*, *'winair'*, *'winen'* and *'winie'*. Salonese is a phonetic language, he explained. Thus, the words would be spelled 'wut', 'wair', 'wen' and 'wie'. Then you transformed them be inserting an 'in' after the first consonant.

Our time together that night was not like usual. He didn't invite me to go shopping or look at wigs. Instead, he took me to see a film at a movie theatre in the new Summarecon Mall in Serpong, which had just opened a few months before. This was only the second time in my life I had been to a movie theatre. The first time had been with my sister Yati and a guy who was hitting on her at the time. We had gone to see *The Conjurer*, a horror film.

Paris took me to see an American love comedy called *P.S. I Love You*, about a guy who writes letters for his wife to read after he's dead. Because I couldn't understand the English, I had to spend most of my time reading the subtitles in order to keep up with the storyline. Sometimes when I found myself unable to understand the gist of a conversation, Paris would be laughing.

After the film, Paris asked if I wanted to go somewhere else or if I wanted to go back to the pesantren. I saw on the dashboard of the car, that it was only 9 pm, so I decided to let Paris make the decision.

'I'll go wherever you want,' I said in a faithful tone of voice. We left the parking lot of the mall and were soon on the main street of Serpong, heading back towards our home city of Tangerang. I didn't know where we were headed, but we talked about this and that, nothing of particular importance. He also gave me additional instruction in Salonese: how, for instance 'B' stands in for all 'to be' verbs and with the use of an 'en' suffix on a verb, all tenses are covered. What an amazing and funny language, I thought.

When the car finally came to a stop, I found myself in a familiar location.

'What are we doing here?' I asked.

'I need to take care of something,' he said without explaining further. 'Do you want to come or wait in the car?'

'I'll come with you,' I replied.

On Saturday nights apparently, the Tangerang Public Hospital was much busier than on other days; the place was almost always jammed with visitors. Ignoring the bustle, I followed Paris, not asking where he was going. Finally, at the in-patient ward, the quietest section of the hospital, Paris found the duty nurse he had been looking for. The nurse spoke briefly with Paris and asked him to sign some forms. After that we were taken to the third floor of the hospital, the VVIP section, where rooms had air-conditioning and were equipped with mini-refrigerators and other amenities.

'The patient has been ready since evening,' the nurse said with slight chastisement in her voice.

'There's no one at home, and I've been busy. I only found time just now,' Paris lied easily.

'Are there any outstanding expenses?' Paris asked.

'No. Just the cost of a check-up, when he comes back in.'

We went into the room where I saw the figure of a male sitting on the edge of the bed and watching television, his body turned away from us. When he turned, I saw a look of irritation on his face. Maybe he was irritated from having to wait. Or maybe, I thought, it might be the sight of me.

Paris smiled and went to him. 'Let's take you home, but first let me introduce you to a friend,' he said looking from the man on the bed to me.

'We already know each other,' both Oskar and I answered at the same time.

Not surprisingly, Paris was confused.

'Long story!' I said when Paris looked at me in confusion. 'I'll tell you on the way.'

I carried Oskar's bag of belongings while Paris pushed Oskar who lounged in his wheelchair. Recalling my first meeting with Oskar as we made our way through the hospital's halls and waiting rooms brought back to me vivid memories of the night Yusuf and I spent there.

In the car, Oskar sat in the back, and none of us spoke a word during the ride from the hospital to my pesantren. At the end of the lane, I got out and said a brief goodbye to Paris and Oskar. I had been prepared to tell Paris the story of how I had met Oskar, but since he didn't ask me, I thought he might want to hear the story from Oskar himself. I guessed that Paris felt closer to Oskar than to me.

While I was walking to my cell at the lodge, I mulled over this strangely coincidental meeting. I never thought I'd see Oskar again. Never in my mind had it occurred to me that there might be some connection between Oskar and Paris. By this time, I had almost put Oskar out of my mind. Was Paris keeping him too, I wondered?

The world is not large after all. Often, when you meet someone, it turns out that you have mutual friends. There are a limited number of degrees of separation between one person and another. Now I realize that this kind of relationship is in every way linked to matters of fate and soul mates. We might not know who we're going to meet in this world, but it's all been destined, and there is a meaning to everything.

Weed

By 11 pm that same Saturday night, when I fell asleep, Yusuf had still not returned to the pesantren. When the call to prayer at dawn sounded from the majelis I decided to pretend to not be in my cell and didn't turn on the light. What a wonderful feeling it was to skip collective prayers sometimes or not even pray at all. But then, with a creak, the door to the cell opened slowly, and Yusuf crept into the room. He shut the door and lay down on the bed, unaware that I was in the room. I should have been at prayers, after all.

'Where have you been?' I asked hoarsely.

Yusuf jumped in fright and stifled a girlish scream. 'Just having some fun,' he then said. 'And where were you last night? You weren't around.'

I wanted to tell him about Oskar, but I still wanted to sleep and merely echoed his response – 'Just having some fun' – and then fell asleep again.

At 9 am, the two of us woke at the same time. We also yawned and rubbed our eyes at the same time. I quickly fixed the position of my cock because in the morning I usually woke up with a hard-on, which was something I definitely did not want Yusuf to see. The first thought that came to my mind was food.

'Want to get something to eat?' I asked.

'I'm still tired,' he moaned but then seemed to reconsider. 'OK, I'll come with you.'

At the *nasi uduk* stall, we ate our fill, though Yusuf's every bite alternated with a yawn.

'Let's buy a lock for the door to our room so that not just anyone can come in,' Yusuf suggested at the end of our meal. 'If you buy one, I'll pay you back later.'

'Sure, as if you have the money to pay me back,' I smirked while drinking my hot tea.

Yusuf gave me a scornful look. 'Hey, I'm working now, and in a week or two I'll have plenty of money.'

We went to a home-supply store near the market where I bought a latch for the door and then we spent quite a while attaching it on the inside in a way that we could lock it from the outside. Somehow, I managed to get the job done. Even with the lock, I knew the door could easily be pushed in, but at the very least, it would give an unwanted visitor pause to think.

Yusuf looked around the place. The pesantren was quiet because most of the residents were home with their families; others were hanging out at the food stall and watching TV. I watched Yusuf as he checked the results of my work.

'Now we're safe!' he announced when locking the door dramatically. He then took his bag and removed from it a small packet of something, no larger than a baby's fist and wrapped in white paper.

'What's that?' I asked.

His eyes sparkled. 'Ganja!' he said forthrightly.

'Are you crazy!' I screamed at him. 'You're going to smoke that stuff here? You'll be out on your ass or worse.'

'I'm not smoking it, stupid, I'm selling it,' he said while removing a thin rectangular-shaped packet from his bag: rolling papers. Because the use of ganja was illegal and against Islamic religious strictures as well, I couldn't think of what he was going to do with the stuff. Yet he maintained a look of complete innocence.

'This is your "business"?' I asked. Yusuf nodded.

'Are you sure you want to do that?' I asked. He nodded again.

'It's dangerous, you know. If you get caught, you could spend years in prison,' I told him, thinking of what had happened to a couple of guys I knew at my school.

'Don't worry. Iwenk told me he has police backing.'

I shook my head. So this is the 'business' that Iwenk had hinted at the night we ran into him at the food stall two weeks earlier. From the frying pan into the fire, I thought. Free from a banci's clutches, he'd become a drug dealer instead.

'What do you intend to do with that stuff?' I asked. Just looking at it made me nervous. In days past, before brawls between my school and another, the leader of our gang would usually pass a few joints around. He told us that it would calm us down and make it easier for us to fight. I myself never tried the stuff. I was afraid of what getting high might do, and that if we were attacked I might not be able to run and would just stand there like a stone.

'We'll make little joints and sell them …'

'We?' I interrupted.

'If you help me sell them, I'll give you a commission,' Yusuf answered.

'No way. I've got other work.'

'Come on, don't you want to help your friend?' he coaxed. That was new. Since when did Yusuf consider me to be his friend? I watched him as he tried to roll a joint but he was a complete amateur. His joints were lumpy and leaves stuck out of the papers. The mat on which Yusuf was sitting was littered with fallen weed.

'Here, let me show you how. You have to twist the ends so the leaves don't fall out.' I didn't like the notion of this business, but Yusuf was so hopeless, I felt forced to help him.

'How much for one joint?' I asked.

'Twenty thousand.'

'Wow, that's expensive.' From what I knew, the street price was around five thousand.

'Well, the stuff is hard to come by,' he reasoned.

I helped Yusuf roll until he had a pile containing a few dozen joints. He then divided the pile into units of three and put them in little zip-lock bags, the kind prescription drugs come in. Each bag contained three joints.

'Budget packets,' Yusuf announced with a smile. 'Buy three for fifty thousand.'

'Where are you going to sell them?'

'Here, to the other residents,' he said immediately. I blinked, 'Are you out of your mind?'

'Or to the ustadz before recitation lessons. Wouldn't that be something! A stoned kiai?'

I shook my head, reluctant to humour him further.

'You know, don't you, that not all the guys here follow the straight and narrow,' he said, as he concealed the joints beneath a pile of clothes in the cupboard.

I said no more. It was up to him where he sold the stuff. It wasn't my business anymore, and though I had just taught him how to roll a proper joint, I had no intention of getting involved in that kind of business. I didn't want it messing up my life. After thinking about it, I decided that maybe that is what had been making Yusuf so anxious of late. Maybe he'd been trying to decide whether to do it or not. Or debating with himself as to whether it was a sin. Whatever the case, in the end money had won out. His need for money made him determined to do whatever necessary to get it, including selling ganja.

It was the end of a dreary November, and Yusuf had been selling his joints for a week now. Some days he came home with a happy look on his face, other days with a not-so-happy look. When asked about it, he said that sales weren't good or that a teacher had almost caught him. Another time he was happy because sales were good and he had made a big profit. In that seven-day period I helped Yusuf roll his wares several times. How ironic, rolling joints in a pesantren, but Yusuf didn't seem to give the matter too much thought. He was only selling the stuff, he reasoned, nothing more than that. Ganja was a transferable commodity, which resulted in a profit for him when it changed hands. Was it a sin for a guy to sell goods in the marketplace? I'm sure that deep inside himself, Yusuf knew that it was wrong, but money had closed the door to that.

Ali seemed to know that something was not right with Yusuf. At the week's end, he said to me, 'Yusuf seems to have stopped his memorizing.'

It was true. Of late, Yusuf had been spending little time memorizing texts. But what with him skipping out at night to pay Iwenk and to pick up a new supply of ganja, when did he have time to memorize? He spent most of his free time rolling joints.

'I've not memorized anything either,' I said to Ali.

'I know,' he said, 'but everyone knows you're lazy. The laziest resident here.'

'I don't see the use of memorizing something I don't understand,' I said in self-defence.

'Knowledge is not something one immediately understands. What's important is first to know. Understanding can come later.'

'Yeah, yeah,' I muttered then walked away. I didn't want to argue with Ali, and I also didn't want him asking me about Yusuf. What was I going to do? Tell him that his brother was a dope dealer? No, I decided, it was best that Ali didn't know. Yusuf was right: the fewer secrets one knows, the less the risk of getting hurt.

By coincidence, just after that meeting with Ali, Yusuf arrived at the lodge. He was sweating, as if he had been running. I thought perhaps it was because isya prayers were about to begin.

'Your brother was just asking about you,' I told him.

'Ignore him,' Yusuf said as he took off his shirt. He shut the door to the cell and locked it. After that he took out a roll of money from his pocket, then sat down beside me and lazily counted the notes.

'Three hundred thousand,' he said with a big grin on his face.

'What are you going to do with it?' I asked.

'I'm going to buy myself a nice sarong,' he said, without a hint of guilt in his voice.

I was surprised to hear him say that: to sell something illicit in order to buy something used for prayer? Was that permissible? Was it a bit like stealing something to give to the poor? Was it right or wrong? Was Yusuf even telling the truth? I simply didn't know.

A Treat

Seconds gather into minutes, minutes combine to form hours and hours are woven into days, which, standing abreast, become weeks that form months. One month passes, and then two and three follow it. Fourteen weeks had passed since I'd moved to the pesantren. At times, life there felt devastatingly dull: the same routine every day with the same people in the same place, with the same clothes and conversations, repeated time and again. There was little variation in our recitations or discussions about them. A person who was used to independence would likely find the situation stifling. But the pesantren was not meant to be a place to make one happy. It was a source of guidance for the road to heaven. And, as everyone knows, the road to heaven is not an easy one.

Luckily, during that period of my life, I had other, outside activities. Because I was still in school, I was able to see and discover the world beyond the pesantren. I had the opportunity to meet different kinds of people, which made it feel less confining. Now I lived in Paris's world as well. Not a single lesson I received at the pesantren provided legitimacy for what I was doing, for being a kept boy, but what the hell, I thought. I was still young and didn't care.

One night in early December, after isya prayers, I was sitting by myself in the doorway to my cell, my legs hanging over the side into the pedestrian pathway below. It had rained earlier, and the air felt refreshing. While swinging my legs, I watched the residents pass back and forth in the space between the two units of the dormitory. Some of the boarders were in their cells, memorizing texts; others were engaged in enunciation exercises; others were engaged in conversation. There was nothing odd about the scene except the visitor with the crew cut who came looking for me.

It was his voice that first caught my attention: 'The guy is fairly tall, a student, with kind of wild-looking eyes,' I heard him say to another boarder.

'You must be talking about Ricky,' my fellow boarder said to the visitor and pointed towards me. 'There he is, squatting over there.'

Hearing my name, I stretched my head like a bird and went to greet the visitor. It was Oskar.

'All healed?' I asked. We shook hands. He had no brace on his arm.

'Just about,' he answered. 'Stitches come out tomorrow.'

'Want to come in?' I asked, pointing to my cell.

Oskar nodded and followed me inside. 'Who did you come with?' I asked.

'Alone,' he told me.

What is this, I wondered. Why had he come to the pesantren looking for me? It was now close to 10 pm.

'I'm surprised to see you,' I said after inviting him to sit down. 'What are you doing here?' I asked him point blank.

'No particular reason.'

Coming here at night, I doubted that.

'Where's your friend, the banci-like guy?' he asked.

'Don't say that. You remember how angry he got the first time you called him that. Why are you asking, anyway?' This was the first time I'd actually talked to Oskar.

'I just wanted to tell him thanks,' he said lightly.

'So, you want to thank him but not me?' I said snidely.

'Yeah, you too,' he said with a blush, not looking at me.

As I mentioned before, I believed that my meeting with Oskar was destiny, something that was meant to happen. On the day of the brawl, if Oskar had hidden in another boarder's cell after he was stabbed, this story would be altogether different.

Oskar removed a pack of cigarettes from his shirt pocket, took one out and lit it, and threw the pack to me. I took one out and lit up too, even though it was forbidden to smoke at the pesantren.

'And how's Paris? Is he your boyfriend or something?' Oskar asked, yet another non sequitur.

I didn't know what to say. I felt confused and embarrassed.

'Fess up. No need to be embarrassed,' he laughed.

'If you came here to make fun of me, then you'd better go home,' I said angrily but this only made Oskar laugh louder.

At that moment, Yusuf stuck his head inside the door and looked around to see who I was talking to.

'Hey, a visitor!' he said excitedly, but the look on his face suddenly changed when he recognized who the visitor was. Stone-faced, Yusuf came into the cell carrying something.

'Hey, shake hands, OK?' Oskar said, holding out his right hand. 'You look like you want to choke.'

Yusuf barely touched Oskar's hand. 'What are you doing here?' he asked in a rude tone of voice but once again, Oskar just laughed.

'Got a little temper, don't you!' he said, but added more seriously, 'I just wanted to say thanks.'

'I'm surprised you know the words,' Yusuf harrumphed.

Oskar wrinkled his brow. 'And to apologize as well!'

'Wow! Another surprise,' Yusuf remarked but with a lower voice.

Watching the scene, I could only shake my head.

'What's in the bag?' Oskar asked, perhaps just to change the subject.

'As if that's your business,' Yusuf shot back. 'And put out that cigarette. I can't breathe in here.'

Neither of us put out our cigarettes. Yusuf then opened the bag he was carrying and removed a small box.

'Hmm, a mobile,' Oskar remarked, to which Yusuf did not reply.

I looked at the box in Yusuf's hand. So, he had spent the money he made by selling ganja not on a sarong but on a phone.

'I've wanted one forever, and now I have one,' Yusuf said with a blush of pride.

'That one we'd use as a doorstop,' Oskar said with a sneer. Yusuf's eyes narrowed, and he shot Oskar an angry look.

'I need to buy some call time. Want to come along?' he asked me, ignoring Oskar's presence.

'Sure,' I said. Yusuf was right. With all the smoke, it was getting hard to breathe in the small room.

The three of us walked down the lane towards the main road, where all kinds of vendors plied their wares. I was surprised to see a familiar-looking car parked near the intersection. Oskar had lied. He wasn't alone. Paris had driven him here.

Paris got out of the car and walked in our direction. Yusuf had a look of incomprehension on his face but said nothing. I still hadn't told him about Paris and Oskar, and he didn't know that I had helped him bring Oskar home from the hospital.

'Where are you going?' Paris asked.

'Buying some call time for Yusuf,' I answered.

'So, girl, you have a mobile now?' Paris asked Yusuf.

'Sure do, ma'am,' Yusuf replied with a look of pride on his face.

Oskar and I looked at each other.

After Yusuf bought some call time, Oskar invited us to eat. Night had fallen, and the sidewalk was now covered with tents, makeshift warung where food was sold. We passed a couple of our regular haunts – the eel place and the fried-rice stall – until we came to a seafood warung. Oskar's treat, this big meal of ours, was his way of saying thanks to Yusuf and me for having saved his life. Quite a trade, I thought: a boiled crab for saving his life.

While we ate the crab cooked in red pepper sauce, Paris and Yusuf nattered away to each other in whispers. I guessed that Paris was probably explaining his relationship with Oskar. Meanwhile, Oskar and I concentrated on our food. Oskar told me that he and Paris were related but not by blood; his mother was married to Paris's father. So, the two of them were stepbrothers! And here I'd thought that Paris might be keeping him, too.

The evening ended with Yusuf and me walking back to our pesantren, but Yusuf didn't sleep until much later. He couldn't stop looking at the new mobile in his hand. Maybe he thought that someone might call him, even though his address book was still empty.

A Promise

I'm not the kind of person who always has to know what's going on; I let things happen without getting involved. I don't like the bother or aggravation. Problems with my family, for instance: rather than dwell on them, I buried what feelings I had. The same was true of my life at the pesantren. I didn't particularly care what the other residents thought about me, and I had little interest in getting to know about them or their lives. I didn't want to be friends with the kiai. I didn't want to become his favourite santri. That was me at the time: I didn't know what I wanted.

After that evening with Oskar, Paris didn't ask me out for more than a week. Maybe he felt embarrassed because of Oskar. So when he asked me towards the middle of the month if I wanted to go with him 'into the city', meaning Jakarta, I breathed a sigh of relief. I had almost gone through the last instalment of money he'd given to me.

I left the pesantren at 2 pm and waited for Paris at the end of the lane. Soon we were on the toll road heading to Jakarta. We arrived at a garment centre not far from Pasar Senin, the city's largest market. The building was multi-storied like a mall, but the interior was more like a traditional market with small shops and narrow aisles. The place was crowded and felt claustrophobic. On the other hand, the clothes that were being sold there, which had originally been intended for the export market, were incredibly cheap.

'What are we doing here?' I asked Paris, even though I had nothing against being in a place like that.

'You can find clothes here that you never find at the malls,' he said.

Most of the people shopping there haggled and bargained beyond belief. Not Paris! He bought whatever he liked and paid the price that was asked. I became his porter, lugging jam-packed plastic shopping bags. Around magrib, after we'd had something to eat, we drove back to Tangerang and Paris took me home.

My hands and arms were stiff and so was my back. Paris gave me another two hundred thousand, which I took and pocketed quickly. That way, I didn't feel like I was his kept boy or paid boyfriend. Instead, I felt more like a personal assistant.

When I entered my cell, I found Yusuf preparing to leave. He was wearing his best shirt and the cell smelled of hair oil and cheap cologne.

'Going out?' I asked.

'Come with me, will you, please?' he whined. 'It's just down the road to Lippo Karawaci Mall.'

'I'm tired,' I told him.

He gave me a pleading look. 'I have an appointment with a client. It's important. Take me, please. I'm afraid to go alone,' he begged.

The pleading look on his face made me feel concern. Was he off to sell ganja? And why at a mall? Wasn't that just looking for trouble?

Despite my pissing and moaning, in the end I agreed to take him – not because of his whining but because he said he was afraid. I always feel sorry for people who are afraid. Fortunately, the mall wasn't far: two thousand rupiah for one public van, and you were there.

At the mall, we waited in the food court. Yusuf took out his mobile and typed a text message. Shortly afterwards, the telephone rang.

'Yeah, I'm already here. A little early. I'm at the food court. Wearing a blue shirt. Yes, I'm alone. I'll wait.'

He clicked the phone off then said to me. 'Ricky, would you sit over there, please?'

'What do you mean?' I was confused.

'The person wants to meet me alone,' Yusuf explained.

I looked at him with disbelief. 'You're crazy, you know that?'

'Please,' Yusuf begged again.

I clicked my tongue. Shit. 'OK, so where do you want me?'

He pointed to a distant table. 'Sit over there but keep your eyes in my direction. I'm afraid something might happen. And if he asks me to go with him, follow us, will you?'

Now I gave Yusuf an angry look. What was going on? What kind of business was this? Despite my irritation, I went to a table in the corner of the room, just as Yusuf had requested. From there, I watched as he picked up his phone again. I guessed that he must still be dealing ganja and that he had purchased a mobile to ease transactions. After a short conversation, an older man approached Yusuf's table. I was astonished to think that such an old man might still be imbibing in marijuana. But then another thought came to mind: he was a policeman, working undercover. This was bad.

As they spoke to each other, I waited for Yusuf to do something: to take something out of his bag or pocket and slip it to the man. Maybe the deal was off, I thought. Suddenly, the man stood but Yusuf remained seated. The man tugged the arm of Yusuf's shirt, a sign for him to follow. I was growing more suspicious and watched carefully to see what would happen. The man didn't seem to be using force; simply inviting Yusuf to follow. But the look in Yusuf's eyes told me that he was too nervous to go with the man. At that point, I decided to make a move. I got up from my chair and approached Yusuf's table. What if the man really was a policeman who was trying to entrap Yusuf? An even worse scenario popped into my mind: maybe the man was a member of a gang and had been sent to kill dealers outside the gang.

When I was close enough, I asked, 'Where are you taking him?'

Both Yusuf and the man looked at me in surprise.

Yusuf had a worried expression, which I didn't comprehend. His hands were partially raised as if to say silently not to come close, but it was too late; I was already there.

'Who are you?' the man asked me.

I was surprised by the tone of his voice. 'I'm his friend,' I answered, pointing to Yusuf.

'You brought a friend? You said you were alone,' the man said to Yusuf.

'I was alone. We came together but then he left,' Yusuf lied easily.

The man was now looking at me, assessing me, it seemed. It was a look I now recognized.

'Do you want to come too?' the man asked.

'Where are you going?' I asked Yusuf while signalling with my lowered hand that he should not go along.

The man answered instead. 'To my place. It's not far from here.'

I got a bad feeling. 'Why not do your business here?' I suggested.

'What are you talking about?' the man asked.

'You pay and he gives you what you want,' I told him.

Yusuf rose uncertainly as if to speak, but I stopped him. I pictured him going to the man's place but it turned out to be police headquarters where he was thrown into a cell very different from the one he was accustomed to. If this was police entrapment, I would be the witness. No, better to finish the business here.

'Here?' the man said as if not understanding me. 'Yeah, do your business in the toilet,' I told him.

I watched the man as he turned the suggestion over in his mind. 'Hey, why not?' he then said with a big grin. 'Sounds fine to me!'

Now I was the one confused. Why was the man smiling so broadly? I looked at Yusuf who had a distressed look on his face, like a puppy who knew he'd done wrong.

Paying the man no attention, I pulled Yusuf a distance away. 'What's going on? What does that old man want?'

'He's not an "old man"!' Yusuf declared loudly. 'He's a daddy!'

'A "daddy"?'

'Yeah, you know, a sugar daddy. We were chatting together this afternoon on MIRC,' Yusuf explained.

I still didn't understand. 'And you're selling marijuana to him?'

'No! I'm not selling marijuana,' he answered.

'So then, what are you selling?'

Yusuf seemed afraid to answer. I glared at him as if to say that if he weren't straight with me, I would report him to his brother. 'I promised to meet up with him is all,' he answered, his voice trembling, like that of a naughty child wanting forgiveness.

Finally, the penny dropped.

'And after meeting up, what then? Were you hoping for

money?' I asked.

'He said he would give me some if I went to his place with him.'

'What the hell! You were going to sell yourself?' I swore while smacking my fist against my hand.

Mr. Sugar Daddy was still waiting for us. I could see that he was nervous.

Yusuf wasn't going to give in. 'I'm not selling myself. That's what people do when they are forced to. I'm doing this because I want to do it!'

Angry now, I put my hand around his wrist and squeezed tightly. 'Stop lying. You were going to sell yourself to that man!'

'How is that so different from what you're doing?' Yusuf screamed. 'You sell yourself to Paris! Who do you think I learned it from?'

I was stunned into silence.

'You're the one who told me to make some money!' he added.

I wanted to take him by the hand and drag him home, but instead I loosened my grip and thrust his arm away from me. Who was he to me? We happened to share a room at the pesantren is all. I had no right to tell him what to do.

Saying no more, I turned and left him standing there. I walked home that night, feeling confused, trying to convince myself that what I was doing with Paris was different.

Clubbing

Whether my feelings were justified or not, I felt angry with Yusuf and gave him the silent treatment for the next few days. I found it appalling that he would sell himself but, to tell the truth, I also resented him for having the gall to say that I had sold myself to Paris. I still hadn't been able to settle that question of difference in my mind.

It was a Saturday in mid-December and I decided to go for a walk by myself outside the pesantren. On the main street, I stopped at an iced *cendol* vendor, and ordered myself a glass. For me, there was no better way to beat a funk than this concoction of palm sugar syrup, coconut milk, and gooey shreds of mung bean flour.

Quite unexpectedly – as always seemed to be the case – Iwenk suddenly appeared at the same warung. Why did I keep running into this guy, I wondered.

'Where's Yusuf?' he asked.

'Don't know, don't care,' I quipped as I slurped my drink.

'I have a new business for him. It's sure to be even better.'

'Whatever ….,' I said.

Iwenk ordered a glass of iced cendol too. Not interested in speaking to anyone at that moment, I wanted to leave him there on his own, but my glass of cendol was still half full. And as the kiai said, wasting food gave sustenance to the devil. Waste when you're young, die poor when you're old. So I felt compelled to sit and talk to him.

'Do you like coke?' he suddenly asked.

'What, Coca-Cola?'

'No, cocaine, meth, that kind of stuff.'

'I don't do drugs,' I said firmly.

'What, can't afford to?' he said snidely.

'What I can't afford is more time with you,' I shot back.

'You have a big head for someone who's selling himself,' he said with a sneer.

'I've never sold myself!' I snapped angrily.

'Everyone knows that illegit banci is keeping you,' he spat.

'Don't compare me with yourself!' I growled at him and then stood. I wanted to throw the glass I was holding at his face. Maybe he was just trying to get my goat, as seemed to be his custom, but I wasn't in the mood.

'You talk like you think your shit don't stink,' Iwenk said, gulping his cendol.

'And all you say is shit, so eat it yourself!' I told him. I paid for my cendol and left.

'Just like a peanut that's forgotten its shell,' he said loudly as I walked away.

As the days passed, I spent almost no time with Yusuf – not that I really tried! – but then he was gone all day, not coming home until late at night, and always skipping Quranic recitation after magrib. Because I knew Ali wanted to find out what his brother was up to, I did my best to avoid him. At night, when Yusuf did come home, he'd spend all his time on his mobile, either texting or calling people. Even on the few occasions he participated in recitations, he had his mobile with him, hidden beneath his sarong, and surreptitiously sent text messages. It was a different story in our cell. There, until late at night, he'd be hurriedly whispering into the phone, apparently not wanting me to hear what he was saying. He didn't know how irritating I found his stifled giggles.

Life at school proceeded as usual. The days passed until, at December's end, the time for national exams, a college-entrance requirement, grew near. There was no special counselling at my school; few vocational school graduates intended to go to college anyway. Instead, around exam time students would be given a kind of cheat sheet, so everyone would pass. As a result, the consensus was why waste your time studying?

One day, while my class was on study break, Paris came into the room with a look of annoyance on his face.

Plopping himself down on the chair next to me, he put his hand on mine. 'What is it with you of late?'

I pulled my hand away and avoided his stare. There were too many classmates watching. Sure, they might seem to be preoccupied with their own conversations, but Paris being Paris was always a magnet for attention.

'There's nothing wrong,' I answered with a whisper, embarrassed to be overheard.

Paris gave me a sharp look. 'After school, come shopping with me. Full stop,' he said in a loud voice before leaving the classroom. I couldn't say no. Another scream would have attracted everyone's attention.

After school, I went to the parking lot where Paris was waiting in his car. I got in and shut the door quickly. A group of students had seen me get into Paris's car and I was sure they were now making remarks about us. In fact, one of them whistled and another hooted.

'Are you embarrassed to be seen with me?' he asked me in a flat tone of voice as soon as I had settled in my seat.

'No, I just want to leave. Let's go,' I said.

We went to Matahari Mall. I asked Paris if I could wait for him at the McDonald's. I wasn't in the mood for following him around while he shopped. Paris consented reluctantly. The mall was busy that day, and while I was sitting there sucking on a mocha float, I started to people-watch. I noticed two guys walking so closely beside each other they appeared to be joined at the hip. They were walking in my direction. Then I recognized one of them and wanted to hide, but it was too late. He'd already spotted me. It was Yusuf.

'Hi! Are you here with Paris?' he asked bluntly.

'Yes,' I said.

'Where is he?'

'Shopping,' I answered.

'Why aren't you with him?'

Yusuf's friendly tone of voice made me suspicious. Weren't we at odds with each other? I guessed his behaviour had something to do with the man at his side. He wanted to impress this man as being friendly and kind hearted.

'I was tired and wanted to rest,' I told him.

'Oh ...'

I studied Yusuf. His appearance had changed completely. He had on a new T-shirt. His pants were skinny and tight at the bottom but loose at the waist, revealing the brand of underwear he was wearing. He also had new shoes. At this time of day he should have been in his school uniform. He must have skipped classes.

'I'm going to the bathroom,' Yusuf said to the older man as his side.

'Alright, I'll wait for you here,' the man said.

'Watch him for me, will you?' Yusuf said with a smile to me.

I was uncomfortable and didn't want to talk to the man. Judging from the way he looked, he was old enough to have a few kids of his own. What was it with this kind of man, hanging out with a guy young enough to be his kid?

'Are you a friend of Yusuf's?' the man asked me.

'Yes.'

'Same boarding house?' he then asked.

Since when did Yusuf live in a boarding house?

'Different rooms,' I answered.

'But you're still in your uniform?'

I looked at him out of the side of my eye. 'Well, if I wasn't in uniform, I'd be naked,' I said.

He chuckled. 'Now *that* I would like to see. How about if I buy you some clothes and you change into them in front of me?'

'That's all right, thank you,' I said as politely as possible.

'Want to give me your mobile number?'

'Sorry, I don't have one.'

'Oh, that's too bad. Would you like me to buy you one?'

'No, thank you,' I said again.

He smiled, then said, 'You have luscious-looking lips, you know. They look yummy.'

Yuck! I wanted to throw up. Fortunately, Yusuf reappeared, and the man didn't dare say anything more.

'Well, we have to go,' Yusuf said to me. 'We're going to see a film.'

Who cared?

After the two of them left, I ordered another mocha float. Then, over the next hour, as I waited for Paris, I sipped on my float and thought about Yusuf and his new life. I wondered as well about my own desires and what the future would bring.

I didn't really start talking to Yusuf again until the new year. For me, it was kind of a new year's resolution: I decided to try to make myself new, too. A cliché, I know, but by then, my anger at Yusuf had faded anyway. He could do as he pleased. No skin off my back. The important thing is that he was alive, and, to be honest, he looked far happier than he ever had before.

On New Year's Eve, Yusuf disappeared from our cell without a word and did not return until after dawn with a party hat on his head and a trumpet in his hand. Not wanting him to know that I was already awake, I watched him through half-closed eyes as he tiptoed about the cell, singing to himself, before gently storing his trumpet in the cupboard. Even though he said nothing to me directly, from his light-hearted mood I knew that he was happy, which brought an unforced smile to my lips. I had passed New Year's Eve by myself, with no company but the other santri, reciting prayers.

A couple days later, Yusuf and I were in the majelis after the recitation exercises that followed dawn prayers, and I noticed that he looked absolutely glowing. He wore a new watch on his wrist. Of late, he'd been acquiring lots of new things. But that no longer surprised me, and I didn't want to know where they came from, either.

'Are you still with Paris?' he suddenly asked.

'What do you mean?'

'Just answer,' he said.

I looked at him suspiciously. 'Yeah, why?'

'Why don't you see if he'd like to go out this coming Saturday night?' he asked.

'Ask him out where?' I asked.

We spoke in whispers because many of the santri were still in the gazebo, some memorizing verses, others lying around or nodding off.

'Clubbing,' he said.

'What?'

'You know, dancing, disco …'

'Yes, I know what that is. What I mean is are you sure that would be all right?'

'Why wouldn't it?' he asked.

'Well, to start with, you're a santri.'

He raised his eyebrows so high his forehead crinkled. 'So what if I am. Can't a santri go clubbing?'

Yusuf picked himself up from where he was sitting and left the majelis, leaving me in a state of wonderment. I mean, clubbing? That didn't seem at all appropriate for a santri. But what did I know? After all, neither was his new profession.

Yusuf's request was like a relay message. At school the next day, Paris came looking for me and suggested, 'How about if we go clubbing this Saturday?'

'Why do you want to go clubbing?' I asked, half against the idea, half curious.

'To dance, you know. It would be fun!'

As he batted his eyelashes, I caught the scent of expensive cologne.

'You want to get drunk or something?'

'No. Does going clubbing mean you have to get drunk?'

'Well, on TV …'

'You get too much of your information from TV! A lot of stuff you see on TV has nothing to do with reality,' he argued.

'But most of what is shown on TV is based on real life,' I argued back.

'Oh, whatever!' he said in exasperation. 'The point is, this Saturday night, we're going clubbing. If not, it's over.'

With that said, there was no arguing with him, not if I hoped for any additional allowance.

On Saturday evening I left the pesantren wearing my best clothes: an Ocean Pacific T-shirt which had cost Rp. 200,000 and a pair of dark blue, low-waist Lee Cooper jeans for which Paris had paid close to half a million. Not wanting to be outclassed, Yusuf wore new clothes too, plus he slathered himself with a cologne whose scent made me want to gag.

'Where are you going? A wedding?' I asked while holding my nose.

'Zip it,' he told me. 'You leave first.'

On my way out of the pesantren I ran into Ali. 'Where are you going?' he asked.

'Roll call!' I answered.

'You play around too much, and your recitation skills are still poor,' he commented.

'Well, if my recitation skills were perfect I'd never have time to play around,' I said by way of an answer.

Ali just looked at me, as if unable to speak. But then he asked, 'You're keeping an eye on Yusuf, aren't you?'

I merely nodded and went on my way.

At the end of the lane, I waited for about fifteen minutes before Yusuf finally appeared with a look of panic on his face.

'Omigod! I almost couldn't leave. Ali's had his eye on me all day,' he complained.

Apparently, Yusuf didn't know that Ali was keeping his eye on both of us.

Yusuf pulled out his mobile and punched in a number. The conversation was quick: '*Hae, gerl, we B waiten for Yoelandu! Heree!* Hey girl, we're waiting for you. Hurry!'

'Who was that?' I asked.

'Paris.'

Of course the two of them had cooked up this clubbing plan together. That mobile of Yusuf's would be the end of me.

About five minutes later, a familiar car appeared with the front window on the driver's side rolled down.

'*Yoelandu B linaet!* You're late!' Yusuf grumbled but then ran around the car, opened the door to the front seat, and jumped inside.

I had no choice but to sit in the back. When I got in, I was surprised to find Oskar there, stone-faced and silent, slouching against the back seat.

'Who invited him?' I said to Paris, while pointing at Oskar.

'Don't talk like a person's not here,' Oskar said.

'He wanted to come along,' Paris replied, ignoring Oskar.

'That's great. If he starts a fight, we'll be the ones to pay,' I said off the top of my head.

'Hey, I'm sitting here, you know,' Oskar again reminded us.

'Besides, I thought he might cry if we didn't invite him to come along,' Paris continued to jest.

'Not funny!' Oskar snapped.

'Well, I for one, don't like the idea of spending another night at the hospital,' I added.

'Oh, shit!' Yusuf suddenly cried. 'My student ID is still there!'

At that, the three of us broke into laughter, the first time we had laughed together.

'Hey, where are we headed?' Oskar asked as Paris drove onto the toll road in the direction of Jakarta.

'You'll see in good time,' Paris quipped.

Jakarta-bound traffic was relatively sparse that night, and in less than thirty minutes Paris exited the toll road and entered the Kuningan district of central Jakarta. At one of the major hotels, he drove into the basement garage. I'd never been in an underground parking lot like that. The place was well-lit – no fifteen-watt bulbs here – and the walls and floor were crisply painted. Most of the cars were shiny and new, parked in neat, orderly rows.

Not too far from where we parked, another car pulled in. Its passengers, three men in expensive-looking clothes, got out and walked with assured steps towards an entrance to the hotel. Because they looked like they knew what they were doing, we scurried to follow them. When they went into a foyer and entered an elevator, we were there, just behind them. When one of them pushed a button, Yusuf flashed the man a simpering smile, which he ignored.

When the elevator stopped the trio exited and our quartet followed, trying to look as cool and casual as the men ahead of us.

'I'm sure they're going to the same place,' Paris whispered to Yusuf, who merely nodded.

Up ahead, just in front of us, a small neon sign hung over a wide open doorway that said, Pronto. From the outside, the place looked classy and expensive, with dark marble walls and shiny wooden wall features. I was feeling both excited and afraid. This was the first time I had been to a nightclub.

Yusuf looked even more nervous, and kept pestering Paris with questions: 'How are my clothes? How do I look? How should I act?'

At the counter just inside the doorway, Paris said to the attendant, 'Four, please.'

'Six hundred thousand,' said the cashier.

Paris took the money from his wallet. Oskar, Yusuf, and I just watched. That was a lot of money!

'Have an ID?' the cashier then asked.

When Paris blinked, Oskar stepped up and pulled out an identification card from his wallet. That's when I realized why Oskar had been invited to come along: he was the only one of legal age – or at least the only one with an ID card to prove it.

'Just one?' the cashier asked. We nodded in unison.

'No one underage gets in,' the cashier said.

'I'm almost eighteen,' I told him.

'And I am thirty-eight,' Yusuf announced, 'and have fourteen kids!'

'I don't care if you're one hundred,' the cashier said in a firm and humourless voice. 'If you don't have an ID, you don't get in.'

'So what can we do?' Paris asked.

The cashier looked at us. 'Another three hundred ...'

'Two hundred,' said Paris as he took the extra money from his wallet and then snatched the entrance tickets from the cashier's hand.

The four of us entered the inner door to the club, which was apparently soundproofed, because when we walked into the club, it was just like discotheque scenes I had seen in films. The place was dimly lit and the music blaring. We found a place at the bar and sat down. People looked at us as we seated ourselves, and I felt my heart suddenly beating faster than normal. The smell of alcohol and cigarette smoke filled the air.

The bartender came to where we were seated.

'I want to try a beer,' Yusuf said.

'You'll have Sprite. Don't start getting ideas,' I said to him, with Ali's request clearly in mind.

Yusuf smirked.

'Four Cokes,' Paris said in English to the man.

I didn't know how to behave, didn't know what to do in this unfamiliar environment, and I kept glancing at Oskar, thinking that he might be able to provide advice. He seemed relaxed and enjoying himself. He pulled out at pack of cigarettes from his shirt pocket and began smoking one cigarette after another. I began stealing his cigarettes and doing the same. Yusuf and Paris, meanwhile, huddled together, looking here and there.

Scattered around the room were groups of people, some of them laughing in loud conversations, others slouched in lounge chairs, smoking and sipping on drinks. The pounding music, which I could feel in my chest, seemed to be merely the background for their personal interactions. People were lost in their own groups, unaware of any others.

A few people were on the dance floor, two or three couples, but at that point Yusuf and Paris decided that they wanted to dance. They walked stiffly to the dance floor where, for about two minutes, they danced by themselves, raising their arms in the air and hooting, like two girls having fun. When no one else joined them on the floor, they began to laugh hilariously, but their cheer rang false. Yusuf then put his right arm around Paris's shoulder and they looked like a couple, which caused a few heads to turn and stare at them. Yusuf soon dropped his arm, and they began to dance separately again.

It made me uneasy watching them, especially Yusuf, who seemed to be trying to imitate dancers he had seen on TV but failing badly. Finally, they stopped and returned to our place at the bar, shame-faced. Oskar broke into laughter.

'What's so funny?' Paris screamed, trying to make himself heard above the pounding music.

Oskar just shook his head in reply. For the next ten minutes or so, which felt like ten hours to me, the four of us just sat there in silence until Oskar rose and took out his wallet and asked the bartender for the bill.

Bill paid, he said in a voice that bridged no objection, 'Let's go!'

'But we just got here,' Paris complained. Even so, we made our way out of the bar and to the underground parking lot.

With Paris's consent, Oskar got into the front and took the wheel. Because Paris didn't want to sit beside his stepbrother, I got into the front too. Oskar pulled the car out of the lot and then drove toward Thamrin Avenue, the city's main street.

'So that's what they call "clubbing"?' I grumbled out loud but, at the same time, was secretly relieved that nothing strange or untoward had happened in the half hour we were at Pronto.

I kept smiling to myself, thinking of Paris and Yusuf on the dance floor, and Paris would kick the back of the front seat whenever he saw me smiling in the rear-view mirror, as if he knew my smiles were because of him. Since Oskar was driving, the front windows were down, which allowed us to smoke as Yusuf chattered with Paris in the back seat about the sugar daddies he had met online.

Oskar and I said little as the car went round the Hotel Indonesia traffic circle and proceeded to Sabang Street, where we decided to stop and eat.

In the back seat, Yusuf was complaining, 'Hey, I cancelled all these dates just to go out with you. How am I supposed to make any money this way?'

'Such a slut you are,' Paris said in jest. 'A banci and a whore beside. You're sure to go to hell. I thought you were a santri in a pesantren!'

Oskar and I grinned.

'Shut your trap, will you? Have you never had your eyes scratched by a queen? Come on, Oskar, help me scratch his eyes out,' Yusuf said.

'What the F? Are you calling me a queen?' Oskar snorted.

'No, you're not a queen,' Paris reassured him. 'You're still a princess!'

At that comment, I laughed so hard that I thought I was going to wet my pants.

What I most remember about our meal that night was not the food but the convivial laughter, the jests as Paris and Yusuf made fun of each other, and the fun in hearing them banter in Queens' Speech. '*Naat inoenlee Yoelandu B ina paeshint, Yoelandu B ina kween!* Not only are you queer, you're a queen!' said Paris to Yusuf. To which Yusuf immediately replied, '*Binich!* Bitch!'

Maybe because we had been there for so long or maybe because there were other customers trying to find a place to sit, the waiter at the food stall where we were eating began to clean our table, a sign that it was time for us to pick our butts up from off the chairs and make a move to the street.

On the curb beside the car, we stood irresolutely for some time, wondering what to do next. There was a silent consensus among us: none of us wanted to go home.

Finally, Oskar said, 'I know a place you might like.'

'Nothing too strange, OK?' Paris said from the back seat.

Wherever it was that Oskar was taking us, it took a while to get to there, because he was unsure of directions and made some wrong turns in the Mangga Besar district. In fact, we had passed our destination a couple of times before he finally turned into a dimly lit but crowded parking lot.

We parked next to a row of rundown shophouses. Outside their shuttered doors and windows, beggars and homeless people were sleeping and itinerant street vendors hawked food in a manner that suggested they owned the place.

'Where are we?' Paris asked suspiciously as we got out of the car and looked around the vicinity.

I wasn't sure what I felt, but it was neither nervous, anxious, nor strange. The same with Yusuf. The setting, with its uncomely look and all the various kinds of street people, was one that was familiar to us. It was only Paris who seemed to be in a panic.

Overhead, on the top of the three-story building we faced, was an array of lights shaped to form the word 'Starlight'. Only some of the lights were flickering; many were dead. To the right of the light display was a long horizontal billboard with the same name.

'There are other places nearby, but I think this one is the best one for your sort,' Oskar announced. 'Let's go inside.'

I did as Oskar ordered and entered a smelly, poorly-lit hallway with a stairway at the end. As we walked towards the stairs, Paris clutched my T-shirt and I could feel his fingernails on my skin. The first landing was a makeshift reception counter, behind which there was a bank of small lockers for storing things.

'How much?' Oskar asked the man at the counter who appeared to be Chinese.

'Thirty-five thousand per person,' he answered.

Oskar thrust an open hand towards Paris who hesitantly removed the required amount of bills from his wallet.

The man then told us, 'You can exchange your ticket for a soft drink or mineral water.'

Paris hurriedly whispered to me, 'So cheap and a drink besides! Didn't even ask for an ID. Can it be safe in here?'

We climbed another flight of stairs, where we were greeted by music very unlike that at Pronto. It was a medley of currently popular songs remixed with a beat that was fun to dance to and sing along with. The professional DJ and upper-class clientele at Pronto with their trance music would probably have turned their noses up at the sound. I smiled to myself. There was something different about this place – or maybe it was just me feeling more comfortable in a dirty place.

The lighting was very basic. In fact, it was almost completely dark, with flashes of coloured light reflecting off a mirrored globe revolving overhead. I could feel Paris yanking on my T-shirt, now harder than before.

'I don't know if I like it here,' he said with a lilt in his voice. Oskar had disappeared, and a wave of worry washed over me as well because the room was so dim and crowded. When someone grabbed my arm, I yanked it away, only to realize that it was Oskar, who pulled me toward a lounge chair he had found.

Unlike at Pronto, here there were no islands of tables and chairs around the dance floor, each one separated from the other, just a row of worn-out sofas and lounge chairs lined up against the wall. The place was filled with people on their feet, most of them guys like us, talking, smoking and drinking. The bar itself, situated at the back of the room, was barely visible, with a lonely low-watt bulb hanging listlessly over the barman. Even so, no one seemed to care. The atmosphere was friendly, and people were laughing. Meanwhile, Paris stuck to me like a lost child. Even in the dark, I could see Yusuf turning his head this way and that, excitedly casting his glance around the room.

'So, do you like it or not?' Oskar shouted to make himself heard above the sound.

'What's there to like?' Paris shouted back. 'It's a bit seedy.'

After a few minutes, my vision had grown accustomed to the dim light, and it no longer seemed as dark as it did when we came in. The dance floor was jammed with people dancing however they wanted, with no fear of making a wrong move. Male couples were hugging each other as they danced, not caring what impression they made. A number of them had taken off their shirts because of the heat.

Seated with his legs crossed, Paris kept shaking his right foot in a display of discomfort. Finally, he stood and then pulled me to my feet. 'Come with me to the bathroom.'

I didn't know where the toilets were, but we finally found them off a long open-air walkway behind the bar, which apparently served as the emergency exit as well. This area was much quieter and brighter, and people were able to talk there without having to shout.

In the men's bathroom, the urinals stank, and the tiles were stained and soiled, and slippery from splashed water as well.

Because Paris couldn't make himself piss in such a place he went to see if the women's bathroom was in any better state. I stayed put, waiting for my turn at a urinal. In front of the stall was a small line of guys waiting their turn to pee in privacy or for more serious business. The man at the head of the queue kept rapping his fist impatiently on the door to the stall until, finally, the door opened and two men emerged. The guys in line looked at them in annoyance. 'Can't afford to rent a place, huh?' one of them said.

It was obvious why Oskar thought that this bar might be more appropriate for 'your sort'. He meant guys who liked guys. More specifically, I suspect, he had been referring to Yusuf, because I didn't think I fell into that category, and it definitely didn't seem like Paris's kind of place.

That first night at Starlight was a riveting and eye-opening experience for me. The place was full of male couples, hugging and kissing and a few even groping each other. There were also a lot of banci as well, dressed to the nines and dancing and writhing with uninhibited gusto. There were a few older women, not quite middle-aged but definitely older than the median age of the clientele, who were cuddling with much younger men. There were some young women as well, normal-looking girls our age who seemed to be there just to dance and enjoy themselves.

'This place is filthy and smells bad. It's creepy here,' Paris said to me in the open-air hallway after we had used the toilet facilities. That in itself was not surprising. What was surprising was that we were in a gay club – the first time ever for the both of us – and his first remark was about its level of hygiene.

'Well, you're right about that,' I remarked while signalling with my head that I wanted to go back inside. Paris said he would prefer to hang out in the hallway for a while.

I agreed with him about the cleanliness of the place, but I didn't agree about the atmosphere. I liked this place much better than the previous club, that luxurious den with its expensive cover charge, where we had had to bribe our way to get in. Despite the heat and squalor, I was much more comfortable here. The people seemed much more down to earth.

I found my way back to Oskar, who was sipping on the soft drink he'd gotten with his entrance ticket.

'Where's Yusuf?' I asked, remembering my promise to keep an eye on him.

'He's out there, dancing.'

Indeed, there he was in the middle of the floor dancing and hopping around with people he didn't know. Meanwhile, at the edge of the dance floor, men were hustling drag queens and drag queens were hustling men. Everyone seemed to be flirting with one another. The music was constant, with the DJ changing disks one after another.

'Do you like girls?' Oskar suddenly asked me. 'There's a couple of them over there. Want to say hi?' Oskar pointed to two younger women who had just sat down on a lounge chair not far away. Perhaps overheated from dancing, they were fanning themselves with their hands.

'I think they're a couple,' I said to him. At least it looked that way to me.

'What do you mean?'

'I mean they're *together*.' I couldn't bring myself to say 'lesbians'.

Oskar frowned. 'Just because two girls are together doesn't mean they're a couple.'

'But given the place they're in …'

'You mean a dance club for people like you?' Oskar interrupted.

I didn't answer him. I didn't agree with him saying 'people like you', but I didn't want to argue.

'Not everyone in a queer bar has to be queer,' Oskar said. 'Well, if they're straight, what are they doing here?' I argued. Oskar said nothing for a moment as he sipped his soft drink.

'Not everyone in a particular place has to be the same. Individuals have their own agendas.'

I didn't reply.

'Girls come here because they feel safe,' he suggested. 'They can dance and have fun and not worry about being harassed by men.'

'Or maybe because the place is cheap!' I posed.

In the end, we didn't approach the two girls or anyone else, for that matter. Oskar didn't seem to have any real interest in doing so, and I was overwhelmed by all the new sensations. When Paris came back inside, I asked him to join Yusuf on the dance floor. I was embarrassed, but it was something I wanted to do.

We danced until three in the morning. I was sweaty and tired and barely remember what happened after that. Somehow we ended up sleeping in the car, because the next thing I remember is being wakened in the morning by someone pounding on the car window and telling us to move the car from the side of the road.

Self-Defence

The headache I had that Sunday morning was unlike any I'd ever had before. I've told you the part of the story that I remember – our visit to Starlight – but after that, my memory is blank until we were rudely awoken in the car and Oskar drove us back to the pesantren.

That whole day I spent sleeping in my cell, my body feeling feverish and sore. I had never stayed out so late in my life. Yusuf, too, slept like a log and said not a peep until magrib. I had woken some time before, but it was already dark outside, and no one knew that we were in our cell.

'I'm thirsty,' Yusuf moaned.

I looked around the room but couldn't find any bottles of water. Usually, Ali took care of supplying his brother with water, but today all our water bottles were empty. Stone dry.

'Water, I need water,' Yusuf kept repeating

I opened the door of the cell and looked around but saw no one there. The other boarders, I figured, were probably engaged in recitation exercises. I stepped out of our cell and began to peek into other boarders' cells but found no spare bottles there either. I went to the back of the pesantren, to our makeshift kitchen. No pots of tea there, and the kettle we used to boil our water was completely dry. We'd have to go out to the main road to a stall to buy water, but I was too lazy to do it. As I was bitching and moaning, Yusuf took off in the direction of the latrine. Suddenly feeling the urge to piss, I followed.

Just beyond the latrine was a well and next to it an old carved stone basin, square in shape and lined on the inside with moss. When water was in it, the water always seemed cool and fresh but, usually, the basin only got filled at the time of the call to prayer. We used the water in it for our ritual ablutions. The basin had no faucets, just tapered pieces of wood that were used to plug the water spouts just above the base of the basin. There wasn't much light, but I could see that there was some water in the basin. When Yusuf proceeded to remove one of the wooden plugs, I assumed that he intended to wash his face and feet so that he might pray. He cupped his hands and let the water flow into them. When he raised his hands, I thought he would wash his face but, instead, he drank the water right down. And then, still not satisfied, he lowered his mouth to the base and drank directly from the water spout.

'Don't drink that!' I screamed at him. 'It's not been boiled.'

'I don't care. I'm thirsty,' he whined.

'Yeah, well you're not going to like it when you get the shits,' I told him.

But then he looked at me and his appearance seemed to have changed. His skin glowed and his eyes shone brightly.

'Don't worry,' he told me. 'Allah watches over the people here.'

Hesitantly, I followed Yusuf's lead and drank water from the basin too. It tasted fresh, better than any water I had ever drunk, not at all like water that had been boiled or filtered.

Refreshed from the water we'd drunk, Yusuf and I lounged near our cell. The quietude of the pesantren continued to surprise me. Where had all the other boarders gone? I looked over at the empty pavilion. Soon the other boarders began to appear, very noisy and sweating and all dressed in black. They drew water from the well and filled the basin, then drank the water from the spouts just as Yusuf and I had done earlier. Yusuf and I looked at each other in surprise.

'Where have you been?' Yusuf asked Hamzah, a fellow boarder.

Suddenly, Ali appeared from behind the group. 'Where have you two been?' he asked.

Yusuf gave his brother a look but said nothing, as if he couldn't bother to reply. Instead, he heaved a sigh and moved behind me.

Ali raised his eyebrows and looked at me, as if hoping that I would tell him where his brother had been. Not knowing what to answer, I said off the top of my head, 'With a girlfriend.'

'He has a girlfriend?' Ali asked.

I didn't want to lie for Yusuf. 'No, I do,' I told him. 'Where were you all?' I then asked, in the hope of steering the focus of attention to another subject.

Ali looked dissatisfied with me but answered, '*Pencak silat* practice.'

'Really? Where?' I'd always been interesting in studying that form of self-defence.

'Behind the kiai's house. Tonight was our first night, but it's going to be every Sunday night after magrib.'

I decided then and there that I would study pencak silat too. Having little interest or aptitude for Quranic recitation, I thought that learning pencak silat might be a more interesting way to fill my spare time. So later the following week, when Paris invited me to go clubbing again, I politely turned him down. Not Yusuf, however, who had no interest in martial arts. He jumped at the chance for another night at Starlight.

At my first session, the pencak silat students were made to run around the perimeter of the pesantren complex thirty times – which was equivalent to about seven or eight kilometres – until we were exhausted and could not run anymore. Then we were made to stand in place with our arms raised in front of us for a full one and a half hours – that being the initial position one had to master. When in that position, with your two legs spread apart, you had to concentrate on not moving, even when the instructor kicked you in the calf.

Ustadz Asman, our silat instructor, was a former boarder at the pesantren. After he left, two years before, he had studied *kebatinan*, a kind of mysticism or spiritual power. Now he had returned to the pesantren to teach its residents meritorious work practices, recitation skills, and other disciplines of little interest to me. As an extra, he taught pencak silat.

Two weeks later, after returning to the lodge after my third silat practice, I was in my room, massaging my weary legs, when suddenly Ali appeared and came into my cell.

'You'll get used to it in time,' he commented, seeing me massage my legs. I said nothing.

Yusuf, who was also there, busy sending text messages, sniffed with annoyance to see his brother appear.

'Why don't you study silat?' Ali asked him.

'Not interested,' Yusuf answered without looking at him. 'It's good to learn self-defence,' Ali continued.

'I can defend myself without all that stuff,' Yusuf said.

'Right, with a mobile?' Ali mocked.

'What are you doing here? It's cramped enough in here as is,' Yusuf said by way of trying to get his brother to leave. Obviously uncomfortable to have him in the room, Yusuf had initially tried to conceal his mobile. He'd never told Ali how he had been able to purchase the phone. But Ali didn't seem interested in learning the answer to that question.

'I just came to tell you that if you're going to go outside, not to come back so late. This is a pesantren, after all.'

Yusuf's attention was fixed on his mobile and the text message he was writing.

'And if you are going to go out, you are to ask for my permission.'

'OK. Is that all?'

Ali took a deep breath. I just sat there, trying to pretend to be invisible as I massaged my sore calves. It was uncomfortable for me to be involved in this confrontation between the two brothers. Ali apparently cared for Yusuf and wanted to know what he was up to, but Yusuf already felt himself to be old enough not to have to report to anyone.

'I also came to tell you that the teacher is going away for a while, to Egypt, so for the time being at least ...'

'There will be no recitations!' Yusuf immediately concluded with enthusiasm, while lifting his eyes from his mobile for a moment.

'No, that's not it,' Ali said.

Hearing that, Yusuf immediately returned his attention to his mobile, not interested in what his brother had to say. I silently asked myself, if Yusuf didn't like living in the pesantren, why didn't he move out? What was stopping him?

'While the teacher is gone,' Ali continued, 'Ustadz Asman will be leading recitation practice.'

Ustadz Asman was much younger than the old teacher, and I was pleased with this news. Ever since our first meeting, I'd taken a shine to Ustadz Asman – despite the beatings my calves took.

I'm not sure why I was so interested in learning pencak silat, but the image of my body, muscles hardened and glistening with sweat, held a certain appeal for me. As an added plus, I wouldn't have to run away from a brawl. My goals differed from the original purpose of pencak silat, to be able to defend oneself. I saw it as a way of increasing my self-confidence. I wanted to be macho.

Self-Awareness

My expectations didn't prove to be completely accurate. After the kiai left for his trip to Egypt and the reins of leadership at the pesantren passed to Ustadz Asman, recitation lessons were modified to include a number of additional texts he wanted us to study; they increased in frequency as well. He had us memorizing *nadzhom* verses from the *Al-fiyah*. Most of the santri didn't object; in fact many were enthusiastic. Ustadz Asman had become a kind of celebrity among the boarders. During breaks or in times of relaxation, he was always surrounded by a flock of admirers hanging on to his every word as he told them stories about strange, mysterious experiences.

However, I soon found the new schedule very taxing. I was going to school, after all, doing practical training, and I had to tend to Paris as well. Soon Ustadz Asman had us practice pencak silat every three days, not just once a week as before. He also encouraged us to fast regularly, every other day, the so-called 'David fast', named after the prophet David. In fact, he made fasting a requirement for those who were of sufficient means and had no physical impairment. That, however, was one thing I refused to do.

The only thing I really liked was pencak silat. I hated fasting and memorizing texts. In a week's time, I might at best be able to memorize just four lines of *nadzhom*, each consisting of eight rhymed sentences in Arabic. I did the best I could, but it seemed that whenever I managed to memorize a new line, I'd forget the previous one I had learned.

Yusuf was even worse: he didn't try to memorize anything at all. In fact, he stopped going to recitation lessons altogether. He seemed to disappear into the woodwork of the pesantren. He didn't care. For him, the pesantren was now just a place to sleep at night. For him, Ustadz Asman was not like the kiai, who commanded a certain level of respect. Yusuf would leave in the morning and return in the evening, always speaking loudly when he met anyone so that his brother would know that he was around. Once in our cell, he would lie around, sending text messages and speaking in whispers on his phone.

One evening in mid-February, Paris called me on Yusuf's mobile.

'I never hear from you anymore,' he began with a sigh.

'We see each other at school,' I said.

'But we don't go out anymore. You're always rushing to get back the pesantren.'

'I've been super busy,' I explained. 'The new man in charge, Ustadz Asman, is a killer. He doesn't know the word for fun.'

'But you live in the same pesantren as Yusuf and he gets out,' Paris challenged.

I didn't want to have to justify my action. 'Listen,' I said, 'Yusuf can tell you all about it.' With that, I handed the mobile back to Yusuf and they talked merrily about clothes, the men they had met, or whatever.

A few days later, Ali invited me into his cell and abruptly asked, 'Do you know where Yusuf goes at night?'

My eyes focused on the dust motes alighting on the thick books that lined Ali's wobbly shelf.

'You know I don't like having to ask you about him,' Ali

added slowly.

'I'm not sure where he goes,' I confessed. 'He doesn't tell me either.'

I looked outside the window and then back at Ali. His eyes, with their soft look and long lashes, resembled Yusuf's. I saw in them a bright glow, a cry for help, which stirred my sympathy.

'I don't think Yusuf likes living here,' I opined.

'Well, if he didn't live here, where would he live?' Ali asked, as if to himself.

I started to play with my thumbnails. 'Doesn't he – or you – have a family home somewhere?'

'This is our home. If there's any place for him to call home, this is it.'

I said nothing. There seemed to be a sad story behind Ali's statement, but one I wasn't sure I wanted to hear. Suddenly I felt a feeling of growing concern for Yusuf, the same one that Ali seemed to be feeling.

'Yusuf isn't just a kid now. He can take care of himself,' I said, trying to ease Ali's worry.

After a pause, Ali replied, 'Maybe you're right, but even if he is older now, for me he's still my little brother.'

I nodded as if in agreement but wasn't completely convinced of the sentiment. I had three older siblings and they didn't seem to care about their little brother. If Ali was speaking truthfully, then Yusuf was very lucky, I thought.

'When Yusuf was little, he would always cry when he saw a grown man and ask me to get him a daddy.' Ali smiled wistfully. 'It makes me sad to think of that. Yusuf is still, in my eyes, the same little boy he was then.'

I didn't know why the young Yusuf had wanted a 'daddy,' and I didn't want to find out. I was not a friend of his from the past; he was my friend in the present. All I knew was that he had neither parents nor home, that he didn't like living in the pesantren, and that he was happy with his current life. That was enough for me. The past was no more important than the dirt beneath my toenails.

At that moment, Ustadz Asman came into the cell. Since he had returned to the pesantren and took on the teacher's role, he had been living in Ali's cell. At first I wondered why he didn't live in the teacher's house, but at one point he told me, unasked, that he wanted to be closer to the santri.

Initially I'd had a very positive impression of the man, but with the passing of time I came to view Ustadz Asman more critically. He did as he pleased with little concern for or consultation with the boarders, and what I disliked worse was his constant gung-ho attitude. It never varied. Nonetheless, he did possess a greater magnetism than any of the santri. There was a scent of glamour about him; even his clothes smelled of money.

'What are you two up to?' he asked. 'Am I disturbing you?' he asked, after neither Ali nor I offered him an answer. He sat down in front of Ali.

I said the first thing that passed through my mind: 'I came here to ask Ali about the power of invulnerability.' Of course I hadn't planned to ask Ali about *ilmu tekbal*, but recently the residents had been talking about the knowledge of self-awareness, or *kanuragan*, which Ustadz Asman seemed to possess. I was, in fact, curious about it.

'Are you serious?' Ustadz Asman asked enthusiastically. For a moment I glanced at Ali, whose glare was a warning for me to stop.

'Yes. One reason I ask is because of the brawls between the kids at my school and other schools.'

'You're studying pencak silat now. That should prepare you to be able to defend yourself,' Ali said.

'But pencak silat alone doesn't seem to be enough,' I countered. 'It's just a series of positions, and it takes so long to learn.'

'You're right,' Ustadz Asman nodded. 'If you want, you could study *kebatinan* and the kinds of knowledge that come from inner power. Would you like to do that?' he offered. 'There are numerous kinds. There's one with no physical contact at all, which is called spiritual contact. With that one, even if someone stabs you, you'll not be hurt. That's what's called *ilmu tekbal* – invulnerability.'

This sounded interesting to me. I'm not the kind person who generally believes in superhuman powers or such, but I know that some of those forms of knowledge do exist. Look at the people from Banten, for instance, who are known for *debus*, being able to pierce themselves with swords and not come to any harm. I'd seen that one with my own eyes.

'I'd like to be invulnerable to stabbing,' I said, thinking of the incident with Oskar.

'That's possible, as long as your will is strong,' Ustadz Asman told me. 'But to acquire that knowledge, you'd have to do something, undertake some kind of sacrifice or perform a good deed. It wouldn't have to involve *mahar*,' he assured me.

Mahar is a kind of tribute or monetary recompense one paid the person who provided such knowledge. The thought of not having to pay Ustadz Asman made my face brighten with pleasure. 'I'd like that, I would.'

'But you don't need that kind of thing,' Ali again insisted. 'Better that you learn your recitations and the knowledge will come on its own.'

Ustadz Asman ignored Ali's comment. 'If you want the

knowledge, I can provide it, but you have to be able to do what I ask.'

'What would that be?' I tried to guess.

The man's eyes sparkled. 'First of all, you must white-fast for forty days.'

'What's that?' I asked.

'That's when you eat nothing except white foods. Rice and cassava, for instance, are OK, as is water. And, if possible, to wear white clothes the whole time.'

'I could do that,' I said enthusiastically.

'And there's a prayer in Arabic that you must read aloud ten thousand times a night without dozing off. If you fall asleep, you must repeat the prayer from the beginning.'

My mouth dropped open so wide I must have looked like a buffalo.

'After that, you must undertake a complete fast – *puasa patigeni* – with no food, drink, or sleep for two days and two nights.'

'Are you serious?' I asked.

'You're the one who must be serious. This is no game. Obtaining such knowledge is not easy.'

'And you need to be constantly on guard. Late at night, after prayers, evil spirits will come to disturb you.' That was Ali, trying to frighten me.

I said nothing, but the thought of staying up all night with evil spirits lurking around was unsettling. And reciting a prayer out loud ten thousand times? Plus fasting and not sleeping for two days? No way. My enthusiasm deflated instantly like a flat tire.

'Well, what about it?' Ustadz Asman asked with a smile. Judging from his expression, I knew he didn't think me able.

He'd obviously been planning that from the very beginning.

OK, maybe I did want some kind of superhuman power, but not that way.

'No, I don't think I'm in the mood right now,' I said, and got up to leave.

Hearing my answer, Ustadz Asman smiled broadly. Crap.

Shoes

The sound of the bell that signalled the end of the last class for the day caused my entire class to jump up and leave the classroom, completely ignoring the teacher, who was still standing before them.

My classmates scattered, moving noisily and joking raucously as they drifted towards the school entrance. I hung back a bit from the rest, moving more slowly, content to take my time, when suddenly I felt someone slap me on the back. I turned in surprise and then smiled. It was Paris.

'Hi,' he said and then began to walk beside me but said nothing more.

Glancing at him out of the corner of my eye, I could see him staring intently at me. There was a look of jealousy in his eyes. I knew why, of course, and what with all my frequent absences, he probably had a right to sulk. Even so, I also felt a little irritated and finally stared back at him.

'What?' I asked as we walked towards the parking lot.

'You're bored with me, aren't you?' he asked coyly, just as if he really were a girl and I was his boyfriend.

'What are you talking about?'

At that remark, he pouted.

'Don't be mad, honey ...' I teased and seeing him suddenly blush made me want to laugh. I took his hand but he immediately slapped my hand away. His face was now almost magenta.

He took his wallet from his back pocket, removed a number of bills, and gave them to me.

'Here, this is for you, but Saturday, after school, you have to be there for me. Period.'

Two hundred and fifty thousand.

I quickly pocketed the money, afraid of being seen by another student. 'Not Saturday,' I said unconsciously. I had pencak silat practice Saturday night. We had just learned the proper stance for fighting and a number of new moves as well, and I was at the stage where I was beginning to enjoy it. My hands were bruised and my knuckles were calloused and blistered from all the push-ups we had to do and from punching a rice bag filled with sand, but I didn't want to miss the next practice.

'Up to you, then ... but if you're not there, it's over,' Paris said, and got in his car and drove off without asking me if I would like a ride.

I could do nothing but take a deep breath.

Saturday morning I went to Ustadz Asman to ask his permission to go and to tell him that I wouldn't be able to attend pencak silat practice or recitation lessons that day. He just nodded, as if not caring whether I came or not. His attitude perturbed me but then I remembered what he had once told the boarders at a recitation session: 'The ones who need knowledge are you. If you want to be smart, you have to study. You have to follow recitation, you have to memorize. If you don't, you may as well leave. There is no one forcing you to hear me speak. All of you are free to determine your own way though life.' His tone was adamant, and what he said made sense.

On Saturday I took a change of clothes with me to school so that I wouldn't have to go back to the pesantren afterwards. In the parking lot after school had been let out, I found Paris waiting for me in a new car of a different make and colour.

'Wow! New wheels!' I said. The car, a Nissan Terrano, had a kind of rugged look to it. A number of other students – younger ones, mostly – watched this little scene with a look of wonder on their faces. Even though I felt a twinge of discomfort because they saw me going off with Paris, I also felt proud to be in the category of people who rode in cars that people oohed and aahed over.

'It's Oskar's,' Paris said breezily. 'Look: even his key chain is tasteless,' he said, pointing to a miniature mummy on a chain. 'How is he anyway?' I asked. It had been a while since I'd seen him.

'Yesterday, he borrowed my car and scraped the paint on one side. So, today, I have his and I intend to wreck it!'

'You don't have to go that far,' I advised, fastening my seatbelt.

'At the very least I'm going to get rid of this tacky key chain,' Paris said jokingly, yet I detected a tremble in his voice. He seemed nervous for some reason.

'Where to? The mall?' I asked lightly, trying to chase the look of worry from his face.

'No, a hotel,' Paris said lightly.

'Serious?' I asked while taking the sunglasses that he was wearing and putting them on my head. I looked in the car's front mirror and saw a good-looking young man stare back at me.

Paris just smiled. I knew that he would do nothing about it.

Fighting traffic, Paris drove to Serpong where he parked the car at the International Trade Centre, a place we'd never been to together. Silently, we headed towards the food court. As we walked, I jokingly took Paris's hand in mine. Of late, I had begun to feel more comfortable about myself and didn't care what other people thought.

When walking past a sporting goods shop, I spotted in the

window a pair of Converse shoes I coveted. Slowing down my stride I squeezed Paris's hand and then whispered in his ear. 'I'd love a pair of Converse shoes,' I said, though I pronounced the name 'Kon-ves.'

'It's pronounced *Kon-vers*,' he said, stressing the *r*.

'OK, but I'd really love a new pair of shoes,' I said again, this time with more stress on the word 'love'.

Paris looked down at the shoes I was wearing: an old pair of Warriors that were full of holes and soles that were ready to fall off. I remembered when my mother purchased them for me: a cheap pair, black in colour with rubber soles that had been so stiff all of my toes blistered the first time I wore them. Now their colour was a shade similar to that of an old wash rag, and the big toe of my right foot was peeking from a hole at the shoe's tip.

Without another word, Paris pulled me into the store, which was shoe heaven. I looked around in heightened envy, inspecting the shoes pair by pair. Nice lines, well made, comfortable-looking. I waited for an order from Paris to choose which one. I myself couldn't make a choice, because I liked all of them.

Paris looked at me and I looked back with the gaze of a baby shrew.

'This pair,' he said pointing to a black-and-blue, double-soled pair with backs above the ankle. I tried them on. They felt comfortable and looked good: they were meant for me. But then I looked at the price tag – Rp. 900,000! – and shook my head with dismay. They were much too expensive! Watching me, Paris clicked his tongue impatiently and then took the shoes from my hand, strode to the cashier and paid for them. I put them on straight away and threw away the skeletal remains of my old pair into a trash bin. 'Stuff the poor-boy act,' was the comment I kept hearing in my mind.

With new shoes on my feet, we continued our walk to a KFC outlet, where I ordered chicken as well as a hamburger and a large order of French fries. Paris ordered pudding and a soft drink. He looked increasingly impatient. Guessing that he wanted to do more shopping, I quickly finished my food, stuffing the rest of the bun and burger into my mouth.

I then chugged the rest of my drink and pulled on Paris's arm. 'Let's go!'

'Where?' Paris remained in his chair, thinking about something.

'Shopping, right? Isn't that what you want to do?' I asked.

He shook his head then pulled on my arm until I sat down again.

Something wasn't right. 'What is it?' I asked, my shoulders raised.

'I don't want to shop.'

I felt guilty. Maybe he was out of money from having bought that pair of shoes for me.

'Sorry ... short on funds?' I asked hesitantly.

'No, that's not it.'

'What is it then?'

Paris looked down at the floor, as if afraid to look me in the eye.

I was becoming impatient.

Finally, he spoke: 'I want to go to a hotel.'

Hotel

I looked at Paris anxiously. All of a sudden, my throat felt dry and my muscles stiff. 'A hotel?' I repeated, as if not sure what I'd heard. Paris nodded in reply. Why, I don't know, but the tension I was feeling suddenly spread to the hairs on my thighs, causing them to tingle. But Paris looked even more forlorn than me. His facial muscles twitched and he began to nibble his lips. His eyes looked moist. I felt sorry for him, and that shooed away my hesitation. I came to a decision: to act like more of a man for him.

'Come on,' I said between heavy intakes of breath.

Paris looked at me, afraid. I was nervous, too, but could sense that he was in a far greater quandary. I moved closer to him, put my arm around his shoulders, and again suggested that we leave. Our steps were heavy, but we finally reached the car. He was silent. I said nothing either. I didn't want to look at him, because I was afraid that would make him more nervous. 'Do you already know the hotel?' I asked.

Out of the corner of my eye, I saw Paris nod. He started the engine, and we left. The car smelled of apples – an air freshener, I suppose – and the sense of Oskar's presence became sharper: the seats were worn and there were coffee stains and cigarette burns everywhere.

We turned back in the direction we had come from earlier and headed towards Karawaci, traversing the same traffic jam we had confronted earlier. After about a half hour, we arrived at the

Aryaduta, a 'four and a half star' hotel, located not far from the Supermall. Unless you count the time I went to Pronto on my first night of clubbing, I had never been in a hotel before. For a moment the feeling of worry in my chest was replaced by the astonishment of a kid from the kampung. I gazed up in wonder at the place before me. After I removed a large suitcase from the truck of the car, we entered the hotel and registered at the front desk.

'Room 219,' said the receptionist and handed over the key. A man in livery took the key and led us to our room. I lagged behind, studying the hotel's architecture and its furnishings with a look of awe. The walls and floors were all of shining marble. Small trees in oversized decorative pots dotted the room. A grand winding staircase led to the second floor. Sculptures made from large chunks of alabaster looked very expensive. And the people there, walking leisurely through the lobby, seemed to exude a special aroma: the scent of wealth.

In short time, we arrived at our room, a Deluxe-class room with a king-size bed, walls painted in soothing shades of cream and beige, and coffee-coloured curtains and furniture. The porter motioned for us to enter and then placed the suitcase on a low table. His ever-present smile looked forced; I guessed he was hoping for a tip. I glanced around the room, not sure what I was feeling. I had never imagined myself being in such a place. I stood silently in place, like a statue, until I heard Paris thank the porter and close the door. I heard the lock click loudly in place.

I walked to the farther side of the room, with floor-to-ceiling glass windows. After surveying the scene outside, I turned and looked at Paris, who was standing on the other side of the bed from me, but he avoided my eyes.

I felt a rattle in my chest like the sound of a tin can being kicked down the street. My fingertips began to strum against my outer thigh of their own volition. Paris moved slowly from where he had been standing and then sat down on the edge of the bed. I moved towards him uncertainly. My feet felt heavy. I looked at my shoes, my new shoes. Finally, I reached the bed and sat down beside him.

Paris's fingers played with the hem of his shirt. I leaned back on my elbows, and stretched my legs widely. It felt like a bomb was ready to explode in my heart. Even though the room was cold from air-conditioning, I had begun to sweat. My whole body felt damp.

I'd never thought our relationship would reach this stage, though I shouldn't have been surprised. Paris was keeping me, after all, wasn't he? He bought me clothes, treated me to meals, and gave me pocket money regularly. And he had just bought me a very expensive pair of shoes. He had the right to touch me. Though I silently objected, I did realize, deep in my heart at least, that this day would come. I just didn't know that today would be that day.

I would surrender and let it happen. He could touch my thighs. He could grope my crotch. He could kiss my cheeks, forehead, neck, and lips – whatever he wanted. I didn't have to enjoy it. But I knew that afterwards, our relationship would never be the same, and that I would leave him.

Secretly, I was disappointed that Paris wanted to have sex with me. We had become friends, and I thought that was how he, too, wanted our relationship to be: friendship. For that, I respected him.

The two of us just sat there on the edge of the bed, like a pair of herons waiting for fish to pass. Silently, observing each other. I didn't know whether I should make the first move or to wait for him to touch me first. I coughed.

'I hope ...' he said hesitantly, but stopped, his voice catching. 'I hope you won't think bad of me.'

The sentence had been very difficult for him to say.

I shook my head. OK, I got it. I understood. I thought of Yusuf who had been right about me after all: I was no different from him. I was a sex worker, even if only an amateur one, and Paris had the right to my body. It was I who had asked him to keep me, and now he was asking for payback, which was his right. Again, I thought of Yusuf who had accused me of selling myself and how angry I had become, maybe because I knew he was right, and I was just too ashamed or too embarrassed to admit it.

'I've brought you here because this is something I have wanted to do for a long time,' he said sadly, in explanation.

I nodded my head, still unable to speak.

'I just never had the nerve to do it before.'

I trembled in my silence.

'It's only you, you see ... It's only you that I can trust.'

Only for me that he had feelings? Sexual feelings? The entire time I'd known him, he'd never shown any desire for me.

'You can think what you will, and afterwards you can leave me if that's your choice. I know that's the risk of doing this. But I want you to understand that this desire I feel is not something new; I've always wanted to do this ... I just have never known with whom. It's only you,' he said again. He paused, then began again: 'I don't want you to hate me. I just want to be myself ...'

I could take the melodrama no longer. It was only sex, after all. I wanted to get it over with quickly and then get beyond it, without the prolonged preliminaries. Whether I hated him or not afterwards would be a different story. It would be my story.

'You don't know how hard this decision was for me to make.'

174

Paris, with his feminine alter-ego, didn't want to be ashamed of losing his virginity. Maybe that was the dilemma!

'OK, let's do it!' Those were the only words that came out of my mouth – a sign of my agreement that he could do whatever he wanted to do.

'Are you sure?' he asked, still afraid.

'Yes, do whatever you want to do,' I said in as manly a voice as possible.

Rather than let this preliminary act go on forever, I decided to make the first move. I wanted this nightmare to be over. But when I moved closer to him, ready to embrace him, Paris suddenly rose from where he was sitting.

I looked at him surprised.

'Are you sure you're ready for this?' he asked.

I nodded, but before I could do anything he stepped away from me and grabbed his suitcase.

'I'm going to the bathroom,' he said, lugging the suitcase with him.

As in a soap opera, I imagined a crying session taking place in there.

I tried to relax as much as possible. Maybe you won't believe me, but in this situation, as weird as it was, I sniffed my armpits for body odour and tested the smell of my breath. Then out of the blue a strange thought occurred to me: I didn't want Paris to be disappointed in me.

I waited five minutes, then ten. I tapped my new shoes on the brown-coloured carpet and felt it with my fingers. I'd never seen a floor completely covered with carpeting. I took off my new shoes and then my socks. Fifteen minutes passed … Feeling stiff in the shoulders, I got up and walked around room, absorbing the room's atmosphere. I sniffed the air, I felt the walls, I opened the curtain to view the cityscape outside. I lowered the temperature of the air-conditioning and played with the lights. I was like a spinning top. Nearly half an hour must have passed before I finally lay down on the mattress. Wow, I had never slept on a mattress as nice as this one: soft, nice-smelling and clean. I resisted the thought of rolling around on top of it with Paris.

I began to get worried. What was Paris doing in the bathroom? God forbid he wanted to kill himself. Or maybe he was already dead. I jumped up and went to the bathroom door.

'Paris!' I called.

I heard the sound of rustling inside. 'Just a second. I'm not ready yet.'

My heartbeat slowed. At least he wasn't dead. Though I did ask myself, what kind of preparations for making love took thirty minutes of time alone in the bathroom? I hoped he didn't want to do anything too weird.

I turned on the flat plasma TV attached to the wall opposite the end of the bed. Cable TV. I skimmed through the listings but didn't find anything of interest, until I finally decided to watch a SpongeBob cartoon in English. I didn't understand much of what was being said, but I laughed at the characters' expressions.

And then the door to the bathroom cracked open.

Woman

I never thought that I would lose my virginity to a man – and to a friend of mine at that. I tried to think about what we might do. I knew how my sex organ worked, but I had never given serious thought to having sex with a man before.

The bathroom door opened wider, and I turned my head. My heart was beating so fast I thought it might explode.

Slowly, a figure emerged from the bathroom that caused my eyes to open wide. My heart, which had been pounding before, suddenly seemed to stop, as if suspended. I was thunderstruck and unable to speak. I was dazzled by the bright light, but it wasn't a bright light. It was Paris, who looked like … Wait, was it Paris? Maybe it wasn't, but I knew it had to be. I knew his face and his features – but before me I saw a woman.

'Are you freaked out?' he asked stiffly.

Unconsciously, I nodded but then quickly shook my head. 'Is that you?' I stuttered.

Paris nodded, as confidently as possible but his legs were shaking.

I frowned as I opened my mouth to speak: 'But, but why are you dressed like that?'

My eyes first noticed the high heels; I remembered having helped him pick them out. And then the black mesh stockings. My eyes rose to a clinging blouse tucked into a closely fitting skirt. I remembered him shopping for those items too. Around his waist was an oversized belt made of fake snakeskin. And then the hair, a wig he had purchased at a secondhand store, and the face, which was covered with a thick layer of powder along with mascara and rouge. His lips were a flaming shade of red.

'Do you think I look pretty?' he asked hesitantly.

It was like I hadn't heard the question. I was confused and felt caught off guard. 'Why are you wearing women's clothes?' I asked.

'Do they look good on me?' he asked, now annoyed. I shook my head.

'They don't look right on me?' He sounded surprised.

Instead of answering, I snapped at him: 'What are you doing? What's this about?'

'All I'm asking is if the clothes look good on me.' He now sounded worried.

'You want to pretend to be a woman? You want to have sex in those clothes?' I asked him. I could hear the voices of SpongeBob and Patrick laughing on the flat TV screen. They seemed to be laughing at me.

Paris suddenly looked shocked. 'Sex? What are you talking about?'

Now I was confused. 'Well that's why you asked me here, isn't it?'

'Are you crazy!' he screamed so loud, I thought his false eyelashes were going to pop off his eyes. 'You idiot!' he again swore at me with a trembling voice. 'I don't want to have sex with you! Are you out of your mind?'

I blinked. My stomach lurched. 'Then why did you ask me?'

'For you to see me is all! To tell me if I'm pretty! Whether I look good or not! All I want is your opinion, not sex, you moron!'

He then moved close to me, sticking his face in mine: 'Do I

look good or not!'

'Nooo …' I answered. Paris glared at me. 'You're a guy. Why do you want to dress in women's clothing?'

'So what if I want to wear women's clothing? Is that wrong? I want to be a woman!'

'Even if you do put on women's clothing, you're still going to be a guy,' I argued hesitantly. 'You were born that way.'

'Don't you understand?' Paris huffed in front of my face. 'I want to be a woman!'

I didn't know what to do. Whatever I said was sure to be wrong. Paris's face and my eyes were only two centimetres apart and I could feel the heat of his breath. Suddenly, he collapsed on the floor, on the soft carpet. Covering his eyes, he began to cry.

I stood there awkwardly as he cried and sobbed like a rejected woman in a soap-opera. Silently, my eyes searched the room. I let him cry until finally he raised his head and looked up at me.

His face was like a frightening mask. A rivulet of black flowed from his eyes. The rouge on his cheeks was smudged. His eyes were bloodshot, powder stained his hands, and his teeth were smeared with lipstick.

'Go on, look in the mirror. You look scary,' I said honestly. 'You look like a cartoon character, not like a woman.'

Paris stifled his sobs, then rose and retreated to the bathroom. I laid down on the mattress and stared at the ceiling, using my arms and hands as a pillow. Crazy!

When he finally came out of the bathroom, I told Paris that he didn't look pretty, that his clothing was over the top and that he looked like a hooker. At that remark, he finally laughed, if only between his sobs and tears. I then ordered him to change, which he did, along with repacking his wig, which really did look fake, and all the other accoutrements that he had brought in the large suitcase.

'Why do you want to be a banci?' I asked him.

'I don't want to be a banci! I want to be a girl!' he protested. 'I'm tired of being a guy.'

'That's a reason? That you're tired of being a guy?' I asked.

'You don't understand. You're a guy. Guy's never understand. The only thing guys do is make trouble. I don't want to be a guy. I hate guys.'

'I'm a guy, aren't I?'

'I know, but I don't hate you,' he said softly, packing up to leave. Hmmm, that was too bad, I thought; Paris had already paid for the room and we weren't even going to use it. I wanted to see what it would be like sleeping in such a luxurious place.

The atmosphere in the car was strained. Paris was as nervous as when we had arrived.

'Don't hate me,' he said with his hands on the wheels.

'Neah, neah,' I said, no promise at all.

To break the silence, he turned on the CD player, rock music by the band My Chemical Romance.

'What trash!' Paris swore as he switched off the CD player.

After he dropped me off at the pesantren, I lay around in my cell, waiting for the evening to pass. It was quiet. Most of the other residents were still at pencak silat class. I felt a little chagrined for having skipped the lesson that night, but, on the other hand, I was happy that I hadn't lost my virginity. Even better, I now knew that Paris was not attracted to me. That was a relief, but the question for me was, why did Paris want to be a woman? Was it because of his feminine mannerisms? Did all guys with feminine mannerisms want to be women? Did Yusuf want to be a woman, too?

While I was staring at holes in the ceiling of my cell, Yusuf suddenly came in. I looked at him; it felt like I hadn't seen him for a very long time. He tossed his bag into the corner of the room and shut the door.

'Look at this,' he said. He held a sarong, a very expensive one by the sight of it. 'You'll never be able to afford one,' he added snottily, neatly refolding the red cloth with black stripes into its original shape. 'I'm going to give it to Ali, a little bribe for him to stop asking questions and spying on me.'

'But won't that make him even more suspicious?' I argued.

'I thought of that already,' he answered, his eyes narrowing as he looked at me. 'I'm going to tell him that I'm working, which is the reason I'm not at the pesantren so often.'

'What's your job going to be?'

'I'm going to tell him that it's a secret,' he answered with little concern.

'But what if he asks me?'

'Tell him I'm working as an SPG! See how clever I am?' he asked with a dramatic flair.

I wondered if Yusuf knew that an SPG was a Sales Point Girl. A truer lie might be SPB.

'On Wednesday I'm going clubbing again, and I want you to come along. I want you to meet some rich people.'

'Forget it,' I told him. 'What kind of guy do you think I am?'

'You're a money boy. Come on, the reason you started seeing Paris was for the money, wasn't it?'

Yusuf knew exactly where to get me. He'd hit the mark. With his eyes studying me, I turned away.

Too much information that night: one friend wanting to be a woman, another one trading his body for favours from older men.

Bedroom

When Paris didn't come to school the next day, I thought it was because he might be embarrassed to see me. On Wednesday he appeared in his car outside the school gate but didn't come into the school. Instead, he waited for me to finish classes. When I appeared, he flashed his lights at me and called for me to get inside.

'You smell,' was his greeting as I got in the car.

I sniffed my shirt which did smell of grime and sweat from my work in the shop.

'What are you doing, skipping school? Exams are coming up,' I said, ignoring his comment about my smell.

'I want to quit school,' he said as he started the car.

'Yesterday you wanted to stop being a guy, and now you want to quit school. What about tomorrow? Are you going to want to stop living?' I joked.

Paris didn't smile.

'I don't need a degree,' he explained. 'My business is good, and I have savings.'

That much was obvious from his shopping trips and spending money on me – unlike yours truly, who was dependent on his largesse. As the car moved away from the curb, I finally asked: 'Why did you come to pick me up?'

'I want to go out. I'm feeling stressed.'

'I didn't bring a change of clothes,' I said.

'We can find you some clothes at my house.'

So we went directly to Paris's house. By that time I'd already given a number of reasons for not coming along, but he refused to listen.

Paris's house wasn't what I had expected. I'd imagined a house on a large plot of land with a huge blue swimming pool and an imposing gateway. Such was not the case. He lived in an elite housing section of Bumi Serpong Damai, or BSD City as everyone called it. The house was two-stories high and large enough, to be pretty much the same. All of them were inhabited by people with money, evident in the expensive cars parked in front and the large pure-bred dogs that were being walked by servants.

When we went inside, I saw the stereotypical housemaid of a modern Indonesian home. Dressed in a T-shirt much too small for the size of her breasts and tight calf-length jeans, her braided hair was pulled back, and her face was much lighter in colour than her neck. She didn't look friendly in the least, and Paris didn't even greet her.

'Ignore her. Consider she doesn't exist,' Paris said to me as he climbed the stairway to his room. I guess the servant was the one who had answered the phone the first time I called the house. When Paris opened the door to his room, my first impression was that the place had no character – which was not at all what I had expected. I had imagined a room with pink walls, lots of dolls, and other things a teenage girl might like. I also imagined a large array of photographs of Paris in various poses with decorative frames, and a scent of perfume in the air. In fact, the room was plain and ordinary, like the cubicle of an office employee who didn't care about his job. The walls were a plain white discoloured with age. The clothes cupboard was a simple upright rectangular wooden box with a large mirror on the door. On the desk was an aged and scummy-looking computer which Paris had apparently forsaken for his new laptop. The ivory-coloured tile floor was marked with beverage stains and candle wax. It was a large room with no personal touches. The air-conditioning made the place feel even colder than it was.

'Welcome to Tara,' Paris said softly, stretching out his arms as if to announce that this was his room. The mattress on the bed, which might have once been firm and comfortable, was now lumpy and uneven. Without thinking about it, I unbuttoned my shirt because that's what I usually did when I went into my room after school.

'I don't have a key. I don't even have a key to my own room!' Paris said loudly, while looking in the mirror. 'My life is shit – born in a wrong body to a fucked-up family.'

'Does your father come here often? Is that it?' I guessed.

Paris curled his lips and remarked sarcastically. 'He doesn't just come in; he goes through my belongings and anything he thinks is girly, he throws out.' He then smiled slyly. 'What do you think his reaction would be if I became a real girl?'

At that point, the door opened and Oskar came in. He looked at me lying on the bed with the buttons of my shirt now open.

'Oh, you have a guest,' he said as he turned up his nose. 'Sorry to disturb!' His tone and smile said differently.

I wanted to throw the large vase in the corner of the room at him, but he had already retreated and closed the door.

'He's crazy, you know,' Paris said while staring at the door. He then turned to me with a strange and unexpected glow on his face. 'What would you like to drink? Are you hungry? I'll cook something for you!'

'Up to you,' I said surprised by the offer.

'Go through my cupboard and find some clothes that fit you

and take a bath,' he said pointing to a door to the bathroom before leaving the room.

I bathed quickly, afraid that someone might be watching; stupidly, I imagined that his father had placed hidden cameras in the bathroom. I picked out a T-shirt and a pair of shorts but dismissed the thought of borrowing underwear. Paris and I were about the same height, but he was slimmer, and his form-fitting clothes were tight on me. I found a stick of deodorant lying on the countertop and applied some to my armpits. It was a men's brand, but the stick had never been used. The only other thing on the counter was a comb. Maybe the place was bare because Paris's father had thrown away everything. If his father knew that Paris had a warehouse of women's clothing and makeup stored at one of the salons he supplied, he would probably force his son to drink a can of mosquito repellent.

After brushing the comb through my hair, I opened the door to look around. Directly in front of Paris's room was another room, the door to which was open. Curious, I stuck my head inside and heard rock music playing at a low volume. There was Oskar on his bed, flipping through a magazine. He turned and looked in my direction and gave me what seemed to be a sneer.

I entered his room without asking.

'Oh, you've washed up.' His tone was still cynical.

'Up yours,' I answered. 'And here you are in your underwear, flipping through a magazine. What are you doing?' I sparred in kind.

'These are what you call boxers and this is a music magazine, not *Playboy*,' Oskar pointed the magazine in my direction.

'Sure, whatever,' I said in a tone of disbelief.

Unlike Paris's room, the atmosphere in Oskar's room was one of comfortable dishevelment. The floor was covered with a thick carpet. On his single bed was a thick blanket and comfortable pillows in disarray. At the foot of the bed, his high-school uniform lay in a heap. Next to it was a CD and cassette player with a set of large speakers, with a pile of CDs and cassettes next to it. Leaning against the wall was a guitar. Across the room was a large screen plasma TV with a PlayStation on the floor in front of it. And on one wall was a poster of a man with his tongue stuck out wildly.

'So?' Oskar asked, seeing me study his room.

The smell of the room also said something: it was the smell of Oskar. This is what I wanted my room to be like. Envious, I sat down on the carpet in front of the TV. I had fallen in love with his room the moment I set foot in it.

'Want to try the PlayStation?' he asked.

'Don't know how,' I answered.

'Want to watch a DVD?' he then asked.

'Not really,' I said.

'Do you play guitar?'

'No,' I said.

Oskar took the acoustic guitar leaning against the wall and strummed a tune. 'That was in G,' he said, 'my favourite key.'

He then sang three verses of a song in English, whose words I had also memorized but hardly knew the meaning of. I stared at him, fascinated.

After finishing the song, he looked at me and smiled: 'Easy as pie!' He handed the guitar to me and I tried to imitate him.

Just as Oskar was righting the position of my fingers, Paris came in. Hands on his hips, he said, 'I leave you for a second, and immediately you start to stray. And with my stepbrother besides. Ungrateful wretch!'

Boy Love

'Let's go clubbing tonight,' Paris said as I was stuffing my mouth with a large slice of pizza in Oskar's room. Paris had been kidding about cooking for me. In fact, he had ordered a take-out pizza and when he left the room it was only to go outside to wait for the pizza to arrive. No protest from me, of course. The pizza was delicious, but a meal without rice didn't feel quite like a meal to me.

'But this is only Wednesday night,' I said with surprise.

'Yusuf says that Wednesday night is the most fun time to go,' Paris answered, sticking a hunk of garlic bread in his mouth.

'But I have practice tonight.'

'What kind of practice?' Oskar asked.

'Pencak silat.'

While Oskar blinked with surprise Paris burst into laughter.

'Why are you laughing?' I demanded.

'It's just funny is all, in this day and age, studying silat.'

I argued, frowning with annoyance, 'It's for self-defence!'

'People these days are studying aikido or capoeira, something with a little class but here you are studying silat. So last century!'

When Paris rolled his eyes and flipped his hands up, I wanted to force-feed him the cardboard box the pizza had been delivered in.

'You study silat at the pesantren?' Oskar inquired between Paris's chortles. (Ah, good, Paris almost choked on his pizza and was coughing.)

'Yeah.'

'What's your teacher like?' Oskar then asked.

'He's great. Been all over the place, Java and Madura anyway,' I said of Ustadz Asman.

'Introduce me to him, will you?'

'What, you want to study too?' I asked.

Oskar nodded but I thought his nod seemed suspicious.

Maybe Paris found the idea humorous, but in my opinion a man does need to be able to defend himself. But remembering that Paris didn't want to be a man, I guessed that was the difference between us. I suppose for him hairdressing was more important.

I spent the next three hours in Oskar's room. He taught me how to play on the PlayStation and a few basics on the guitar. We exchanged stories about our brawling experiences. He told me how once, when an opponent of his had been knocked down on the street, he had stepped on the guy's head to keep him down and his friends had pulled on the guy's legs, scraping his face on the asphalt. I related how a friend of mine had hit an opponent with the leg of a bench full of protruding nails, ripping the kid's flesh. At first we laughed when telling these tales, but after a while we fell into silence. The stories didn't seem as funny anymore. Too much blood had been spilled, and with Oskar himself having been a victim, we seemed better able to understand the wages of being in the loser's position.

Sometime after magrib, Paris made a call on his mobile: '*Winair B Yoelandu? Winaet for Ieris, OK? Ieris B kumem tinue Yoelandu.* Where are you? Wait for me, OK? I'll come to you.' He clicked the phone off and said, '*Ieris B goeen for inu sek.* I'm going out for a sec.'

'Stop talking like a banci, would you?' Oskar shouted. 'We

don't understand!'

His comment was not completely correct, because by now I was able to understand much of the language. Also, I now knew that his stepbrother wanted to be a woman, and I was tempted to tell Oskar to refrain from using the word banci around him.

'A few moments later Paris came back to the room with the right person in tow to complete our menagerie: Yusuf.

'Helloooooowwww,' he said, his head peering inside the room, with a wide, weird smile on his face.

Paris pulled him into the room and looked at Oskar. 'We'll leave around eight, OK?'

I waited for Oskar to bathe and watched him as he dressed. He ordered me to change into clothes from his closet. I chose a long-sleeved shirt with large purple checks and a pair of narrow-cuffed jeans. Oskar threw at me a pair of underwear he called boxer briefs.

'Put these on. Who knows you might find yourself with your pants down!' he laughed.

I threw the pair back at him but he threw them back at me. 'I'm serious,' he said. 'The ones you're wearing look like a washrag.'

In the end, I did put them on, but I wasn't about to pull my pants down for anyone.

Oskar and I stood beside each other comparing ourselves in the full-length mirror in his room. I was taller than him and my posture more erect. He was shorter but better filled-out. I had short, curly hair; he had straight hair in a crew cut. He was dressed in a black pin-striped shirt and stonewashed jeans with tears through which his thighs were visible. He had more chiselled features, but I judged myself to be better looking. He had lighter skin, while my skin was deep brown from the sun. He sprayed some cologne on his body and then on mine.

'Tonight we're going to have some fun,' he said, looking in the mirror.

I didn't know what he meant by that and didn't have a chance to think about it, because he yanked my arm to go.

We knocked on the door to Paris's room and then let ourselves inside only to find Paris and Yusuf still trying to decide on what to wear. We were forced to wait for them as they powdered their faces with the powder that Yusuf had brought in his bag.

Precisely at eight, we left the house. Some of the lights in the house were on, but there were no signs of life. Not even the housemaid was visible.

'Where are your folks" I asked. 'Still at work?'

'Probably,' Paris answered.

Oskar took his car. I noticed that the mummy figure on his keychain was misshapen. Maybe Paris really had tried to throw it away. While Oskar and I, in the front seat, grumbled about traffic, Paris and Yusuf were busy in the back talking about other things.

'*Hinue Yoelandu B meeten hineer?* Who are you meeting here?' I heard Paris ask Yusuf.

'*Ieris B meeten inu ginei Ieris meeten inaan Manjam.* A guy I met on Manjam.'

I know now but at that time I wondered why, if Paris didn't want to be compared with banci hairdressers, had he mastered their language? Didn't that signal one's identity as a banci?

Twenty minutes later we stopped at an Oh La La! café near Starlight on Mangga Besar – more to hang out than to eat, because it was too early for the club. Since I hadn't had my portion of rice for the day, I would have preferred eating at a food stall, but I wasn't going to object. While Paris and Yusuf busied themselves looking for new acquaintances on internet sites, Oskar and I smoked and traded our own stories.

At around 10 pm, when we finally left the café, Yusuf whispered, 'Tonight we look for the jackpot!'

I almost stopped in my tracks. What was he talking about, I asked myself.

The parking lot at Starlight that night was not as busy as it had been on the Saturday night we'd first gone there, and the price of admission was even lower, only Rp. 25,000. The main room of the bar was not nearly as full either, plus there was now a kind of long and narrow T-shaped stage that split the centre of the room. I didn't know its function but could see that it got in the way of the people who were on the dance floor. Blinking lights signalled an invitation for people to dance, but the music seemed just so-so that night.

The four of us sat in a row at the bar. Paris excitedly whispered something to Yusuf.

'He's here,' Yusuf said calmly, showing Paris a text message on the screen of his mobile.

'Got a date with someone?' Oskar asked, interrupting their conversation.

At that moment, Yusuf's mobile rang. When he answered, he was forced to speak very loudly: 'Yes, we're inside. At the bar. White T-shirt.'

Oskar tried to get me to order a beer but I didn't want to. He ordered one and began to drink it alone. 'It's just beer,' he said. 'It's not dangerous,' he said, handing the glass to me.

Hesitantly I raised the glass and took a sip but then immediately put the glass back down on the bar. It was bitter to my taste.

Then I noticed a man coming in our direction. He looked at us and asked hesitantly, 'Yusuf?'

'That's me,' Yusuf said, stepping down from his stool and smiling broadly.

I suddenly noticed that something about Yusuf looked different: it was his smile; he was wearing braces! How had I not noticed them before?

Yusuf and the man shook hands, and then Paris introduced himself. They started chatting, with constant smiles. At one point, however, this older, clean-shaven fellow studied me and Oskar before turning back to Yusuf. 'Are those two your friends, too?' he asked. 'Are they boyfriends?'

Yusuf laughed and shook his head. 'No, nobody's boyfriends here. They're just here for the money!'

I couldn't believe what Yusuf had said and wanted to kick him in the groin, but seeing that Oskar didn't react, I also did nothing. Even so, I was irritated. Saying something like that to a perfect stranger, even in jest, seemed rude to me.

'Oh, that's a nice coincidence,' the man said while giving Oskar and I a thorough up-and-down.

'What's a coincidence?' asked Oskar in a low and, to my ears, flirtatious voice.

'It so happens tonight is our Boy Love contest, and there's a pretty good winner's pot.'

'Boy love?' I repeated as a question.

'It's a kind of male model contest,' Yusuf put in. 'It'll be fun to watch.'

The older man said to us, 'Because you're Yusuf's friends, you won't have to pay to sign up. If you want to join, just tell me, OK?', and walked away.

'What was that all about?' Paris asked. Apparently he didn't know either.

Yusuf clarified: 'Every Wednesday night there's a special event. This week it's a Boy Love contest. Last week was Miss Drag, which was really something. There was a lip-synching contest, and it was a hoot. You got to come here on Wednesday nights.'

'Well, *you* seem to be up to date,' Oskar mocked.

'That man was Uncle Bram. He's the manager of this place, and he's loaded. You two should enter the Boy Love contest. There's a big prize,' Yusuf told us.

'How much if you win?' I asked.

'A million or so, I think,' Yusuf said with a shrug.

'And then what do you have to do? Sleep with Om Bram?' Oskar asked.

'Get out of here! He's mine. You two leave him alone,' Yusuf threatened. 'At most, you'd just have to take a turn on the catwalk,' he said, rolling his eyes wearily.

Oskar nodded and looked at me. 'Want to try?'

'Are you serious?' I asked him.

He nodded.

The four of us went together to a large rectangular shaped room behind the bar, which looked to be about thirty square metres. The longer walls were lined with five makeup stations, each with a shelf and a chair beneath and with a round mirror ringed with small light bulbs on the wall. In the middle of the room was a narrow table with a couple of chairs on either side, and at the far end of the room, against the back wall, was a tired-looking sofa with a derelict coffee table in front of it. In the back were also a few box-shaped metal frames with curtains, which functioned as changing rooms, with racks of colourful-looking costumes.

Om Bram was waiting for us there. 'Well, are you in?' he asked.

Oskar nodded. 'All four of you?'

'No, just those two,' Paris spoke on our behalf.

'Hey, I thought you were going to do it too,' I whispered to Paris.

'I don't need the money,' he replied curtly.

After we registered our names, we were each given a number to put on the back of our shirt and told to take a place at one of the makeup mirrors. Around us were a number of other guys around our age who were getting dressed and putting on makeup. 'It's a good thing I brought powder,' Yusuf said, stepping in as our personal stylist.

'Not so much,' Oskar told him.

Meanwhile, my eyes fell on Paris, who seemed forlorn, though his eyes were shining brightly.

I looked around and saw that a number of guys were dressing up as women.

'There's going to be banci tonight too?' I asked Yusuf.

'They're not banci. They're drag queens, just guys in women's clothing. They're going to *lipsing* a song at the start of the show,' he said, mispronouncing the word.

'A guy in girl's clothing is what you call a banci,' Oskar stated.

'Hush or I'll turn you into a banshee,' Yusuf whispered loudly.

A little while later, Yusuf turned his attention to me. He mopped the sweat from my face with a cloth and then powdered my features. My eyes were still on Paris, who seemed to be sinking into a whirlpool, one that was both inviting but also troubling. His attention was on the guys who were dressing up as women.

'Aren't they pretty,' Oskar said with a jeer. Paris huffed when he heard that.

It was close to midnight when the show began. Lights came on and the pounding music suddenly died. The MC was a well-known transvestite who often appeared on TV. I hadn't thought that anyone famous would be willing to set foot in a place like this, but Yusuf informed me that many TV personalities got their start here.

The show began with a comic sketch by another transvestite, who warmed up the audience with his patter and got them to laugh. Then, as Yusuf had said, several drag queens came on stage who took turns lip-synching songs. They hopped around with their mouths yapping soundlessly as they tried their best to mouth the lyrics of the song and mimic the moves of the singer who had made it famous. This act had everyone in stitches, me included, but when it dawned on me that I was going to be up there, on stage, I felt my stomach cramp.

'All we have to do is walk. No need to panic,' Oskar said when I asked what we were supposed to do.

But it didn't happen that way, not exactly. First, we were called, one by one, and told to walk down the catwalk as if we were professional models. My heart pounded and my face felt as stiff as wax when suddenly my own name was called.

'Ricky!'

I wanted to flee that instant. Oskar, who had just finished his turn and had somehow managed to smile throughout, pushed me towards the top of the catwalk.

When the spotlight fell on me, I turned to stone, but gradually the blinding bright light and the pulse of the music reduced my fear, and I began to walk, though hesitantly at first. When I finished my walk and came down from the stage, I was given a modest round of applause. I guessed that I hadn't been too bad.

After a number of other guys had made their appearance on stage, Om Bram came over to Oskar and me.

'Time to get ready for round two,' he said pulling on our arms.

'Round two?'

'Yes, round two,' he repeated, pushing us into the changing room.

Inside were all the other guys, a couple dozen or more, taking off their shirts, exposing their bare chests.

'You want us to take off our shirts?' I stuttered.

Om Bram nodded perfunctorily. 'Yeah. You can stick your number on your pants,' he said before disappearing.

I turned to Oskar who had begun to unbutton his shirt. 'Go on, take it off,' he drawled.

'I don't want to.'

'Come on. Do you want me to take your shirt off for you?'

I thought better that I take off my own shirt than have Oskar putting his hands on me. In a short time we were both bare-chested, and looked at each other. Oskar had a good chest, with well developed lats, but my body wasn't bad either, the result of mechanical work at school and pencak silat practice.

After all the guys who had preceded us in the first round walked the walk – I noted that some were either too skinny or too fat and looked much better in clothes – it was Oskar's turn and then mine. I wasn't as panicked as I had been in the first round and was self-confident about my body, though I'd never shown it to a crowd before.

After the second round, I stood beside Oskar who was beaming with pride. I was hoping he might compliment me, but then we were told to return to the dressing room to prepare for the third round. What now, I wondered.

In the dressing room we found the other guys removing their pants.

'Get ready for round three!' a transvestite said loudly.

'Taeken auf Yoelandu pinants, ninou!' he ordered.

'Take off our pants?' I asked Oskar.

Oskar too seemed hesitant but then said, 'Good thing I told you to wear my boxers instead of that rag you were wearing.'

I decided to leave the contest right then and there. I wasn't going to walk around a crowded room almost naked. The boxer shorts might help a little, but not enough. Oskar and I looked at each other, waiting for the other to decide. We looked around and saw all the other guys now showing off their underwear. Unlike the two of us in boxers, most were in bikini briefs which clearly showed the size and shape of their dicks.

All of a sudden, I felt someone pulling hard on my arm, nearly knocking me off my feet.

'What are you doing here?' the guy screamed at me.

Stunned for a second, I narrowed my eyes to focus on the person who had just shouted at me: it was my long-lost brother, Edi.

Instantly, I felt angry. 'What about you?' I asked him cynically. I never thought I'd run into my brother, the jewel thief, in this place.

'I work here!' he shouted.

His tone of voice revealed anger but an element of pride as well. 'What are you doing here?' he asked again.

At once I felt both offended and irritated. 'I'm a contestant!' I informed him.

'Are you queer? What are the folks going to say about that?!'

I looked at him angrily. 'What I am is not your business. And why are you asking about our folks? Since when did you start caring what they thought?'

I yanked my hand from his grasp and then quickly removed my pants, right there in front of him. Oskar, who was standing nearby, did nothing to interfere.

'Take off your pants,' I ordered, my voice now trembling with anger.

I threw my pants on a chair and then pinned my number to my boxers. My brother just stood there, watching. Of all the things that could have happened in the world, why did I have to meet my brother now? I didn't know why I was so angry. Maybe it was because he was trying to tell me what to do, maybe it was because of his accusation. Whatever the case, before I could figure it out, he turned and walked away.

'Who was that?' Oskar asked as he removed his pants.

I wanted to forget the incident had even happened. 'My brother,' I said shortly, 'but I haven't seen him for a long time.'

Oskar just jutted his chin, as if he didn't care.

Our appearance in round three excited a response in the crowd far more enthusiastic than the previous rounds. There were whistles and catcalls and long rounds of applause from the audience: gay men, drag queens, aunties, and lesbians too. On the catwalk I walked with new confidence and felt myself to be a winner when I stood among the row of participants for the final evaluation. Self-pride may not be an admirable quality, but I did think myself to be good-looking. Or maybe it was just the anger being channelled through me that way. It was as if I could see my brother staring angrily at me. And making him mad gave me great pleasure.

The transvestite MC pinched Oskar in the stomach as he went down the row, eliminating one contestant after another. In the end, I was named runner-up and Oskar came in third place.

The winner was a guy whose underwear was so skimpy he might as well have worn nothing at all. His pubic hair and the sausage-like contour of his cock were visible for everyone to see. I guess that's what swayed the jury's verdict. I beamed when given a fake crown and a certificate on which was written, 'Runner Up, Boy Love'.

The Boy Love contest was a one-night-only show, not a series with quarter- and semi-final contests. One of the drag-queens in the changing room told us that Om Bram was looking for new faces and the show that night was a talent search more than anything else.

My face flushed red when I entered the changing room, and Paris and Yusuf slapped me on the back. As runner up I was awarded a cash prize of Rp. 750,000. Oskar, who seemed chagrined for having come in third place, was awarded Rp. 500,000. On top of that we were also awarded free lifetime membership at the club.

After we finished dressing, Om Bram approached with a broad smile on his face.

'Congratulations,' he said to both Oskar and me.

'Thanks,' I said, also smiling, but wondering what he might now expect us to do for him.

'Come again next week, will you?' he said. 'I'd like to hire you to appear on a regular basis. You'll get paid for what you do. Try it out, and if you like it, you can stay on.' He took Yusuf's hand and started to leave.

Yusuf waved to us and then hurriedly whispered to Paris, 'I'll text you.'

It passed through my mind that maybe Yusuf was the reason that we were selected as winners, but I didn't think about it for long, because my long-vanished brother reappeared, and my feelings changed immediately. I thought he'd probably come to steal my winnings.

'What do you want?' I barked at him.

'Like to get something to drink?' he asked.

I looked at him momentarily, trying to discern a hidden intention, but I could detect nothing suspicious. I asked Paris to take care of settling my business including picking up the prize money for me. I signalled to Oskar that I had to talk with my brother. He just nodded.

Edi and I hadn't seen each other for three years or more. Now he looked like a typical Jakarta low-life, his body full of tattoos and mysterious scars. The last time I'd seen him he had shoulder-length hair; now it was very short.

We found a place to sit at the bar and for a time said nothing, our eyes on the transvestite on stage who was re-enacting a scene from a well-known soap opera. The audience was laughing loudly. The smell of alcohol bothered my nose and caused my throat to constrict.

After ordering a soft drink for me, my brother began our conversation: 'How's Dad?' he asked.

'Don't know. I'm not living at home anymore,' I told him.

'What, did you run away?'

'I'm living in a pesantren.'

Edi almost choked on his laughter. I felt stupid for having given him an honest answer. I should have followed Yusuf's example and told him I was staying at a boarding house.

'If you're at a pesantren, what are you doing here?' he asked with a sneer.

'Just trying to earn some money,' I answered honestly. In my head I was telling him that he'd be better off taking a look in the mirror than lecturing me.

Edi took a deep breath and patted my shoulder. 'If anything happens, tell me. I work here. You can do what you want, but you have to watch yourself here. There are a lot of people here who are not to be trusted.'

I said nothing, didn't even look in his direction. Instead, I sipped on my drink and acted as if he were a stranger.

'I need to get back to work,' he said, then got off his stool and walked away.

After he had gone, Paris and Oskar came to join me. It was already 3 am, and the show was almost over. Paris handed me an envelope of money. He now seemed happy to be there. His eyes were fixed on a gaggle of cross-dressers who were still in the room.

Tribute & Tips

In the following days at the pesantren, many curious stares were directed at Yusuf or, more precisely, his brace-covered teeth. I can still picture it clearly: Yusuf walking around the pesantren with an MP3 player attached to his ear, his face bright and shining, his wired smile glowing as he sang popular English-language songs.

At the pesantren, most of the residents were behind on current technology and gadgets. But not Yusuf, however, who now owned an array of expensive electronic devices. The good thing about Yusuf is that he wasn't possessive and would willingly lend his new toys to other residents to try them out. However, that did little to conceal the question that hung in the air: 'How does he manage to buy all those things?' Though he didn't know the answer, Ali was, I could tell, apprehensive about the kind of work his brother was engaged in, but Yusuf refused to be open with him. The only person he could count on to serve as a liaison with his brother was me. But when Ali asked me where Yusuf was working, all I could do was lie. If I had told Ali that Yusuf was trading his body for favours, he probably would have put his brother in stocks. And the fact was I didn't know if Yusuf was actually selling himself. All I knew is that he was often going out with his so called daddies.

'I know I'm not that close to him,' Ali confessed, 'but that doesn't mean I'm not concerned. That's why I'd like you to keep your eye on him.'

I wasn't sure I was up to the task. How could I look after another person when I couldn't look after myself? Besides, by all appearances, Yusuf was not a person who wanted to be watched over. He was a wild deer.

One evening in early March Oskar showed up at the pesantren. 'What's up?' I asked when I saw his crew-cut head.

'Do you have silat practice tonight?' he asked.

'No,' I told him. Practice had been the previous evening, and my body was stiff and sore to prove it.

He seemed disappointed. 'Is your teacher here?' he asked.

'He's gone to Egypt,' I told him, and saw the look of enthusiasm disappear from his face. I added with a smile, 'but if you mean my silat instructor, yes, he's around.' I had already guessed that that was the reason for Oskar's appearance that evening, and sure enough he regained his good spirits.

'Take me to see him, will you?' Oskar asked.

'If you want to see him, you have to bring him something – a tin of cookies, at least,' I said, pulling his leg.

His forehead wrinkled. 'Really?'

I laughed and shook my head, then led him in the direction of Cell Ten. There I found Ustadz Asman seated cross-legged on his prayer mat. In his hand was a string of prayer beads made from a very expensive kind of wood, which people believed would harden to stone over a long period of time.

'*Assalamualaikum,*' I said in greeting from the doorway, but Ustadz Asman didn't move. I repeated the greeting twice more, but still he didn't respond. Finally, I decided to nudge his shoulder a bit and when I did he jumped in shock. He'd been asleep.

'*Salamualaikum,*' I said again, with stress in my voice. '*Waalaikumsalam,*' he answered. He might have been irritated with me for having disturbed him, but seeing a guest at my side, he didn't bark at me.

'What are you doing, surprising me like that?' he asked.

'I brought a friend of mine to meet you,' I explained and nudged a grinning Oskar forward.

'May I help you?' Ustadz Asman asked in a not unkindly tone of voice.

Without an invitation or request, Oskar immediately plopped himself down on the mat in front of Ustadz Asman, the typical behaviour of a city kid with no manners. Rather than standing there like a bodyguard, I too sat down. Oskar gave me a look of annoyance, but I didn't care. I wanted to know why Oskar had been so insistent about meeting my silat instructor.

'Ricky told me that you teach self-defence,' Oskar began.

'Yes, pencak silat. Would you like to study too? Just come here with Ricky,' he said, nodding in my direction.

Oskar thought about this and said, 'Listen, I really want to study, but that sounds like it would take a long time for me to learn. It's not easy for me to spend so much time outside the house,' Oskar lied, with a pleading look in his eyes.

Ustadz Asman said nothing for a while and finally said, 'Oh, so you want to learn extra fast. Is that it?'

Oskar looked pleased. 'Yes. That's possible, isn't it?'

'Yes, it's possible, but the prerequisites are difficult to fulfil,' Ustadz Asman answered without looking at him.

'If it's a question of money, that's OK,' Oskar remarked.

I could sense that Oskar's comment had piqued Ustadz Asman's interest but that he was restraining himself from showing interest. It would have been unseemly for him to have reacted like a money grubber, although that is what he seemed to be.

He stared at Oskar for some time: 'Because you are a friend of Ricky's, I will fulfil your request as long as the tribute you provide is appropriate to the task. Prepare the *mahar* and then come back to me in forty days,' Ustadz Asman told him.

'But how much is it?' Oskar asked.

Ustadz Asman stared at him for a second, then said, 'There, you have it. I just whispered the amount in your ear. If a certain amount now comes to mind, that is the amount you must bring to me as your mahar. Are you able to do that?'

The man's words were a challenge, causing Oskar to fall silent, but then he nodded.

I felt completely stupid and didn't understand what was going on. I hadn't seen Ustadz Asman move from where he was sitting and certainly didn't see him whisper into Oskar's ear. But then, all of a sudden, Oskar was nodding? Had I missed something?

After that, Ustadz Asman indicated for us to leave, which we did immediately.

'What did he whisper to you?' I asked Oskar as I walked him to his car, which he had parked beside the lodge.

'He didn't whisper anything, but I know the amount,' Oskar answered, sounding equally perplexed.

'But how much was it? Fifty thousand? One hundred thousand? More?'

Oskar said nothing, just kept on walking.

'You know, don't you, it's not easy to obtain such forms of knowledge,' I warned.

Still Oskar didn't answer my question. Instead, he patted my shoulder and said, 'Thank you. But you should buy a mobile, so it's easier for us to keep in touch.'

That is just what I did! With part of the money I won in the Boy Love contest, I bought myself a cheap mobile, like Yusuf's first one. Yusuf had changed phones several times – always trading in the one he was using for one that was more sophisticated: a Blackberry, a touch-screen phone, whatever. I was trying to figure out how to work my phone when Yusuf came into our room and surprised me with a high-pitched scream: 'Oh my god!' I almost threw the box the phone had come in at his face.

'Give me Oskar's number, will you?' I asked. 'And Paris's, and yours, too.'

As he read out the numbers, I typed them in. 'It's good you finally have a cell; it will be easier to promote you to other people. A mobile is a communications gateway, a business tool.'

'Don't lecture me.'

He sat down and began to remove his school uniform. 'At the very least, you have to learn how to use PS,' he advised.

'Why?' I asked.

'Because with PS you can meet guys who will buy you free phone time, which is a lot better than having to buy them yourself.'

I'd heard Yusuf using phone sex and found it disgusting. While I was sleeping, or trying to sleep, I kept hearing him moan, 'Oh, oh, oh!' until I finally kicked him. Another time he switched on the speaker to his phone so I could hear his chat partner talking to him in a breathy voice – 'Oh, darling, oh, honey' – which caused me to laugh but also drew the attention of another resident, who shocked us by suddenly putting his head around the door.

'Who's he talking to?' the resident asked.

Yusuf immediately switched the phone off. How idiotic of him! Our hearts were pounding: What would happen if another resident found out that we – or Yusuf, more accurately – were engaging in phone sex with men? After he left, we burst into laughter.

Having never owned a mobile before, or even a pager, I truly was in the Stone Age when it came to telecommunications technology. But what happened when I purchased my first phone? I couldn't believe myself, but I turned into Yusuf, forever checking the screen of my phone to see if I'd received a text message or call. In a short time it became an addiction.

I saved the numbers for Paris, Oskar and Yusuf in my phone's contact list, and made my first call to Oskar. Hearing the ring tone on my phone made me break into a smile. He picked up after the fifth ring.

'Hello,' he said in a bored voice.

Knowing he didn't have my number yet and hoping to fool him, I whispered breathily, 'Let's PS, honey ...'

He was silent for a moment and then said, 'Why phone sex? Why not real sex – Ricky?' Shit!

Then I heard Oskar inviting me to go to Starlight on Wednesday night. Yusuf screamed happily when he heard that.

One problem with going out on a Wednesday night was that Thursday was a school day, but what troubled me more was that I would have to skip silat lessons. Despite my reservations, I decided to go along.

Oskar and I got in free on Wednesday because the attendant at the entrance recognized us and knew that we'd been given lifetime membership. The day before, I had asked Paris to take me to a mall, where I bought a few pair of boxer shorts similar in style to the ones that Oskar owned but with different motifs. I chose ones with cartoon characters on them. If I had to take off my pants again, I didn't want to be embarrassed by wearing the same underwear I had worn the week before.

When we arrived Om Bram approached us and told us to follow him to the changing room. There he told us to take off our shirts. I could smell a heavy dose of cologne on Oskar.

'Now your pants,' he then said. He looked down at the

boxers that Oskar and I were wearing. 'Next time, wear briefs,' he advised. 'Like the ones he's wearing,' he added, pointing to the first-prize winner the week before, who was grinning and looking thoroughly self-confident.

I shook my head. Oskar giggled.

The show that night was nothing special: just a series of songs lip-synched by drag queens. Meanwhile, we, the top five finalists from the Boy Love contest the week before, were assigned the task of walking around the bar and smiling at customers, dressed only in underwear and a bow-tie around our neck.

I didn't object to the work. It was easy. All we had to do was smile; we didn't have to talk to the customers. In fact, people weren't allowed to touch us if we didn't want to be touched. The point of our presence was simply to be eye-candy, to make the customers happy to be there. Mostly I just talked to Oskar.

At around 1 am Oskar and I were sitting at the bar and watching a drag queen sing a Kris Dayanti song – 'Yang kumahu ...jadi wanita ...tapi tak begini ... keadaannya ... All I want is to be a woman but not one like this ...' – when he said to me, 'I need you to help me make some extra money.'

'Sure thing,' I said, but I didn't know how I could possibly help.

We caught sight of Paris who was staring intently at a group of transvestites chatting together in a corner of the room.

'On guard,' Oskar advised. 'If Paris likes one of those banci, it will be the end of you.'

'I'm very certain,' I told him, 'Paris is not into banci.'

At that moment Paris turned towards us and the look in his eyes was one full of a longing for something we could only guess. For a time we said nothing but then, finally, Oskar asked in a low voice, 'Paris wants to be a banci, doesn't he?'

'No, he doesn't,' I told him. 'Paris wants to be a girl.'

Oskar looked at me sharply. I thought for a moment he might laugh, but he sank into serious thought.

'Ha ha ha. Very funny,' he remarked sarcastically.

'I'm serious,' I said, and told him about the incident in the hotel room. I felt like I was betraying Paris, but at the same time I also felt relieved to be able to share the story with someone – and Oskar, I thought, was the best person to share it with.

The next morning, at the food stall near the school where I usually got something to eat before the first bell, I actually fell asleep. My eyelids were so heavy I couldn't keep my eyes open. Oskar and I had each received Rp. 200,000 for our work the night before. Oscar complained about the size of the fee and stressed to me that he had to obtain a great deal more than that in the space of forty days. I didn't know what to tell him. Work every day? We had to go to school, plus final exams were coming up; and with my repeated absenteeism of late, I worried that I might not graduate.

On Saturday night the four of us returned to Starlight. We left quite late, after I had finished my pencak silat practice session. My body was hot and flushed and my muscles were still swollen from all the exercise. Even a prolonged splash bath hadn't refreshed me, but the air-conditioning in Oskar's car made me feel more comfortable.

I had forgotten to buy new underwear, so I was wearing boxers again. When Om Bram saw them, he looked very displeased. On the other hand, Oskar gave him a pleasant surprise: he had on black-coloured underwear with a swimsuit cut. He then took another pair from his jacket and threw them at me.

'Here, I brought these for you.'

It was a white-coloured pair of underwear and the elastic

waistband on which the words 'Calvin Klein' were printed was much wider than that of the cheap underwear I usually wore.

'You owe me a hundred and fifty thousand,' Oscar said. Shit. That was a lot of money for an item of clothing so small.

That Saturday night the atmosphere in Starlight was tumultuous. The seedy club was packed. Loud music blared at us from every direction, and as full as the club was, customers still kept coming in. Dressed only in underwear, I felt a bit embarrassed among such a large crowd of people, but fortunately Om Bram, gave us each a black Zorro mask to don, which I grabbed from him gladly, for it gave me a degree of anonymity.

At one point, during a break in the music, Om Bram had us preen and prance around in front of the DJ's console. The rapidly blinking strobe lights almost made me dizzy, but it was odd that I, who so recently would have been averse to be caught in such a place and situation, now found myself savouring the experience. I could feel inside me the beat of the songs, and my body moved with the rhythm. When we walked on stage, all eyes in the room were on us. I felt like the centre of attention, which caused my adrenaline to flow. I no longer cared that I was nearly naked.

Afterward, Oskar said, 'There must be another way of making money fast.' Om Bram told us to spread out through the club to serve as eye candy for the customers.

Ignoring Oskar, I began to walk the floor and spotted my brother Edi going back and forth between the entrance of the bar and the changing room. I wondered if he might be looking for me. Stopping at the bar to rest for a spell, I felt someone grab my thigh and thought it must be Oskar. When I turned around, I saw that it was a middle-aged man with parted hair slicked back, whose shirt was open wide exposing his chest and a thick gold chain that hung from his neck. I smiled faintly as he stared at me, even though his touch made me feel on edge. Suddenly and with no warning he pulled the waistband of my underwear and tucked some money inside. I was completely shocked but did nothing. I didn't know what to do or what was expected. Thinking it best to ask Om Bram first, I did nothing.

Fortunately, the creep left immediately, so I didn't have to make a choice.

When I ran into Oskar, I told him what had happened, but he merely complained, 'Damn it. No one's tried to stick money in my pants!'

'Time to go off on my own,' he added and left me.

I looked at the money in my waistband: a fifty thousand note! Instantly, my brain twirled. If I could get Rp. 50,000 from one person, that meant from ten people I would have Rp. 500,000 – just in one night. Suddenly, I felt cheerful and in love with my work, though I said to myself that the following week I had best wear a double layer of underwear for greater protection.

I walked around, showing off myself here and there, but did not immediately find any other generous admirers.

I ran across Paris, who was sitting at a corner of the bar looking a tad forlorn, perhaps because he was alone, I thought.

'Oh, soooo sexy,' he remarked sarcastically when I sat down beside him.

'Where's Yusuf?' I asked. I still had it in my mind that I should be watching him.

'Looking for some sugar daddy to pay for his braces.'

'You don't want to look for one, too?' I teased.

'I don't need one,' he hissed. 'I have enough money of my own.'

Paris tapped his digital watch to illuminate the face and check the time. He looked bored.

'If you have so much money, why don't you get an operation?'

Paris immediately looked up at me. 'What do you mean? What kind of operation?'

'You know, a sex-change operation.'

'That's not funny!' Paris said loudly, then turned his head away.

Even though he was angry, I saw a change in his expression, a sudden glint of spirit, or maybe hope. I didn't know at the time, but it was I who first put the thought of a sex-change operation in his mind. I mean, I'd read about such things, of course, so I thought if he really does want to be a girl, then why not have an operation? With all his money, couldn't he go to Thailand or somewhere?

'So, I guess you don't want to be a girl anymore,' I said.

He glared at me. 'I still do!'

'Well then, next week come here in girl's clothes.'

'You're out of your mind!' he said, then stamped his feet and disappeared.

We didn't leave the club until almost dawn: Oskar and I and the other three eye-candy guys had to wait around until all the customers had left before we pooled and divided our tips. I'd been given Rp. 200,000 that night but I had to put it in the pot with tips the other guys had received, the total sum of which was then divided up equally. Each of us got Rp. 110,000, which was irritating for me because I had made the most money that night. Oskar had collected a large number of ten-thousand rupiah notes but the first-prize winner in our Boy Love contest made almost nothing at all.

Even though I had made some money, I still didn't view the work as a kind of profession. I was doing it as much for fun as for the money.

Wings

For Oskar, the forty days he needed to put together the mahar for Ustadz Asman were passing quickly, and he was constantly calling and pressuring me for ideas on how to collect the money he needed. I couldn't help him. Besides, I thought, wasn't he the one that wanted to acquire special powers?

It was the third week of April, and when Saturday night came around, something funny happened. It all started when we booked a room at a cheap hotel near Starlight, Rp. 75,000 for the night. It was my idea.

That night I forced Paris to bring his wigs and women's clothing in a suitcase to the hotel. At first he flatly refused, and his face had flushed as red as an imported Fuji apple. But I told him, if he didn't start then, when was he going to start? He said he was embarrassed because of Oskar and Yusuf; he was ashamed for them to know. I asked him if he intended to conceal his true self from people forever. If he felt himself to be a woman, then demonstrate that he was one, at least to the three of us, the people closest to him. After thinking about what I said, he finally agreed. At the hotel, Paris froze with apprehension, unsure what to do. At first I thought it was because of the scuzzy room we'd rented – nothing like the Aryaduta – and then maybe because he was just nervous. For five minutes he did nothing but stand there, leaning again the wall, not saying anything, with beads of sweat on his upper lip and forehead. I thought he'd be more relaxed; we were his closest friends, after all; but I was wrong. I turned on the fat-tube television in the room, hoping to relieve the tension, but the static noise it produced helped very little.

Meanwhile, from the bathroom came a series of shrieks from Yusuf when discovering a large number of used condoms in the trash receptacle. Given the price of the hotel room, this didn't surprise me. Oskar was busy playing with a portable PlayStation he had brought along, not paying attention to us at all. I watched as Paris retreated into his snail shell. I sat there, waiting silently, and for a time it didn't look like the tension that had filled the room would ever let up. Then Yusuf, catching us completely unawares, decided to open Paris's suitcase.

'This case is so big. What do you have inside?' Yusuf cried as he began to rifle through the contents. Paris tried to stop him, but that was the wrong move: hard-headed Yusuf always did what he wanted to do, especially when it was forbidden.

'Oh my God!' Yusuf cried as he pulled a bright pink bra from the suitcase and hung it on the crook of his arm. That was enough to get Oskar's attention, and he looked up from his game. Paris tried to grab the bra, but Yusuf was too quick. Yusuf's brain was moving in slow motion, and it was only after a while that it dawned on him. At that point, he stopped trying to evade Paris and stood stock still in front of him.

His face was burning and his eyes moist. 'Oh my God, you want to wear a bra!' Though initially surprised, he now began to smile.

'Give it back!' Paris said with a trembling voice.

The smile on Yusuf's braced teeth immediately faded and he slowly handed the bra to Paris. There was no sound in the room at all. Complete silence. I didn't know what to say. Paris was obviously very embarrassed.

Suddenly Oskar spoke up: 'Go ahead, put it on if you want. No need to be embarrassed with us.'

Yusuf and I looked first at Oskar and then at Paris. As he had done before at the Aryaduta, he collapsed on the floor and covered his face. But I had to give it to Oskar; his choice of words had been perfect.

Yusuf began to inspect the suitcase more closely. I worried that he might worsen the situation by making fun of Paris again, but instead he asked simply, 'What do you want to wear?' His tone of voice was curious and light.

He removed from the case a purple satin blouse. Paris remained silent, his eyes covered with his hands.

'I think I'll wear this,' said Yusuf. He pulled out a white miniskirt and held it up against his waist. 'Do you have stockings that match?'

Yusuf's tone of voice was exceedingly friendly, but when Paris persisted in not speaking I thought that the problem might be me and Oskar.

Oskar must have come to the same conclusion, because he jumped up and signalled for the two of us to leave. 'Let's get something to eat,' he said.

In fact, neither of us were hungry. Instead, we bought a pack of cigarettes from a sidewalk vendor and hung around a bus shelter for an hour or so. Finally we bought some fried cassava to take back to the room for Yusuf and Paris.

In the hotel room, we found Yusuf bewigged and dressed in Paris's clothes, wearing Paris's jewellery, posing in the full-length mirror on the outside of the bathroom door.

'Don't you think I look great in this miniskirt?' he said. Oskar started to laugh, but I kicked him in the ankle.

'Where is Paris?' I whispered to Yusuf.

As he fastened an earring, he said, 'He's in the bathroom and won't come out. I told him to dress up, but he refused. So I decided to dress up myself.'

I knocked on the door to the bathroom. Nothing happened. 'If you don't come out, I'm going to knock the door down,' I threatened loudly. 'One! Two!'

The door clicked, then opened, and Paris emerged. His eyes were puffy from crying. In appearance, he was still a guy.

'Why haven't you changed clothes?' I asked, beginning to grow annoyed. We stared at each other but then he looked at Yusuf.

'Don't I look nice?' Yusuf asked Paris, seeking confirmation. 'Don't worry,' he added, 'I'm not wearing your bra. It's too small anyway.'

Paris blushed in silence but then exploded angrily, 'What do you guys want?!'

His anger surprised me.

'Do you want me to be a banci?' he asked. I still couldn't say anything. 'Are you satisfied making fun of me!' He pointed at Yusuf, who now looked frightened. 'You're being cruel, all of you!'

'It's not like that,' I blurted.

'Don't say anything! This is all because of you! You can't keep your mouth shut! You want me to be laughed at! That's it, isn't it!' he screamed at me.

'That's not it. Really, I didn't mean to do anything wrong.' I struggled to find the words.

'This is all because of you! All because I got to know you!'

I couldn't say anything. Was it wrong for him to know me?

Did he hate me all this time?

'Here, give me those clothes! I'll put them on and be your

banci. Then you can laugh all you want!'

'Nobody wants you to be a banci!' Oskar said loudly, in my defence. 'Who do you think wants you to be a banci?'

Paris stared at Oskar, whose ears had turned red with anger.

'You idiot, we don't want you to be a banci!' Oskar said again. 'We only want you to be yourself!'

Suddenly, Paris's voice changed and he whimpered, as if seeking her stepbrother's help, 'But I'm embarrassed ...'

'For God's sake, why be embarrassed? Look at me! Am I embarrassed?' This was Yusuf speaking. His sense of sisterhood had suddenly emerged, and he put his arms around Paris, stroking his back with one hand to calm him down.

I still couldn't speak. I felt uncomfortable to be caught in a situation beyond my control. I wanted to pretend that nothing was happening.

'You can be whatever you want to be, and we won't object,' Oskar stated firmly. 'I'm not going to tell on you. Besides, we're still young. It's up to us to decide what to do and who to be. And even if you do want to be a banci, so what! The important thing is to be true to yourself.'

'I want to be a girl, not a banci,' Paris said between sobs.

'Yeah, well, that's up to you,' Oskar barked as Yusuf gave him a malicious stare.

In the end, Paris did dress up like a girl and we were happy to see him do so. Thinking about it, maybe it did seem to Paris that we were forcing our own wishes on him, but that's not what we had intended. We only wanted him to be happy. I for one think a person can only be happy if he knows himself. What Oskar had said was correct. So was I wrong to have urged Paris to fulfil a desire he was having difficulty to express?

Oskar and I enjoyed that night. As Yusuf moved to music on his mobile, Oskar and I lounged on the bed eating the fried cassava we'd bought as we watched Paris try on the various outfits he'd brought.

Oskar and I laughed as we took terms making comments on the various outfits: 'Not sexy enough ... like a street peddler ... hmm, no good ... transvestite hooker ... just out of the boondocks ... truck driver in drag ... starlet material ...' Paris finally relaxed and began to enjoy the charade as well. By 9 pm he had finally transformed himself into a faux female. The good thing was that he didn't put on a lot of makeup; the bad was that his choice of clothing fell into the category of drag-hooker. When Om Bram called Oskar and me to remind us of the time, we left. When we exited the hotel, people in the lobby stared at us, making me want to shrink and hide behind Oskar, but Yusuf was oblivious to the stares and sashayed away with nary a care. Paris on the other hand, tottering in high-heeled shoes, looked like he might fall down at any minute.

'No need to pay attention to those people,' Yusuf said once we were in the car. 'They don't know us anyway. And from now on, call me Yessi, not Yusuf, OK?' He played the role well.

When we arrived at Starlight, the club was not that busy, and the four of us hung out in the changing room. Yusuf – or Yessi, rather – made many new friends among the drag queens who were getting dressed there. Paris sat still in place like a river stone.

Om Bram came looking for us.

'A lot of people are asking to meet you two,' he began. 'It's up to you what to tell them.'

Oskar and I looked at each other, not sure of what was being said.

I got the feeling that Om Bram was asking if we'd be willing to sell our bodies to those people who wanted to meet us and that he was waiting for an answer.

No one said anything until Oskar finally spoke, voicing my own feeling: 'Sorry, Boss, not our scene.'

I nodded in agreement.

Om Bram didn't continue the line of conversation. Instead, he gave us each a pair of wings to put on our backs. The wings were affixed to a kind of harness with loops through which to put the arms. At first the outfit felt heavy and uncomfortable, especially in the armpit where the loop snagged my underarm hair when I moved my arms. After a while, however, we got used to them and were able to move naturally.

The wings were made of white feathers and when we put them on, the other people in the room – the performers, drag queens, makeup artists, and the other eye-candy guys – looked at us with a combination of admiration and envy. I later learned that Om Bram didn't give wings to just anyone. The two of us – and only the two of us – had been chosen by Bram as prospective 'Angels', young men whose charm and attraction would serve to increase the clientele and revenue of his club. For me, the garb was just a pair of false wings incapable of carrying us anywhere.

When the bar was nearly filled with customers, Om Bram told Oskar and me to walk around in front of the DJ's console so that people would know we were the club's prospective angels. Paris wanted to stay behind, apparently reluctant to show his face in public, but Yusuf pulled him by the arm and convinced him that no one would recognize him. And there, in the club, even though he did little but sit and sip on his drink, flashes of life and animation gradually began to appear on Paris's face. Finally feeling safe – with no one calling him a banci or looking at him with disgust – he began to act more natural and carefree. He might have been a socialite in a fancy club.

As Oskar and I strutted around, we smiled at the people who looked at us, and even though I was dressed only in my underwear and Converse shoes with a set of fake wings on my back, I didn't feel embarrassed. I had become accustomed to people looking at my almost naked body and had even come to like it. As I had no intention of selling myself, I didn't see anything wrong with it. I had never thought of myself as sexy before, but with one person after another telling me that I was, I began to believe that I did possess that quality. That night I began to see my work at the club as a profession. To myself, I said goodbye to my former goal of becoming a garage mechanic. I was now an angel.

That night I earned one million rupiah. I had never had so much money at one time in all my life, and these earnings were the result of my own work. Oskar, however, despite having pocketed almost the same amount of money, didn't seem satisfied, which caused me to wonder how large a sum of money he needed for that tribute of his.

Sixty Days

I was experiencing difficulty with my recitation lessons. Not surprising, given how inconsistent I was in my studies! I couldn't memorize even a single verse from the *Al-Fiyah* that Ustadz Asman had assigned me to learn. When it was time for us to recite the yellow books, I would daydream or fall asleep and then awake with drool running down my jaw. I frequently missed prayers. When it was time for meals, I'd either skip out and not help with the cooking or pretend not to be hungry and eat just one or two spoonfuls, and then go to a food stall and help myself to Padang or some other kind of cuisine. I had become accustomed to better-tasting food than was the standard fare at the pesantren. I had also gotten into the habit of spending a lot of my free time at shopping malls. I discarded my old clothes and bought new apparel, including underwear of different name brands. No more Rp. 10,000 underwear for me!

One evening in late April, after I had been awarded my wings, I invited Paris and Yusuf to go shopping with me at Taman Anggrek Mall in Jakarta, the city's largest mall. Yusuf immediately made a date to meet a man there. The man turned out to look old enough to have five children, but he was generous and treated us all to a meal and tickets to a film. Afterwards, when he asked me for my mobile number, I gave it to him.

Later, unbeknownst to Yusuf, I met up with the man on my own, and he took me to eat at an expensive restaurant and bought me some clothing. Not just once, either. We met a few times, and whenever I arrived late he appeared restless. When I told him as an excuse that I was late because I didn't have a watch, he took me straight to a store and bought me a Casio that cost more than a million rupiah. I didn't object to him buying things for me as long as he didn't expect anything in return. I was happy to feel like a person of means. All my possessions were new and expensive. I no longer looked like a poor kid whose family had no concern for his well-being.

'Where will you go to school when you graduate?' the man once asked me when we were strolling around Plaza Indonesia, in central Jakarta. His question was a reminder that I would soon graduate from high school.

'I'm not going to college. Can't afford it,' I told him.

'Well, maybe I could help you there,' he offered, 'as long as you agree to live with me.'

He squeezed my shoulder. I could only grin like a donkey. That was the first time I realized that I had such a high value in the eyes of men who liked men.

As the weeks passed, I have to admit, I began to fall in love with myself. Without shame or embarrassment, I now worked on making myself better looking. I was rigorous with my silat lessons but not for reasons of self-defence; much more so because I wanted a sexy and well-muscled body. I asked Paris to help me with the style and cut of my hair, and highlights soon enhanced my hair colour. I even went for facials with Yusuf on a routine basis, every two weeks. My skin felt smooth and I liked it. I bathed more carefully and frequently. I whitened my teeth; body lotion was never far from my fingertips.

I started going to the gym with Oskar, who had also begun to work out regularly to keep in good physical shape. As an additional incentive, there were many older gay men at his fitness centre which, to us, of course, represented more financial opportunities.

My change in appearance did not escape the attention of other residents at the pesantren. I no longer looked like the kampung kid I had once been, with just one prayer shirt and a wrinkled and threadbare sarong. Now I owned several finely embroidered shirts and expensive Samarinda-style sarongs as well. I dabbed myself with different brands of cologne costing hundreds of thousands of rupiah; many of the bottles were gifts from the men who were pursuing me.

I refused to go out with guys my own age because, generally speaking, they had neither jobs nor money. Thin, short, fat, I didn't care what my dates looked like, as long as they had a stable income and were generous in spending it on me. Winning them over was easy. A romantic look, a pleasing conversation, the ability to listen to them pour out their woes, and sometimes even – though it was something I still didn't like doing – a hand on their thigh were sufficient. And every time I succeeded in winning the heart of another older man, the more pleased I became with myself.

Over time, the material world consumed me. Two or three times a week I would appear at Starlight both to work and flirt – and the following morning go to school with heavy eyelids and doze off in the corner of the classroom. Even though I knew that national exams were coming up at the end of May and I needed to prepare, I didn't worry.

On the last weekend in April, Oskar and I were finally anointed as official angels of the club. The ceremony was an interesting one.

Oskar was given the name 'Angel of Temptation' while I was

called 'Angel in the Know'. We had no idea why we were given such names; only that it was the custom: all the club's angels had their own stage name. With a growing amount of money filling my pockets – or my underwear, rather – I was no longer reliant on Paris to support my living expenses.

The forty-day time period Ustadz Asman had given Oskar to acquire the tribute that was required for his acquisition of special powers had already passed and he was now in a panic. How much did he still need, I wondered. Hadn't he made enough money already?

Yusuf and Paris now regularly came to the club dressed as women, and though to my eyes at least, they still looked like banci instead of real women, they seemed to enjoy it, especially Paris, who had undergone a much more radical transformation. He was no longer the Paris he once had been. Now he was Susan, or Sherly, or Aisyah, a calm, elegant woman not prone to coquetry at all – unlike Yusuf, or Yessi, who used his over-the-top personality to lure clients, but with limited results.

One busy Saturday night at the club in the middle of May, I thought I caught sight of someone who had played a significant role in introducing me to the world I now lived in. As ever, the lighting in the club was dim, but I was pretty sure that it was him …

'Iwenk!' I called, waving my hand. He turned in my direction and looked at me in surprise. I saw his eyes widen as he noticed the wings on my back. They were black in colour that night. After becoming official angels, Oskar and I were given different coloured wings to wear from time to time.

Iwenk scanned me with his eyes, from my highlighted hair to the sturdy Doc Marten's on my feet.

'You work here?' he asked with a grin that made him look like a sneaky hyena. I knew instantly it had been a mistake for me to have addressed him.

'Yeah, why?' The cheerful tone of voice at meeting an old friend immediately changed.

'Such a hypocrite you are,' he said without hesitation. 'Since when did you become a homo whore?'

'Fuck you!' I swore at him loudly enough to cause a few heads to turn our way, but I didn't care. I felt empowered to swear because of my black wings.

'Got some work for me?' he asked, as if not knowing he had just insulted me.

He was skinny and his eyes were sunk in their sockets, which made me sure he was on something.

'There's no work for dealers here,' I said while walking away. Fortunately, he didn't follow. I couldn't understand it. Iwenk had such a knack for making me angry. With him strung out like that, what right did he have to bad-mouth me? And why did I even bother to get so angry?

Oskar noticed the look of irritation on my face and raised his eyebrows.

'Iwenk, that guy over there, called me a homo whore,' I said, answering his unasked question.

'Is that what you feel you are?'

A man had just approached, apparently wanting to talk, and had slipped a twenty-thousand note into Oskar's waistband.

'I'm not queer and I'm not a whore. I'm just trying to earn some money,' I said in a loud voice.

Hearing that, the man who had been hovering next to Oskar immediately backed away.

Oskar raised his hands. 'OK, no big deal. Don't waste your

time getting angry.'

At that instant, a flash, like a bolt of lightning, illuminated us. But it was not lightning; it was the flash of a huge camera and the two of us looked in its direction. The photographer was a woman, dressed in a dark blue flannel shirt and jeans, with her hair rolled up and pinned to the back of her head. Once again she pointed the camera at us and – *pop!* – the lightning flashed again. 'A pair of angry angels,' she said as she held out her hand towards us. 'I'm Dolly.'

Each of us shook her hand.

We were used to being photographed. People liked to take our picture and to be photographed with us. Men and women, both gay and straight, and drag queens too liked to be seen with the club's angels. But never before had a professional photographer taken our picture. Not having asked our permission, however, I for one felt like it was an intrusion.

She stared at us sharply. 'I have a business proposition for you.'

Raffle

I had found my way into a good business, and I was wrong about our fake wings; they did, in fact, take us to another world, one distant from the dark, dim club. Dolly, the photographer we met at Starlight, promised us each a fee of fifteen million rupiahs for a single photographic session. Incredible! We were so dumbstruck by the figure she mentioned that we forgot to ask exactly what the work would entail. She just gave us a card and told us to come to the address on the back, which was in the Pondok Indah residential area of Jakarta, the following Wednesday evening. No need to call ahead, she said; just show up. The date was guaranteed. We nodded and said that we'd be there.

On Sunday we went with Yusuf and Paris to a salon and spa for intensive skin treatment: facials, body scrubs, exfoliation, the works. Then we soaked in a tub of bubbling hot water, a 'Jacuzzi', Paris called it. We spent some time sweating in a sauna and afterwards dined on Japanese food. I kept smelling my skin, which had the fragrance of strawberries. It felt clean and had a golden sheen, a nice contrast to Oskar's fair skin. I had to laugh at myself. When had I ever thought about my skin before? I used to be nothing but a smelly vocational high school student.

Yusuf, too, was surprised by our indulgence. 'This isn't like you. What's going on?' he asked while lifting a piece of sushi to his mouth.

I glanced at Oskar, not quite knowing what to say.

Since I was being so close-lipped, Oskar explained to Paris and Yusuf about our meeting Dolly and her proposition of work.

'But what kind of work did she propose?' Paris asked. All Oscar and I could do was shrug our shoulders.

Yusuf narrowed his eyes and then announced, 'I know what it is! It's a "raffle" club!' He made quote marks with his index figures.

'Yes, I'm sure that's what it is,' Paris agreed. 'A kind of Tupperwear party for rich wives.'

I frowned and looked at Oskar, assuming he might be able to clarify our friends' remarks. 'What are they talking about?' I asked but he said nothing.

'Don't you know?' Yusuf asked. Again, I shrugged my shoulders.

'These so-called raffle clubs are get-togethers for the bored wives of government officials and businessmen,' Yusuf explained, 'but the winner doesn't get money. She gets a young stud, instead – like you or Oskar, for example. Or maybe the two of you at the same time. Oh, yuck!' Yusuf paused and pretended to gag. 'That's a disgusting thought.'

'I don't believe it,' I said, shaking my head, refusing to entertain the thought.

'Well, it's up to you whether to believe it or not,' Paris put in. 'You are being paid fifteen million after all. Maybe you will have to sleep with them.'

I immediately got goose bumps thinking about it, and felt the blood drain from my face. I'd never slept with anyone before, and now I was going to have to do it with a middle-aged housewife?

I turned to Oskar who was still eating. 'Did you know about this kind of thing?'

He didn't answer.

'Well, that's it, I'm backing out,' I decided that instant. My three friends looked at me.

'Why?' asked Oskar, obviously worried about the thought of losing the promised fee.

'I've never done it before.'

'Never done what before? You mean you're still a virgin?' Oskar asked.

'Yes, I am, and for my first time I don't want it to be with some rich guy's wife,' I told them.

'What's the big deal? It's not like it's going to show afterwards,' Oskar joked. 'You'd think you were a girl or something.'

'Well, are you a virgin?' Paris asked his stepbrother.

That would be interesting to know, I thought, but Oskar remained close-mouthed.

'I'm not a virgin,' Yusuf announced, although no one had asked him.

'Do tell!' Paris cried.

'Yeah, it happened at a hotel, a five-star – or was it a seven-star? – hotel. It was five older guys at once, all of them Arabs. Sheiks, you know. An orgy! And I had to service all of them. I felt like a porn star! The next morning my body felt broken, but oh my god, I felt so sexy!'

Paris shivered visibly. 'That is super-disgusting.'

Yusuf went on: 'I mean, I once imagined giving my virginity to a person I loved, making love on the grass beneath a full moon. I thought it would be super-romantic …'

'Wow, and you're supposed to be a santri?' Paris giggled.

'Zip it, would you?' Yusuf ordered. 'I'm human too, you know.'

'Well, I'm no virgin either,' Paris said in a haughty tone of voice.

'Oh, really?' Yusuf interrupted.

'Indeed, I lost my virginity …'

'To vegetables!' Oskar said suddenly. We all turned in his direction.

'Vegetables? What the …?' Paris shook his head with incomprehension.

'How else do you explain the disappearance of carrots and cucumbers from the fridge and then their sudden reappearance under your bed!' Oskar continued, popping sushi into his mouth.

Yusuf and I broke out in laughter.

'You liar! That's not funny at all!' Paris snapped at him but then started to laugh as well.

All four of us laughed until our stomachs ached.

Because Paris was driving, Yusuf sat in the front, and Oskar and I sat in the back. After all that I'd heard, I wasn't sure about things now and was irritated with Oskar because I thought that he was concealing from me what he knew.

He seemed to be aware that I was annoyed and said offhandedly, 'What's the problem? Take it easy.'

'Maybe you don't have a problem, but I do!' I said angrily. 'What, don't you like girls?' Oskar asked.

'That's not it!' I yelled. 'Besides, it's a sin, you know?'

Paris looked at us in the rear-view mirror. 'Hey, guys, cut the talk about sin, OK? We're all sinners, you know. Do you think dancing half naked in your underwear isn't a sin? Or Yusuf selling himself to sugar daddies, isn't that a sin?'

'Who's selling himself,' Yusuf interrupted with a squeal.

'How about you, wanting to be a girl: Isn't that a sin?'

'Good idea: stop the talk about sin!' Oskar pronounced. 'Just admit it: we're all sinners. But we're young and that's normal.

Everybody sins, not just us. We're just trying to make money. We're not hurting anyone.'

'But aren't you afraid of going to hell?' I asked.

Oskar took a deep breath. 'Who isn't afraid of hell? But we have plenty of time to repent. Just do it this one time, OK?'

I turned and looked at Oskar. His facial muscles twitched as he looked at me. Was money that important for him? Was that special knowledge he wanted to acquire that important? But I was his friend and he had just begged me for help. I couldn't ignore his plea, so I just gave in.

'Alright …' I muttered feebly.

On our way back to Tangerang, We stopped at a mini-market and asked an older-looking ojek driver who was waiting there to buy us some Mix-Max Vodka – which he did, for a tip of course. After buying some chips, chocolate candy and cigarettes, we partook of our little feast.

After we exited the toll road in Tangerang, we drove through the red-light district for transvestite hookers, waving to them as they cast sultry looks at us from their haunts in the shadows of trees. We whistled at them, and then sped away in laughter. After that we just drove around, singing in the car, as we explored the night. It was one of the best days the four of us ever spent together.

An Angel's Kiss

On Wednesday evening, Oskar and I drove to the posh residential neighbourhood of Pondok Indah in Jakarta. All the way there, I kept thinking about what lay ahead. To be honest, it wasn't sin I was thinking of: it was the middle-aged women I was expecting to find there. If there really was a raffle, and I was the prize, I wasn't sure if I could bear being in the same room, naked and alone, with a woman old enough to be my mother. Playing Oedipus was not my game.

Even though the air conditioning in the car was on full blast, I was sweating.

'Still nervous?' Oskar asked.

'Fifteen million for my virginity: can you imagine?' I tried to laugh.

'You should be thankful anyone would want to pay,' Oskar joked.

'Up yours!' I told him. 'My first time with an old woman? I've never been with a girl, never even been kissed. How can I have sex if –'

Oskar interrupted: 'Never even been kissed?'

I shook my head.

For a moment, he said nothing. 'Here, I'll show you.' With his right hand on the wheel, and the car going at a constant speed, he leaned over and pressed his lips to my mouth for just a second, and then righted himself again.

I blinked my eyes and nodded my head, the expression on my

face no doubt reading, 'Oh, is that all?'

Oskar merely grinned.

I felt my cheeks blush but I didn't know what I was thinking or feeling. Oskar and I were friends, family of a sort. Whatever Oskar's thoughts were, the two of us suddenly broke out in laughter, and then I was able to relax.

Pondok Indah is the kind of residential area with expansive, well-maintained lawns and swimming pools so often seen in melodramatic films and soap operas. We rang the door bell of a mansion that looked like the White House in Washington, with porticoes and colonnades. I had to crane my neck to see the roof. We waited for what seemed like forever, and finally heard the click of the door as it opened. I was expecting to hear a gaggle of older women welcome us with giggles and screams, but when the door opened, the only people we saw were Dolly, a number of scruffy looking men, and one banci as well.

I looked at them looking at us. Apparently, Paris and Yusuf had guessed wrong. There didn't seem to be any party going on – but was that good? Maybe it was even worse. Maybe the host liked to indulge in weird fantasies involving a multiple number of men and a transvestite.

'Come on in,' Dolly said while leading us inside. Without any chitchat or offering something to drink, she said, 'We'll start right away,' and led the way to a spacious room with a very high ceiling and bright lights shining everywhere.

'Sit down for makeup,' Dolly then told us.

Oskar and I looked at each other as we sat down in front of a brightly illuminated makeup mirror. The drag queen who had greeted us with a grin in the foyer felt our faces with his hands and then began to apply powder and other cosmetics.

The scruffy-looking men turned out to be Dolly's crew. They

were positioning large lamps, ready cables, and strange-looking umbrellas. One of them brought a pairs of wings that looked like the ones we wore at Starlight.

Finally, I coughed. I had to ask. 'Excuse me,' I said to Dolly, who was fiddling with lenses on her camera. 'What is it we're going to be doing here?'

She gave me a look of surprise and wrinkled her brow. 'What, you don't know?' Didn't I tell you?' She slapped her brow. 'You silly boys, why didn't you ask?'

It was my first experience working as a model. Dolly told us that our appearance with wings at Starlight had given her the idea for this shoot. But she refused to tell us where or for whom she worked. She said the important thing is that we were being paid well and that our photographs would not be seen in Indonesia.

During the first part of the photo shoot, I was very nervous, stiff as bamboo, but after about twenty minutes and who knows how many frames, I finally began to loosen up and let myself follow Dolly's orders. I felt relieved – I wasn't going to lose my virginity! – and my body flushed with warmth as my blood coursed through my veins.

One of the men served as choreographer and suggested a number of poses, but gradually I was able to pose on my own by following Dolly's suggestions. She kept saying that we had talent, but truthfully, little true talent was required. We were dressed only in underwear and leather boots plus wings – which were much lighter and looked more realistic than the ones we wore at the club.

After each session, they changed our makeup, one time with temporary tattoos, another with streaks of body paint, and so on, but in all of them we wore nothing but underwear – but different kinds, of course.

You can guess what the photos were intended for. Oskar and I were told to tease, tickle, hug, and even kiss each other. My objections were tempered by the thought that compared to the thought of making love to an older woman, feigning attraction for Oskar was nothing.

In the final shoot, Dolly told Oskar and I to take off our underwear and pose naked in front of the camera. She promised that our genitals would not appear in the photographs and that, as much as possible, she would shoot from an angle that did not show them. Bullshit, I thought. In fact, a number of times I sensed that she was zooming in on our crotches.

For this final session, Dolly took charge of the choreography, and in one shot she had Oskar carry me in his arms. 'Very good! Brilliant!' Dolly kept saying, or 'Let's repeat that shot with your body like this. Your lip is sweaty. Move your body this way,' and so on.

I feared what might happen to the photos, but at that point I decided there was nothing I could do about it. Whatever will be, will be …

The session finally ended at around eight o'clock that night. My cheekbones ached from hours of posing with different kinds of expressions on my face and having to hold them for minutes at a time. It almost hurt to smile. We showered at the house, scrubbing away glitter and fake tattoos from our bodies. After we'd changed into our street clothes, Dolly invited us to dinner at a restaurant, but exhausted and just wanting to rest, we begged off politely.

Once we were in the car, Oskar laughed and said, 'Well, that was quite a raffle!' He patted the thick brown envelope resting on the console between our seats. I smiled in return and leaned my head back against the headrest. I was one tired Angel in the Know, for whom the only remedy now was sleep.

Power

More than two months had passed since Oskar's initial meeting with Ustadz Asman. It was almost the end of May now, far past the original forty-day deadline for his payment of tribute. During the past few weeks he had been working hard at the club. Om Bram had to reprimand him for annoying – as opposed to enticing – the customers. Bram ordered him to be the Angel of Temptation he was supposed to be, not the tinsel angel he was becoming. Yet Oskar's efforts were paying off. He was constantly going back and forth from the bar to the changing room to stash his tips.

For one full week after our photo session, Oskar appeared at Starlight every night, ready to flap his wings. He forced me to accompany him. He also asked Yusuf to find him other admirers. Oskar hoped that one of the lonely aunties or the wife of a rich official would adopt him, but he found little success with that and had to settle for escorting the daddies that Yusuf found for him, mostly on Manjam and chatting on MIRC. However, that wasn't lucrative enough for him; at most he might make Rp. 300,000 for spending time with these men. Of course, that was because Oskar refused to do anything except escort them, work out with them, go to see a film with them, or whatever. No sexual activity whatsoever.

I had no idea how much money Oskar had managed to put together by this time, but given how much I had made during the same time period, I guessed that it was a little fortune. I began to worry and wanted to warn Oskar that the knowledge he was buying would, in the end, require more than just money as payment. I was certain that Ustadz Asman would also demand that he undertake a special kind of fast or something like that. I felt sorry for him just to think about it, but I did not reveal my fears to him.

On the last Sunday of that month, Oskar came to the pesantren. We had just finished pencak silat exercises and were hanging out near the well, drinking water from the stone basin. I remember the happy look on Oskar's face when I found him sitting alone, cross-legged in my cell, waiting for me to return.

'Is Ustadz Asman around?' he asked straight out.

'He's bathing,' I told him, then plopped on the floor in my cell. I was still breathing heavily.

Oskar gave me a kind of sneer. 'Tired, are you? Better my way, I'd say. Instant power!'

I smiled cynically. 'You still don't know what else will be required of you. You just wait and see.'

After waiting for a while longer, I took Oskar to Cell Ten to see Ustadz Asman, who was now smelling good and neatly dressed in his best Samarinda sarong.

'I knew you'd be late,' Ustadz Asman said to Oskar. Oskar merely nodded.

'Are you ready?' Ustadz Asman asked.

Oskar nodded again and sat down cross-legged in front of Ustadz Asman, who held a string of prayer beads in his hand.

I sat behind Oskar, hoping that I didn't smell too bad since I still hadn't bathed.

'*Bismillah* ...' Ustadz Asman began as he recited something in Arabic. He closed his eyes for a moment and then opened them. 'Where would you like to keep the amulet that I will give you: around your neck, your waist, or in your wallet?'

Oskar looked at me for guidance. I shrugged my shoulders but whispered, 'Try your waist.' I didn't really know what was being asked.

'Your waist?' Ustadz Asman asked. Oskar nodded uncertainly.

'Now take out your tribute, and your wish will be granted.' Oskar put his hand in his knapsack and removed a thick stack of rupiah notes wrapped in brown paper.

Ustadz Asman looked momentarily at the packet and then closed his eyes. With a movement I did not see, a thin plaited rope appeared in his hand where his prayer beads had been.

'Pray in your heart that your tribute is worthy of your new power,' Ustadz Asman said while extending his hands towards Oskar.

I watched as their hands touched, expecting to see something miraculous: a flash of light or whatever, but nothing extraordinary happened at all. They clasped hands, looked into each other eyes for a few seconds, and then it was over.

'Here, let me put it on. Take off your shirt,' Ustadz Asman instructed Oskar.

Oskar took off his shirt. Ustadz Asman removed the black plaited rope from his hand and then put it around Oskar's waist. When he tied the string together, I noticed that at one end there was a rectangular charm made of black cloth, which looked as if something were wrapped inside it. I guessed that it might be a written mantra.

'I pray to God that nothing will go wrong,' said Ustadz Asman when patting Oskar's stomach.

'What might go wrong?' Oskar asked.

'Wait here a moment. Don't put on your shirt just yet,' he then told Oskar. Still seated in cross-legged position, Ustadz Asman then turned his body around to take something from behind his back. Suddenly, with his right hand, he threw something in Oskar's direction.

This movement was so fast I didn't know immediately what had just happened, but the shining object he had thrown at Oskar was a knife. It struck Oskar's left arm, causing him to shriek in pain. My heart jumped to my throat, but when I looked at Oscar's arm, I saw no blood there or on the knife's blade. I was sure the knife hadn't missed its mark, yet there was no wound. Oskar quickly felt his left arm with his right hand. He was flushed and sputtering, but from fright, not pain. As hard as the knife had been thrown, it should have severely cut his arm, but there was no mark, no blood at all.

Oskar stared at his arm and then looked at Ustadz Asman. 'It's yours now,' Ustadz Asman said, again extending his hand.

Trembling almost uncontrollably, Oskar also extended his hand.

They clasped hands once more, then Ustadz Asman took the brown paper envelope. 'Go now,' he said to us.

The two of us quickly left the cell without even saying goodbye and scampered back to my room where we could do nothing but look at other, completely confounded.

'Wow, I'm invulnerable,' Oskar announced with a grin. His chest swelled with pride.

'Yeah, damn it. Well, that's cool,' I answered with a grin as well.

The Thugs' Share

For the most part, the four of us had achieved what we wanted and were satisfied. Oskar now had his secret power of invulnerability; Yusuf had freedom and money from the men he met, the 'daddies' he had sought since he was a little boy; I had my freedom from my parents and a steady income as well; and Paris ... Well, Paris was different. Although he was more content with himself and who he was, he still didn't feel satisfied. He still wanted to be a real woman. And the more time that passed, the more dissatisfied he became with his appearance.

One day, when he accompanied me to the food stall near our school for lunch, he asked me, 'Do you think my thighs look too big for a girl? What about my arms? I think they're too muscular-looking.'

'You're thin already,' I said without much interest, spooning a meatball into my mouth.

'I've been using this hair remover I found on Facebook, to make my calves and thighs smooth. That way I can wear a miniskirt without stockings.'

I glanced at Paris, but he didn't seem to be talking to me. His eyes were someplace distant, while his hand played with his fork. 'I read on the internet that if I want to keep my body from developing like a man's I have to take female hormones. Otherwise, I'll just look like a drag queen. And do you know what kind of medicine stimulates the production of female hormones?' he asked.

I shook my head.

'Birth control pills! Amazing, isn't it? They can stop male muscular growth and even prevent my beard from growing. Amazing isn't it? I can be slim like a woman.'

I nodded and said facetiously, 'Well if you take birth control pills, you won't be able to get pregnant either.'

'That's all right. I don't want kids anyway. I wouldn't like their playmates making fun of them and calling them banci kids.'

I chuckled but then asked, 'Are you serious about becoming a girl?'

Paris shrugged his shoulders, making me wonder what he was thinking.

'Let's go to the mall later,' he said. 'I need to buy supplies for the salon and some more clothes.'

Paris's choice in women's clothing was more tasteful now. He no longer pretended to be buying clothes for a cousin or gifts for a girlfriend. He would try the clothes on himself in the dressing room.

That day, he tried on several pairs of tight jeans, shorts, hot pants, miniskirts and tightly fitting T-shirts. He tried on high-heels as well, and bought a wig that looked much more natural than the cheap ones he had before. Paris was no longer the frightened creature he once was. I wondered how he had developed such a thick skin. He was beginning to be like Yusuf.

'That was gutsy of you!' I remarked in the car.

'Well, since we don't know how long we're going to live, it's best that we live now. Oskar's right. We are still young.'

The last week of May was the period for national exams. Unlike students at the public schools who were caught up in the paper chase, I didn't study at all. At exam time at my school, a rolled-up crib sheet with all the answers somehow appeared and was passed from one student to another. Where this cheat sheet had come from, I didn't know, but I copied down all the answers. Paris, for his part, didn't even bother to do that.

At the pesantren, I used the national exams as an excuse not to participate in recitation exercises, but the fact is I spent most of the time in my cell talking to or texting with Oskar.

The scores for the national exams wouldn't be announced until the end of June, so the time until then was pretty much a driftless zone. Yeah, the seniors still went to school but didn't really take classes anymore, rather spending their time in class meetings, sporting competitions, and the like.

By this time, I had gotten used to being referred to as 'Paris's boyfriend' and no longer got angry or felt ashamed when I heard the remark. It no longer bothered me to be seen with him. All the tsk-tsks and under-the-breath coughs no longer got my attention. Fellow classmates had become aware of my transformation from the slovenly Ricky I once had been to the good-looking guy I now was. Eventually, they grew tired of taunting me because they knew I didn't care – or maybe it was because I sometimes treated them to cigarettes or a meal. At any rate, the jeering voices were silenced.

During this time, Paris and I frequently skipped school to take care of his salon-supply business. Sometimes Oskar also came along. We had almost an entire month until the announcement of the final exams.

Yusuf had changed the colour of his braces several times, also the style and colour of his hair, each time in a more eye-catching style. As a result, my tinted hair attracted almost no attention at all. Our cell became the focus of attention for the other residents, who thought of us as social climbers, engaging in behaviour that was inappropriate for santri. Sometimes I thought about this. We lived in a pesantren, yet we earned a living by peddling ourselves, but without force and of our own volition. Was that a sin? I displayed my body at a nightclub and made the clientele fantasize about sleeping with me: Was that a sin? I was trying to earn enough money to live. Was that wrong? I didn't want to be a burden to others. I wanted to be able to survive on my own. And now that I was able to earn an income, what was I supposed to do? At times I thought of moving out of the pesantren and renting a place of my own, but a part of me was attached to the pesantren now, and I didn't want to leave. Besides, I didn't want to abandon Yusuf.

The point is, I continued to live at the pesantren even as I continued my work as Angel in the Know. I truly enjoyed the work. The beat of the music had infused my blood, and I was in love with the money I was able to make. I knew what good food was; I knew where to get it and how much to pay for it. I had opened a savings account at a bank and built up a tidy amount of money for myself. I had an ATM debit card and paid for my purchases with it. Except for Paris, no other classmates I knew had cards of their own.

During this period, the four of us had fun exploring the town and spending the cash that customers tucked into Oskar's and my underwear. We went to holiday resorts on the coast and in the mountains and stayed at hotels. We took lots of pictures with Yusuf's pocket camera, hung out at malls, and delighted in being the centre of attention. I felt both loved and desired, something I had never felt before. I had finally found a life of my own.

In the midst of my nights at work, I would occasionally see Iwenk staring hatefully at me, jealous of the money that I was earning while he was forced to furtively sell marijuana and other illegal drugs. My brother Edi was around, too, but he didn't say much. In fact, we rarely said hello or even acknowledged each other's presence when we were at the club at the same time. No one except Oskar even knew that Edi was my brother.

One evening towards the end of the month, Yusuf announced to Paris, 'On Wednesday night there's a Miss Drag contest at Starlight. You should participate,' he suggested.

Paris looked at him in annoyance. 'I am not going to participate in such a contest. Do you not still get it? I want to be a woman, not a drag queen.'

'Just an idea,' Yusuf said.

Paris never deigned to participate in what he considered to be low-class events in which loud-mouthed drag queens made themselves the butt of jokes on stage. Yusuf might, but not Paris. In the end Paris did come to the club that night, but he didn't wear the glam rags that other cross-dressers wore. Instead, he wore body-hugging jeans, a light shift with a bra underneath, and a casual cardigan. His wig was natural-looking. Very different from Yusuf, who went all out, as if getting dressed up for Mardi Gras.

'Watch it, Beyoncé is coming through!' Yusuf screamed.

While Yusuf registered for the contest, Paris sat on a barstool with an elegant air. I suspect he felt pleased with himself because a number of people thought he was a real woman, which gave Paris a real sense of achievement. Yusuf, on the other hand, only used women's clothing to attract attention.

With that small plaited rope around his waist, Oskar looked a little weird. I told him to take it off but he refused. Instead, he tried to conceal it beneath the elastic waistband of his underwear, which was funny because when customers attempted to stick bills into his underwear, their fingers would get tangled in the rope.

The Miss Drag contest was one of the club's most popular competitions, and a large number of cross-dressers registered for the event. Every week, for four weeks straight, the club would be packed with people coming to watch, some to show support for their favourite candidate, others to enjoy the comedy skits between the drag queens' appearances. There were three weeks of eliminations and then the finals.

Yusuf – or rather, Yessi – survived one elimination round after another. Every week he was busy with his preparations for his appearances on stage on Wednesday and Saturday nights. On the day before an event, he always performed a full dress rehearsal in the clothes and makeup he was going to wear. He would stealthily practice his prancing walk at the lodge, miming his song and casting flirtatious glances at the empty air, but broke into laughter whenever he caught sight of me. Over time, he changed from a young gay man to a fledgling drag queen. Paris, who accompanied Yusuf on his shopping trips, came to serve as a kind of dresser and manager for him.

In the third week of eliminations, Oskar and I were sitting together at the bar watching Yusuf on the catwalk, wearing a peignoir he had found at the used clothes stalls near the Senen Market Terminal in Jakarta. Iwenk was sitting beside us. Where he'd come from I didn't know.

'Ain't that something,' he commented as he studied Paris, who was watching Yusuf and smiling.

Oskar and I looked in his direction. Oskar didn't know who he was.

'What's something?' I asked, afraid what he might say. 'One is now a prostitute and the other is a banci!'

Obviously, I was the one being called a prostitute, but I ignored his comment.

'I see that he's a legit banci now,' Iwenk added, as if to provoke me to respond. 'You queers are so weird.'

'What do you mean?' Oskar asked loudly.

'Hey, no need to get mad. Are you into banci or something?' Iwenk smirked.

As quick as lightning, a blow from the black-winged Angel of Temptation's clenched fist landed on Iwenk's face and sent him sprawling on the ground.

Immediately, a little commotion ensued as people rushed to see what had happened. Oskar explained that the guy had been rude to him. Everyone understood. Lots of customers were rude to us, especially when they had had too much to drink. They'd pull on our wings or try to grope our crotches – without even bothering to slip a bill inside.

My brother Edi appeared, picked up Iwenk from off the floor and began to lead him away.

'Don't go looking for trouble,' he said to me under his breath. In the early morning when I went into the changing room to rest and change, I found Iwenk snoring loudly on the floor next to the sofa. Edi was there, too, sitting at the table in the middle of the room, talking to two strangers who looked completely out of place in the club. Both of them sported long, straggly beards and white over-shirts and billowing trousers. I watched them out of the corner of my eye as I removed my wings and put on my street clothes.

I noticed Edi nod to the visitors, as if confirming an agreement about something. The two visitors gave him what I perceived to be a threatening stare but, in the end, they stood, muttered something, and made their way towards the door, with Edi right behind them.

When Edi returned he said nothing about his visitors but

immediately offered some advice: 'Punching a guy in the bar is just looking for trouble, you know.'

I shrugged as I pulled on my T-shirt. 'How's he doing?'

'He's OK. Sleeping it off is all. But that's quite a punch your friend packs,' Edi remarked.

I just smirked. With his super powers, of course Oskar now packed a punch.

Edi pointed to Iwenk. 'You got to be careful with dealers. They're just front guys, you know. They got backers behind them.'

I said nothing as I gave Iwenk a slight nudge. No reaction. Looking into his face, I remembered the night at the hospital when he demanded the doctor check his butt. That made me smile. He should have become a friend, I thought. He had given me the initial push in this direction to earn a living.

'Who were those guys you were talking to?' I then asked Edi, shifting the subject of conversation.

He raised the second and third fingers of each hand, signalling quotation marks. 'Moral guardians.'

'What do you mean?' I asked.

'You know, those people who claim to be moral representatives of the nation, the ones who demonstrate outside karaoke places and nightclubs, and raise their voices about sexy-looking film stars. You know who I'm talking about?'

I nodded slightly, knowing all too well the organization whose name we dare not speak, which operated in the name of religion but was little more than a band of rabble-rousers.

'What were they doing here?' I then asked.

Edi chortled loudly. 'Where do you think they get their money from for their demonstrations?'

I shrugged my shoulders. Indeed, I had no idea.

'From places like this, that's where!' he said emphatically.

'Especially places where degenerates gather. Unless you want to see the place burned down, you have to give the thugs their share.'

'A share of the profits, you mean?' I asked in amazement. If these people really were moral guardians, why didn't they demand that the place be shut down? Instead they were here asking for a cut to ensure the club's security.

Edi mimed a person counting money with his fingers. 'For those people and the police, too, the bottom line is money.'

I folded my wings and put them away. 'How much are they asking for?'

'Twenty million. Said there would be problems with the show if they didn't get it.'

I whistled. 'Twenty million not to shut down the Miss Drag contest?'

On the scale of things, in a city the size of Jakarta with fifteen million people, Starlight was a small club and the contest a minor event, an entertainment for a relatively small group of customers. Moral guardians, I sniffed. Money-grubbers was more like it. Such hypocrisy!

At that moment, Yusuf, who had turned into Yessi, appeared in the doorway and announced gleefully, 'I made it to the semi-finals!'

Not a Virgin

Making it to the semi-finals of the Miss Drag contest meant that Yusuf would have to prepare to lip-synch a new song the following week. Contestants were allowed to demonstrate other talents – magic tricks, dancing with a python, or whatever – but most of them chose to lip-synch, because that was a mandatory skill for the first-prize candidates.

After the bar closed, the four of us went for breakfast to a McDonald's where Oskar and I stuffed our faces.

'With most of the contestants lip-synching Western songs, maybe you should do an Indonesian song,' Paris was saying to Yusuf. 'Something in Indonesian might make you stand out.' He then removed a small plastic bottle from his Etienne Aigner bag and poured a few tablets into his hand and tossed them in his mouth.

Yusuf looked at him curiously. 'What are those? Are you sick or something?'

'These are my hormone tablets,' Paris said, putting the plastic bottle back into his bag.

Yusuf continued to look at Paris, as if not understanding.

Paris ignored him. 'So, what song do you want to perform? I can help you with the moves,' he said.

Paris had begun to delve more seriously into the subject of gender change, poring through articles he found on the internet about the subject. On occasion, he'd bring me up to date on his findings about plastic surgery, genital transformation, scraping of the Adam's apple, and so on. He discussed hair styles: length, cut and style. He plucked his eyebrows and dieted to lose weight and look slimmer. He tried different kinds of falsies for a more natural look. He purchased women's fashion magazines, which he gave to Yusuf to store in our cell.

'I'm going to start getting hormone shots so I can stop taking these awful birth control pills,' he said. Oh, that's right, he also made me go with him to the drugstore to buy those dammed pills.

One evening, when Yusuf and I were in our cell munching on snacks, I thought about Paris and the seriousness with which he was exploring the possibility of a sex change. I looked at Yusuf and asked him, 'Do you want to be a banci?'

Yusuf looked up from the magazine he was reading. Following my lead, he was not bothering to study for his final exams, not because he was lazy but because he was smart. He would ace his exams with little study; far more important for him at the time were his preparations for the Miss Drag contest.

'Hey, keep your voice down when you say things like that,' Yusuf said, his eyes on people passing outside the open door of our cell. 'I don't want to be a banci,' he whispered hurriedly.

He seemed to notice that I wasn't satisfied with his answer. He added, 'I just want to win something! I've never won anything in my life. So I'm not doing this because I want to … No, that's not right, I want to do it, but …' He took a breath. 'I don't want to be this way forever. So don't worry, I don't want to be a banci. I like being a guy better. At first, you know, I was only doing it to make Paris happy.'

Hmmm, back to Paris.

Yusuf's explanation served to ease my mind somewhat. I had

begun to feel guilty about the change in him. Ali was still keeping an eye on me, and though he rarely said much, I found the way he looked at me discomfiting. He was curious about me, or rather about us, what we were doing to become the moneyed social creatures we now were. Yusuf's answer was a relief for me. Ali didn't have to worry that he was going to lose his brother. Only Oskar would have that experience.

When the night of the semi-finals finally arrived, we were back stage, and Yusuf was complaining to Paris. 'I should be performing an Agnes Monica song.'

Paris was in the middle of helping Yusuf attach his false eyelashes. 'What? You're not a rocker! Can you see yourself stomping your feet on stage. *Ieris B choezen inu sinaung for Yoelandu.* You'll sing the one I chose for you. With you as Britney Spears singing "Womanizer", you're sure to win.' I guess he had changed his mind about Yusuf performing an Indonesian song.

It was the third week in June, in the middle of the dry season, and the club felt especially hot that night. I couldn't stop sweating. Neither could Oskar.

As usual, the contest was marked by laughter and loud clapping, but that night everyone seemed to be drinking. Ice was going fast, and the bartender could hardly keep up with the orders. When Yusuf appeared, he forgot his lines in several places, but that didn't seem to affect the audience's reaction. I too laughed and clapped my hands, not because for Yusuf so much, but for Oskar, who was on stage acting as Yusuf's slave. A few days before, Yusuf had entreated Oskar for his assistance: in his performance he was going to play a dominatrix, and he wanted Oskar to be his whipping-boy. To get his way, he whispered, 'You know, I still haven't forgiven you for the comment you made the first night we met. If you really want me to forget that incident, you have to do what I want.'

In the end, Oskar finally agreed. Little did Oskar know that I had given Yusuf the idea.

In the middle of the performance, when Oskar was on his hands and knees acting like a dog and Yusuf was whipping him, Paris came looking for me in a panic. His eyes were moist and there was a worried look on his face.

'Iwenk's here, and he's seen me!' he said loudly.

'So what?' I asked, flapping my wings, hoping to cool down the situation.

'Iwenk's seen me!' he said again.

I didn't see a problem. 'So what?' I asked.

'He laughed at me! That's stressed me out!' Paris's wig bobbed about on his head as he shifted his weight from one foot to the other.

I had forgotten to tell Paris that Iwenk already knew about him and that there was no need for him to feel stressed, but at that moment I had no time to explain, because Paris was as panicked as a drag queen who had lost her wig.

I tried to calm him down. 'Don't worry. People are going to know eventually.'

'No, I don't want him or anyone else to find out!'

I frowned with confusion. 'So what do you want then?' I had had enough of Paris's indecisiveness. Anyway, it was so hot, I just wanted to fly away.

'I want to go home. I want to go home,' he whined dramatically.

I looked at his face. He seemed embarrassed. I didn't understand why. If he wanted to become a woman, then he had to be able to show himself to other people, not just to his close friends.

'Wait for Yusuf to finish,' I told him.

Paris bit his lips and moved about restlessly but did what I said. As soon as Yusuf was finished, Paris accosted him and told him they were going home – even though the contestants who had been selected for the final round had yet to be announced. But I would be there to hear the news. Oskar and I were always there until closing time. We could either take a cab or get a ride back to Tangerang with someone.

With the show nearly over, Oskar and I sat together at the bar: two angels together, a sight that drew looks of admiration or envy from numerous customers. Several men offered to buy us drinks or otherwise engage us in conversation but, because of the heat, neither of us was in the mood. And then, a familiar person appeared: Mulyono, the salon owner whose existence I had long tried to forget. The thought of me being groped in the bathroom at his home immediately came to mind and made my stomach turn. I didn't want anything to do with him, but there was nothing I could do as he came toward me.

'Hi, sexy,' he said in greeting, as he sat down and gave me the once-over. 'How are you doing?' he said with a grin while extending his hand.

I stared ahead, not bothering to look at him or shake his hand. 'Stuck up are you, now that you're a celebrity?' he said.

'Just normal,' I said quietly. I didn't want to deal with him.

Besides, the lecherous look on his face made me angry.

Oskar gave me a nudge, a reminder that I was dealing with a customer, but I ignored him, too. Orders from Om Bram were that even if we didn't like a person or felt bothered by a customer, we were still supposed to smile and at least pretend to be polite.

But with this Mulyono guy, I couldn't fake it. The man revolted me. Had I been able to, I would have flapped my wings in his face. 'Introduce me to your hunky friend,' Mulyono said while leering at Oskar.

Oskar smiled but just barely, not wanting to encourage further conversation. Generally speaking, it was easy to discern a customer's intentions, even when they were veiled, but Mulyono made no attempt to disguise his.

'How much for your time?' he asked straight out.

'Sorry, but I don't do that kind of thing,' Oskar answered firmly. 'You may look but not touch.'

'You like to play hard to get, huh?' Mulyono commented, 'Well I like it even better when it's not so easy.'

Both of us blew wind from our mouths and silently prayed for the man to go away.

'Would you like a drink?' Mulyono then offered.

'No, thank you,' I answered quickly for the two of us.

'Don't be that way,' Mulyono responded. 'I may not be your type, but you could at least let my buy you a drink.'

Not wanting to be overly rude, I gave a slight nod of consent and not too long afterward Mulyono handed glasses of cola to Oskar and me. We took them reluctantly. At first we made motions of just sipping on the drinks, but the night was so hot and the glass of iced cola so refreshing that we both soon drained our glasses.

After standing beside us a while, Mulyono finally nodded and went away. After that, all of a sudden, and for the rest of the night – or at least the part that I remember – I felt extremely happy. All I wanted to do was dance. I grabbed Oskar by the arm and went to the middle of the dance floor to take advantage of what time still remained before the club closed. Oskar and I laughed and laughed. I felt a bit tipsy but also warm. I didn't know if Oskar felt the same, but I felt giddy and strange. We were two happy angels on the dance floor, and we didn't care if our wings got into other people's faces.

When someone pulled on my arm and led me off the floor, away from the crowd, I simply followed, laughing all the while. I was still holding Oskar's hand, and he too followed, also laughing.

'Where are we going?' he called over the roar of the music.

'I think we're flying to heaven,' I answered, letting myself be pulled away from the crowd by an unknown hand. After that, it's a big blank.

The next thing I remembered was the sound of a mobile assaulting my eardrums with its ring tone. The phone rang again and again, dozens of times. I recognized the ring tone, but my eyes felt heavy, as if bricks were on my eyelids. I was half-awake, half-floating somewhere I didn't know. But the mobile kept screaming at me. Finally, I opened my eyes a crack. My vision was blurred, but I was able to spot Oskar's phone, flashing and vibrating wildly. I resisted picking it up, hoping it might stop ringing of its own accord. But it wouldn't stop, and its sound grated against my jagged nerves. I wanted to reach for it and throw it away. I tried to move my right hand, but it wouldn't move. I then tried to move my left, but it wouldn't move either. Something was wrong, very wrong, I realized subconsciously. Maybe I was dreaming. I rested for a moment and tried to concentrate, isolating the sound of the phone in the back of my mind. I tried to gather my wits and return to full consciousness.

When consciousness did return, I discovered that I was in an unfamiliar place. Not only that, my entire body felt sore: my neck, back, waist, chest, nipples, thighs, but especially my crotch and my ass which was a zone of pain. I shook my head, trying to clear my vision, and that's when I saw Oskar, lying naked and motionless across the mattress with his two hands tied to the bedposts. His eyes were blindfolded. Looking around, I saw the remains of our broken wings scattered around the room. I then looked at myself. I was naked and seated in a chair, my arms tied to its arms.

The mobile rang again.

I struggled with all my might to release my arms, ignoring the pain that was racking my brain. I roared as I fought with the bindings. Finally, I managed to break one of my arms free, and then the other. I groped for the mobile and stabbed the answer button with my finger. It was Paris calling.

I heard him chatter: 'Hi! Where are you guys? We've been looking for you since last night. How come you didn't say anything. What's going on? Helloooo! Oskaarrrr!' But I couldn't manage to say a single word.

My eyes fell on Oskar again, and at once I wanted to explode with anger. I untied the rope that was around my waist and moved quickly to Oskar. While I fumbled to untie his hands, I kept saying, 'Wake up …! Wake up …!' but the sound of my voice was that of an injured animal. I couldn't scream; I didn't have the strength. It took a long time for me to rouse Oskar, and when he was finally half awake, we found ourselves huddled naked like two animals in a cage; that was when the fear emerged.

We couldn't speak. We just looked at each other, our eyes welling with tears.

I looked for my underwear and, after finding them, located Oskar's and threw them next to him. Our bodies smelled. The entire room stank. My body felt broken.

Oskar finally managed to return Paris's call: 'Come get us,' he said in a broken voice. 'Come get me and Ricky.'

I knew how dry his throat must have been. My own mouth hurt inside.

I heard a loud cry at the end of the line: 'Where are you?' Oskar looked around the room to find an identifying feature.

On a cheap ashtray was the hotel's logo.

'That hotel ... That hotel where we took you.'

'What's your room number?' Paris then asked.

'I don't know! Just come here!' Oskar screamed in frustration, before he realized that he needed to get control of himself and the situation. Finally, he said slowly, in a calmer voice, 'And bring us some clothes.'

After he clicked off the phone we sat and stared at each other again.

After Paris arrived and somehow managed to find our room, he blinked wildly when he saw us, and his mouth fell open wide. Without a word, we took the clothes he had brought along, dressed as fast as we could, and then made our way to the lobby. But just as we were leaving the hotel, a security guard stopped up. Only a deposit had been paid for the room; we had to pay the rest. Paris took out some bills and handed them to the guard.

At the car, letting Paris serve as chauffeur, Oskar and I got in the back and sank wearily against the back seat. I was glad to see that Yusuf hadn't come along.

'I don't want to go home,' I said.

Paris took the initiative and drove the car to the nearest toll-road entrance and headed westward towards Tangerang; but when we reached the Tangerang exit, he drove straight past it, heading west.

On and on we drove, for hours, it seemed, until we reached a beat-up road jammed with trucks that led through a vast industrial estate with chimneys billowing white smoke. When we got to the other side, the road suddenly emptied, and the drive became peaceful. Soon we came to the white, sandy coast at Anyer. The sea beyond was a canvas of green and pale blue. I looked at the clock on the dash: it had been four hours since we'd left Jakarta. Finally, at a deserted stretch of beach, Paris slowed the car, drove off the road, and parked on the edge of the sandy strip. Oskar jumped out of the car and ran down to the sea. Paris and I followed him.

At the water's edge, Oskar stopped and stared at the horizon. Then he screamed, as loud as he could. No words, just a wounded scream.

Paris looked at me, his eyes full of questions. We still hadn't told him what had happened.

I wanted to scream as well, but I could not. My throat was killing me, and I could only gurgle.

Oskar suddenly tore off his clothes and ran into the ocean. I hesitated but then followed his lead. That was our first bath after the realization, hours earlier, that we were no longer virgins. I thought, not even the water of the entire ocean could wash away the anger, which would haunt us for the rest of our lives.

Clap

A number of days passed before Oskar and I were able to talk about what had happened. When we finally did, we concluded that Mulyono must have engineered our abduction and violation. We guessed that the drinks he had bought us that night were laced with some kind of drug, the same M.O. he had used when he raped Iwenk. And even though he was reluctant to admit it, Oskar had also been a virgin before that night.

On the day national exam results were announced, while the other students were celebrating their graduation by signing one another's white shirts with magic markers or parading around town in a convoy of motorcycles, Oskar and I decided to pay Mulyono a visit instead. We first went to his house but didn't find anyone there. The place looked just like the first time I visited it: haunted and smelling of degradation. Then we went down the list of the salons he owned, going from one to the next. When we finally did find him, at one of his salons, he acted as if he couldn't be bothered with us. Oskar was furious, and his face was beet red, but Mulyono put his hands on his waist, pursed his lips and said to him: '*Yoelandu kinant prueven inu thheeneng.*' You can't prove a thing.

He was right, of course; we had no proof that he had abused us. Oskar didn't care and raised a clenched fist.

Immediately, Mulyono threatened to report us to the police: '*Yoelandu B tuchen Ieris, Ieris B kallen D polenta.*'

Pow! Oskar's fist plowed into the man's face. Mulyono's hairdressers shrieked in horror and threw down their combs and hairdryers and prepared to come to his assistance. I yanked Oskar's arms and pulled him out of the salon to prevent him from doing anything more. Call me a coward, but the last thing I wanted at that moment was to have a raging pack of cross-dressing hairdressers attack me with their nails and high heels.

After fleeing the place, I told Oskar that the only thing we could do now was to try to forget what had happened. Even though we could not change the past, Oskar deserved to be pleased with himself, because Mulyono was going to need an operation on his jaw for sure.

The days turned into a week, and I began to feel a little better, at least less dirty than I had before. I suddenly became more serious about saying my prayers and attending recitation lessons. I was becoming an obedient and faithful santri. I tried my best to forget that night of no memory and thought of the ocean, the wide, open sea. Immersing myself in its waters had represented the first stage of the healing process for me, but the fact was I was still seething inside. I had merely suppressed the memory of what had happened in order to forget. When Yusuf whined and begged me to go with him to the club to rehearse for the finals of the Miss Drag contest, I yelled at him. I told him to shut up and stop whining, because I never wanted to go to that place again.

'Why are you going there?' I screamed at him. 'You said you didn't want to be a banci.'

'I told you I want to win!' he responded angrily.

I stopped talking. Yusuf didn't understand. Oskar and I still hadn't divulged our secret, so he didn't know what had happened to us. He called me a nasty person and began to give me the silent treatment. Even without me, he was still going to go to the club, of course, so unbeknownst to him I called Paris to make sure that he was going with Yusuf.

Then something happened. On the seventh day of my misery, I felt something wrong with my penis. When I pissed, I felt a burning sensation. At first, I thought that maybe I wasn't drinking enough liquids or was drinking unclean water. For a week now I hadn't been buying water or boiling water to drink. I was getting my water from the basin and drank it as if the liquid were bottled mineral water. Pretty sure that that was the cause of my discomfort, I bought a five-gallon bottle of water to store in my room and I drank as much water as often as I could. It didn't help. Whenever I pissed, I still felt that burning sensation the length of my penis. Gradually, it wasn't just urine coming out of the head of my penis, but pus-like liquid as well.

I decided that I had to talk to Oskar about this. We hadn't spoken since tracking down Mulyono. I called him on the phone. 'Oskar,' I began hesitantly.

'Hi,' he said. He sounded unenthusiastic.

'I just wanted to find out if anything is wrong?'

'What do mean?' he asked in a tone that indicated he knew something wasn't right.

I didn't reply.

'Want to meet?' he proposed.

'Sure.'

I almost jumped with joy.

After Isya prayers that night, at the side of the road not far from the lane that led to the pesantren, Oskar and I were leaning like two dolts against the hood of his car. Oskar lit a cigarette then offered me one. I started to take it, but stopped, afraid that smoking might somehow worsen my condition. Noting my refusal, Oskar threw his cigarette on the ground and kicked it away.

For a time, we said nothing.

'How are you doing?' Oskar finally asked.

'I don't know. All right, I guess,' I mumbled. There was another silence, as we looked at the sky. I felt a twinge of pain in my penis.

'Do you think we should see a doctor?' Oskar asked. 'Maybe just to check things out?'

I took a deep breath and then exhaled strongly through my nose. I nodded without looking at him.

'Where?' he finally asked.

'The general hospital,' I answered.

We jumped into the car and took off. On the way, I thought of the night I had run into Iwenk at the hospital and him telling me, 'I want my butt examined. I'm afraid of AIDS.' I felt my colour fade. Now that I thought about it, I was amazed that Iwenk had had the foresight to undergo an examination after Mulyono had abused him. Why the fuck hadn't I thought to do the same?

The hospital wasn't that busy. After Oskar parked the car, I followed him as he sauntered towards the registration desk. I thought he might say something about the last time he had been to this hospital, the day he nearly bled to death, but he didn't. Instead, he put my name down in the registration book for a check-up with a general physician. We sat in the waiting room, skimming through the tattered magazines, while waiting to be called. When finally my name was called, Oskar rose from his seat as well and tagged along behind me.

In the doctor's office, I hesitated to speak. It wasn't until the doctor had said several times, 'Tell me what's wrong,' that I finally was able to stammer an answer: 'When I piss, it hurts.'

'OK.' He nodded. 'Anything else?'

'Well, there's some pus,' I added, embarrassed to say so in front of Oskar.

'All right, we better check it out. Take off your pants and lie down there.' The doctor pointed to a cold, hard-looking examination bed.

I did as he asked. The doctor told me to pull my underwear down, and then he squeezed and inspected my penis. He dabbed the head with a cotton swab, removed a sample of the pus that had emerged at the tip, and smeared the liquid on a small, thin piece of glass, which he said would be sent to the lab. He then told me to put my pants backs on and to return to my chair. Oskar said nothing during this time. He sat not moving in his chair.

'When was the last time you engaged in sexual relations?' the doctor asked.

I fumbled for words: 'Hmm, never … oh, not really, doctor, I mean, I was out of it. Hmm, I can't remember …' I really didn't know what to say.

The doctor gave me a look of surprise. Of course, I could have told him what had happened or what I thought had happened but that, I thought, would have been too much information. I feared that he would suggest that we report the incident to the police. Instead, I said, 'Hmm, two weeks ago, I guess …'

'So, maybe fellatio, then?' the doctor coaxed.

'Umm, umm …'

'In plain words, a blowjob?'

'Umm, maybe, I guess,' I stuttered.

'Oh,' was all the doctor said, and took out a pad and wrote a prescription.

'That can happen with oral sex if your partner is infected in the throat. Next time, use protection,' he said, looking up momentarily and then continuing to write. 'Use a condom,' the doctor spelled it out more clearly, seeing my confused look.

There won't be a next time, I thought to myself. 'But what is it, doctor?' I asked.

'Gonorrhea or "the clap", as you might say – which is what you can get with unsafe sex.' Although he had a hint of a smile on his lips, the doctor's voice was steady and professional sounding.

Seeing that trace of a smile gave me a huge sense of relief. 'Is it dangerous?' I asked.

'No,' he said, while handing the prescription to me. 'I'll give you a shot and after three days of antibiotics, you'll be back in good shape.'

I smiled with relief. Thank you, God! I wasn't going to die. I suddenly felt like heavy chains had been removed from me.

When I stood up to thank the doctor, Oskar said, 'Hey, Doc, would you mind making that two prescriptions?'

The doctor gave both of us an injection of antibiotics and prescriptions for tetracycline, which we purchased at the hospital pharmacy. Once we were back in the car again, we sat there silently for a while but then, spontaneously, with nothing triggering it, we both began to laugh.

'Don't come close to me,' I warned Oskar with mock horror, 'I don't mix with people like you!'

'You're the one who's disgusting! Sit on a towel. I don't want your crotch touching my car seat!'

Laughter does, indeed, seem to be the best medicine. Life is funny. Here the two of us had steadfastly rejected a large number of men who would have been willing to pay a high price for our virginity, but in the end it was taken from us for nothing, with no payment whatsoever, and all we got in return was the clap. How could that not be funny?

The Final Round

Having not fully explained to Yusuf what had happened to me and Oskar that night, Yusuf remained in the dark as to my reason for not wanting to go back to Starlight. After a while, however, I began to become annoyed with myself. The incident was over. I had to get past it. Starlight hadn't been the problem. The problem had been Mulyono. So why was I so reluctant to return to Starlight? Yusuf was right when he reminded me that I liked working there, that I liked making lots of money, and that I liked people liking me.

Then Om Bram called. I had just finished isya prayers and was sitting in my cell. With my right hand leafing through the pages of the yellow book on my lap, my left held my mobile to my ear. 'It's been three weeks since you've been to the club,' he stated in a tone of annoyance. 'No news. You just disappeared. Your phone is dead. And Oskar the same.'

I didn't reply. Indeed, I had taken to turning off my phone when not using it. I didn't want to talk to anyone. 'I wasn't feeling well,' I told him.

At the end of the line, I heard Bram take a deep breath. 'Well, are you going to be well by this Saturday? It's the final round of the Miss Drag contest.'

I hesitated to answer.

'Come on. Please! I need you guys to open the show. It will be busy for sure. You stand to make a lot of money on tips.'

That was tempting for me, of course, and he seemed to realize this. 'I know that money isn't a cure for everything, but help me this one time, will you? Besides, people are asking about you.'

I got the sense that Bram knew what had happened. 'OK, we'll see,' I finally said.

Not long after the call from Om Bram, Yusuf came into our cell and started pestering me again about going to the club with him on Saturday night.

I didn't tell him that Om Bram had just called and that I was in fact considering returning there. Instead, I said, 'Hey, I'm trying to reform.'

'Reform later, after the contest is over. Now I need you to come with me,' he demanded.

'Idiot. Reform isn't something you can delay until a more convenient time,' I argued.

'You're too much, you know. Since when did you get so rich you don't have to work anymore?'

I said nothing. I thought of the money I'd made for that modelling shoot and the tips I made as an angel at the club. I still had plenty of savings, and if I could teach myself to be economical and free myself of my spendthrift habits, I probably had enough to last me for the year ahead. I wouldn't have to go to work in a factory after graduating from vocational high school. I had more money in my savings account than a factory worker might make in a year.

'I have some savings,' I finally said in answer to Yusuf's question.

'Your money won't last. How can you not want to work? Your work is easy. Why do you want to stop? People would kill for a job like yours. Look around you at how many people are out of work. And here you are with a good job and not wanting to work anymore.'

'But it's wrong. It's against the Book, you know, to show your body.' I swear I hadn't planned to say such a thing; I just blurted it out. When had I ever concerned myself with sin or showing the body? I think I just said it to make Yusuf shut up.

And it did make him shut up, at least momentarily.

He frowned at me in irritation. 'All right, but come with me this one last time. It's the final! I want my friends to be there. You don't have to take your clothes off if you don't want to.'

'And what about you?' I asked offhand. 'How long do you want to go on being that way?'

'What do you mean?'

'I mean dressing up in women's clothing and chasing after those daddies of yours.'

At first Yusuf said nothing. I thought maybe he'd decided to stop pestering me. Then he suddenly erupted, spouting things I had never heard him say before.

'If what I'm doing is wrong or a sin, you shouldn't be the one lecturing me. I was living in the pesantren and learning to recite my prayers even before I could walk. I learned about sin long before I could sing an Agnes Monica song. I'm tired of thinking about sin. I want a life of my own. I want parents. I want money. I want a home. Do you think I like living this way? I just want a normal life.'

Why was he so angry all of a sudden, I wondered, and then smiled at him.

'And don't you smile at me!' he said angrily as he pulled the peci I was wearing from my head and threw it in my face before stamping out of the cell.

On Saturday night I stopped a cab on the road outside the pesantren and made my way to Paris's house. Earlier that afternoon I had called Oskar to ask him if he was going to the club to work that night. He said that Om Bram had also called him, and implied that he was.

The house was pretty much like it normally was, imposing but depressing-looking, with few lights on and little sign of life except for the sound of a soap opera coming from the maid's room.

When Yusuf opened the door, he looked surprised to see me. He didn't say anything at first, but I could tell that he was pleased.

I went up the stairs to Paris's room where I found him dressed in hot pants and T-shirt and trying on a wig. It had been about three weeks since I had seen Paris, and I was a shocked by his appearance. He looked different. His face looked more oval in shape and seemed to glow. His skin was lighter, and he was thinner, too.

He smiled when he saw me. 'How are you?' he asked, in a pampered and girlish but natural-sounding voice.

'You're looking ... you look pretty,' I finally said.

He blushed and turned his head away. 'What the ...?' he began, and then pushed me out of his room and shut the door.

Left by myself in the hallway, I opened the door to Oskar's room and went in without asking permission. Standing in front of the mirror with just his underwear on, he turned to look at me but then said nothing and turned away. I plopped my body on his bed, then watched him preen in front of the mirror.

Finally, he shot me a glance. 'What?' he asked. I said nothing, just smiled.

He caught my smile but then turned back towards the mirror to practice his poses.

I noticed the guitar leaning against the wall not far from him.

'Hand me the guitar,' I said to him.

After he gave me the guitar, I placed my fingers on its strings and began to strum.

'Wrong key,' Oskar said to me. After quickly pulling on a T-shirt, he came to me and righted the position of my fingers.

Later, when the four of us were ready to go, we lugged Yusuf's suitcase with his costume inside to Oskar's car and set off for Jakarta and Starlight. It was only 9 pm when we arrived, but the place was already very busy. In the changing room, the drag queens were competing with one another, making cutting, sarcastic remarks as they dressed or helped their friends to dress. As usual, some of their comments and looks were directed towards me and Oskar. We were accustomed to it.

'*Mairilin B aan paar.* They're straight,' said one of them.

'*Poo, methinks, Mairlin B inu ietim.* Don't believe it, I think they're an item,' another added.

We paid them no mind.

I watched as Yusuf transformed himself. His dress was a sexy one – supposing a woman were wearing it. It was deep red in colour with an open back and a slit in the front almost to the navel, which would have exposed his breasts, if he had had them. The hem fell just above the knee and the cloth almost but not quite concealed the bulge in his crotch. Though he had shaved his legs until they were smooth, he wore nylons as well. He wanted nothing more than to win this contest.

I saw that Paris had also changed but not into that of an aspiring drag queen. He was dressed simply, just jeans and a tank-top with a bra and falsies underneath. Looking closer, it seemed as if his breasts were bulging slightly. He was ordinary-looking, almost like a real girl, and at a glance he looked quite pretty.

'Hey, introduce me to your sister,' I said to Oskar, who was taking off his clothes.

'Not by the likes of you,' he said, jabbing his finger at me.

It was almost 10 pm, so I too began to get ready, taking off my pants. Oskar had already removed his and was wearing black Armani underwear.

'Still wearing that thing?' I said, pointing to the black rope around Oskar's waist. He was trying to conceal his amulet beneath the waistband of his underwear.

'I'm lucky I still have it,' he said, indirectly referring to our night of no memory.

'No more free drinks,' I said, more to myself than to Oskar.

'You remember that too,' Oskar said to me.

After applying lotion to our bodies and attaching bow-ties to our necks, I found two new pairs of wings hanging from a rack not far from the makeup table. The wings had our names on them and were much better made than the ones we had worn before, more like the ones Dolly had used in our photo shoot. They seemed to be made of real feathers and were very light. I gave the black pair to Oskar because they matched his underwear, and I put on the other pair, which was grey and white. With our wings now attached, we looked at each other in the mirror. It seemed like it had been such a long time since I'd had wings. Somehow I felt different: I felt I could fly that night.

When Om Bram came into the dressing room, he gave us a look of approval. 'Very nice! Let's get going. The show is about to begin.' He pushed us out of the room and told us to walk around on stage, where the outrageous drag queen who was serving as MC was opening the show.

It was the busiest night I had ever seen at the club, much busier than the night of the semi-finals – my night of no memory. After prancing around on stage, Oskar and I accompanied each of the finalists to the stage. As they took their turns on the catwalk, Oskar and I stepped down from the stage and mingled with the crowd.

It was three weeks since I had been stared at by people in this way. I smiled and evaluated each of them in turn: which ones had money, which ones might have bad intentions, which ones were looking to fall in love. In their eyes I saw lust, love, hate and envy. The messages were clear, even though many of them turned away, pretending not to care when I stared back at them.

My wings fluttered as I walked and brushed people's faces. A number of daddies tried to engage me in conversation – which was normal, of course – but suddenly feeling a need for air, I decided to take a break in the changing room. There, I found Paris seated on one of the sofas alone.

'Hi,' he said with a smile.

I sat down beside him. He moved away to give me more room. 'What are you up to?' I asked.

He shrugged his shoulders. 'I came in to take my pills but decided to sit and relax. It's nice and quiet in here.'

He let his hand fall on my bare thigh. He then looked at me coyly and began to stroke my wings with his fingers.

'My boy now has wings,' he said softly, in a woman-like voice.

I smiled and sniffed. 'Am I still your boy?' I asked. I'd almost forgotten.

I closed my eyes and leaned back, my wings spreading out between my body and the back of the sofa.

'Don't tell me you've forgotten the hand that once fed you,' he said, with no trace of rancour in his voice. His eyes shone brightly, and when he smiled, he glowed. He mussed the hair on the top of my head lightly, and I found myself recalling our initial meeting, when I was just a smelly vocational-school kid from the wrong side of the tracks, when I had no money and was easily angered, when I was hungry for emotion. That was when Paris had appeared in my life.

Thinking about it now, I realized that Paris had been much more of an older brother to me than a master. Much more of a friend, very much like family. I wanted to tell him this, and just as I was about to express my thanks, the door flew open and another person who would influence my future life appeared: Iwenk.

I don't know why but I felt an urge to hit him. He made me feel uncomfortable.

'Having a date, are you?' he quipped before plopping down beside me.

'Zip it,' Paris said tartly, which surprised me. He was calm, unashamed, not trying to hide. Wow, I thought, things had changed in three weeks.

'What are you doing here?' I asked straight out.

'Preparing my sales,' he answered, removing some small plastic bags from his jacket pocket. I then watched as he arranged piles of pills, packets of powder, and other stuff on the table.

'How did you get in here?' I asked.

'Don't you know? I work out of here, and the security gets a share of the action.'

The man he was referring to, I later learned, was none other than my own brother, Edi.

'A dealer,' Paris sneered.

'And you? What are you, a man dressed like a woman but with a poker instead of a hole?' he commented, without looking up. 'By the way, you're looking pretty. Do you have a boyfriend?'

'Thanks for the compliment, but I'm not looking for a boyfriend, at least not one like you,' Paris answered.

'Who'd want to go out with you anyway?' Iwenk huffed.

'That's a lot of stuff you got there,' I said to break up the conversation.

'It's busy out there tonight. They're sure to sell.' He continued to package his wares. He sniffed a few times and shook his head. I wondered if he himself was on ecstasy.

'You guys are something,' he then said. 'Big successes! A banci, a gigolo, and tonight maybe even a beauty queen.'

Despite Iwenk's snide tone, I sensed that he was envious and ignored his comment.

At that point, Paris removed a small bottle from his bag, opened the top, poured a few pills into his hand, and swallowed them.

'Shit, you pop pills too,' Iwenk hooted.

'Beauty pills only!' Paris answered, after washing down the pills with a glass of water on the table.

Those birth control pills, I thought. Maybe that explained his body's changes.

Iwenk didn't believe him. 'Buy from me' he suggested. 'I sell only grade-A shit.'

'Sorry,' Paris said dismissively. 'I get my stuff elsewhere.'

Iwenk was just about to open his mouth, when the door to the changing room flew open and three men came inside: one was my brother, Edi, and the other two were the 'moral guardians' I had seen with him once before. Their straggly beards made them unforgettable. They were talking in loud voices, arguing.

'Not now, the boss isn't here,' I heard Edi say to them as he motioned for them to take a seat at the table in the middle of the room. He then took a chair and sat down opposite them.

'It's been a month,' one of the guardians replied. 'We're not going to wait any longer.'

'But the boss isn't here,' Edi insisted.

'We're not fooling this time. Our people are ready.'

After that I didn't hear what was said because Paris grabbed my arm and pulled me out of the room. Iwenk didn't seem flustered by the situation and continued to do what he'd been doing.

Inside the club, Paris disappeared into the crowd. I went to look for Oskar and found him sitting idly by the DJ's console.

'How come you're not mingling?' I asked him.

He had a broad smile on his face and pointed to the crowd. 'I want to be a real angel and watch over the people down there.'

'What are you on?' I asked derisively.

My wings made my back itch, maybe because of the feathers, but Oskar didn't seem bothered.

Suddenly I spotted Edi coming across the room towards the DJ with a disturbed look on his face.

'Help me find the boss!' he screamed at the DJ who was a good friend of Om Bram.

'I can't!' the DJ shouted back with his hands on the turn table. 'I'm working.'

'I can't find him!' Edi screamed.

'Try his phone!' the DJ called back.

'His mobile's off.'

The DJ merely raised his shoulders and refocused on his music, leaving my brother to handle things himself.

'That's what happens when you look for trouble,' the DJ muttered.

'What's going on?' I asked Edi.

'It's those moral guardian people,' Edi said.

'What? Do they want more? I thought they were already paid off.'

My brother didn't respond. I stared at him, suspecting something was amiss.

'I borrowed it,' he answered, turning away from me.

I clicked my tongue. Un-fucking-believable! Edi was still the delinquent he had been when he left home, using other people's money for his own purposes.

Of course the so-called moral guardians were going to be ticked off. They hadn't gotten their cut. 'So now what?' I asked.

'Maybe you should go home,' Edi said before leaving me.

I watched as he made his way around the room, talking to one person after another, apparently trying to locate Om Bram.

The atmosphere on stage was growing increasingly lively. Several drag queens had already appeared, lip-synching popular Indonesian and Indian songs. The audience clapped and laughed after each appearance.

At two in the morning, Oskar and I were standing on stage, ready to escort the contestants on their final walk around the catwalk. Oskar's wings were getting in my way, so I pushed them aside, but then he intentionally flapped them in my face. I play-punched his stomach, and his wide smile turned into a glowing strip of white as the spotlight fell in our direction. We preened as we walked, grinning and cheerful. We had never been as playful as this with each other before. I plucked at the feathers of Oskar's wings. We punched each other and laughed as we walked, all eyes following us. We were a pair of angels in harmony.

For the final round of the contest, the contestants emerged one by one from behind the gilded curtain at the back of the stage for a solo strut on the catwalk. The jury, seated in front of the stage, beside the catwalk, whispered to one another as the contestants passed.

Oskar and I waited behind the curtain for our turn to appear as the final act of the show. Secretly, I was planning to pull Oskar's underwear down to his knees when we were on stage. That, I thought, would be a super finale.

Just when Yusuf was about to take the stage, we heard a commotion coming from the entrance to the bar. Loud fights between lovers and arguments between drunken customers were normal but this was different. Something was wrong.

Yusuf was walking towards the jury now, ready for their final judgment, but still the noise did not abate. He tried to maintain an elegant pose as he walked but couldn't help but sneak peeks in the direction of the entrance. The commotion stopped momentarily, and I stuck out my head from behind the curtain to see what was happening. A moment later, the clamour grew louder.

'What's going on?' asked Oskar, who was trying to see around me.

'I don't know,' I said rising on my toes. What with the pounding of the loudspeakers, the cheering of the crowd in support of the contestants, and the non-stop applause, it was impossible to know.

But then the cries changed into anguished shrieks. I looked around in panic. The people on and around the stage were unaware of what was going on at the back of the bar, but I could see a mad surge of people near the door. From his elevated position on the catwalk, Yusuf had a better view of what was happening, and I could see on his face a look of sheer terror.

The cries became more distinct. '*Allahuakbar! Allahuakbar!*'

Because everything happened so fast after that, I can't give a detailed description of events. The memories are all mixed together, but as I stood on the stage I saw bearded men in long white shirts wave machetes and knives in the air.

'*Allahuakbar!*' one of them shouted. 'Slaughter the tribe of Lot!'

Drag queens were screaming hysterically as they tried to flee, and the customers jostled and tripped over each other as they sought an exit. Everyone was trying to hide or run away. The bearded men were using their knives to slash the wires of hanging lights and punch holes in loudspeakers and the DJ's console, smashing his records in the process. From the direction of the bar came the sound of breaking glass as the intruders threw bottles on the floor while crying out in the name of God to kill the sinners.

The jurors jumped from their seats and pushed against one another as they fled towards the exit, as the gang of marauders continued to ransack the room. One of them then lit a torch that was in his hand. 'Allahuakbar!' It felt like a nightmare. I squeezed my eyes shut, hoping that it was so, but then Oskar gave me a shove.

We saw several angry-looking men making their way in our direction.

'Run!' Oskar screamed at me, but Yusuf was still standing there, alone and in shock on the catwalk, like a deer caught in the headlights of a car at night. A lanky man in a flowing robe with a sharp machete that gleamed in the strobe light, moved wildly as if possessed. In his sunken sockets, his red and beady eyes looked ready to explode.

'Allahuakbar!' the man screamed while thrusting his knife into the air. Jumping onto the catwalk, he advanced towards Yusuf who remained frozen in place. With my wings on my back, I flew between the two and instinctively forced aside the man's arm with my own. I punched him in the stomach and twisted his arm back, forcing him to drop his knife, then jabbed him in the neck causing him to bowl over in pain.

Then I did what was probably the most stupid thing I had ever done in my life: I assumed a fighting position, confronting a pack of guys with knifes, machetes and torches, ready to attack.

At that point, I didn't feel anything. If I had to die, then die I would. I turned to pick up Yusuf, who had fallen to the floor in fright.

With my back to the attackers, I felt my wings being slashed by sharpened metal. I didn't regret what I was doing: protecting Yusuf. Holding him tightly, I could hear him crying.

I heard the gang of men screaming, '*Allahuakbar!* Sinners, sinners! Kill the tribe of Lot!' But then, at that moment, I stopped being able to hear anything at all: the screaming and shouting, the beating of the clock, even the thumping of my heart. I surrendered myself to my fate and prayed, '*Bismillahirrohmanirrohim.*'

I felt something fall on top of me, something warm and friendly that touched my skin. An angel had fallen on me whose arms encircled me and whose hands held me with all their strength. I smiled as tears formed rivers on my cheeks. For several arrested seconds I could see Oskar smiling back at me – even as knives were tearing at his wings, knocking off feathers and sending them flying in the air.

I suddenly heard the song he had once sung for me: '*Oh, Brother, show me the way to go home ... no one believes me like you do ...*' I sang the song back to him: '*Oh, brother, take me to where I belong. No one believes you like I do ... Oh, brother take me to where I belong; no one believes you like I do.*' [Credit: Oh Brother – Andrea Corr.]

I can still feel the pummel of blows on Oskar's body. He was being jabbed and stabbed and every movement of his body on my own revealed his suffering. I heard him moan with pain. I felt my hot and bitter tears.

'*Nobody needs you like I do ...*' With one strum of the guitar in the key of G, the song finished: in my imagination, Oskar and I were in his bedroom with him sitting behind me as he fixed my fingers in the proper position on the guitar strings. It was almost as if he were embracing me, his chin on my shoulder, his lips near my ears, his fingers leading mine to the proper key of G.

I heard the sound of guns fired three times in the air. Finally, the blows to Oskar's body ceased.

Rest Area

It was the police who were the real angels that night. And it was my brother, Edi, who called them – so I have him both to thank and to blame for what later came. But, whatever the case, that's now the past.

As I later reconstructed that night, the police, after barging into the club, fired warning shots, the three shots I had heard from the stage, which caused the men with machetes to freeze in place. I wish the police had shot those people but, of course, they couldn't do that.

Thereafter, the moral guardians began to disperse, though not without a lot of cursing and the destruction of anything that got in their way. A leader of the group yelled at the police: 'Do not give refuge to devils. It is our duty to destroy them! *Allahuakbar*!' The police shrugged and motioned with their rifles for the intruders to leave. No arrests, of course, but at least they were now gone.

As the mayhem began to die down, I pulled myself out from between Oskar's and Yusuf's bodies. Miraculously, the two of them seemed to be OK – I could see no visible bodily damage. Perhaps in Oskar's case, literally a miracle: I thought of his amulet. Only Yusuf was making any sound, still moaning with fright. I pulled him to his feet, assured him that everything was going to be OK, and ordered him to take care of Oskar while I looked for Paris.

I looked around the place angrily and saw a few little flames still burning at the bar, the curtain on stage, the DJ's console. Broken bottles littered the floor, light bulbs were smashed, the mirrored disco ball was rolling on the floor. Drag queens were hiding beneath tables and behind the bar, some of them crying in fear.

I stuck my head inside the changing room and found Iwenk there, sitting stiffly in a chair and holding Paris's bag tightly against his chest as if it would protect him.

'Hey!' I cried as I came into the room. 'The police are out there.'

Immediately, Iwenk jumped from the chair, threw Paris's bag at me, and fled the scene.

Continuing my search for Paris, I finally found him, huddled in a corner of the women's bathroom. Strangely, he wasn't crying and didn't seem to be afraid at all.

My next image is the beach at Anyer in the morning, the same place we had found comfort and cleansed ourselves not that long before. I can still feel the touch of the wind on that new day, tickling the exposed nape of my neck. A morning wind off the coast, neither cold nor warm but gentle. I inhaled the fresh air. Deeper, then more deeply still. Felt it in my lungs. I waited for the sun to rise.

I sat on the sand, staring at the birds and the waves, watching the clouds change colour, and waited for a red dot to rise in the east. I had never experienced anything so beautiful in all my life. Silently, I thanked God. I was still alive.

I heard the sound of a car door opening then closing. 'I want to see the sun come up,' I said.

'How romantic!' Oskar replied as he sat down beside me. I just smiled and sniffed.

Again I heard the sound of a car door opening and closing. Moments later, Paris and Yusuf were sitting beside us. We sat together, four abreast, wriggling our toes in the sand.

'I'm tired,' Yusuf yawned.

'I'm cold,' Paris said.

We'd almost died, and now all they could say is that they were tired and cold. I had to smile.

The sun grew in size as it rose, and I turned towards Oskar and studied the swollen marks on his back left by the attackers' knives. 'The twenty-five million was worth it, wouldn't you say?' he asked, smiling at me.

'Who could have known?' I answered.

I wanted to throw my arms around him and thank him, but I knew it wasn't necessary: he knew I was happy without me having to tell him so. And I was thankful, too, for that thin rope around his waist, which I learned for the first time had cost him twenty-five million rupiah. I'd always been sceptical about such things, but not after that night. So, thank you, Ustadz Asman, for that amulet, spell, mantra, or whatever it's called, for giving Oskar a power for which there is no rational explanation but somehow managed to save his life. Without it, the moral guardians would have turned Oskar into minced meat.

We listened to the calling birds until the sun came up.

You might think that my story ends here. And this is where it should have ended, because there's nothing that happened after that I want to remember. The rest of the story causes my stomach to cramp and makes my heart constrict. I wish there was a way I could permanently erase the rest of it from my life. What I thought was the start of a happy ending that morning turned out to be altogether different.

We fell asleep on the sand and didn't wake up until the sun was nearing its peak. With our stomachs growling, we returned to the car. Oscar was behind the wheel; Yusuf and Paris sat in the back, still dressed in women's gear, their wigs full of sand. We made an odd sight: two bare-chested men and what appeared to be two bedraggled young women.

Before we got into the car, I removed Yusuf's suitcase from the trunk and handed it to him in the back seat. 'Both of you, change your clothes and remove your makeup,' I told them, 'I want to get something to eat.' I was thinking of the village near the beach where we had taken refuge. There would be food stalls there, no doubt, but I could see the looks on people's faces if we were to set foot in them. I was famished but not ready to face the embarrassment.

'Let me be, I like it this way,' Paris said. Meanwhile, Yusuf had already opened his case and taken out some normal clothes along with a packet of wet-wipes, with which he began to clean his face.

'Where do you want to eat?' Oskar asked. 'How about at one of the rest areas on the toll?'

As if in agreement with my suggestion, the car rolled towards the coastal highway. I would have to staunch my hunger pains for a while longer.

Looking in the mirror, I saw that Yusuf had already transformed himself into a normal-looking teenage guy. His eyes were drooping with weariness, and his body, I knew, was bruised as well, but that's nothing compared to losing your life, is it?

After we got on the toll road, Oskar turned on the radio to find some music. He rolled down the window and lit up a cigarette.

'Put that out,' Paris complained, fanning himself with his

hand. 'It's not good for my skin.'

Instead of following his brother's orders, Oskar gave me the cigarette and told me to smoke it. The two of us laughed.

'Let's watch Paris getting wrinkled,' Oskar said.

Knowing the trip back to Tangerang would be a long one – at least a few hours – we settled in to enjoy the passing scenery. It would be about an hour before we came to the first rest area on the toll road. It was there we had stopped before. We could be sure of finding hamburgers, French fries and other junk food, washed down with glasses of cold cola. My mouth watered as I thought of the meal ahead.

I looked in the rear-view mirror to see Paris rustling through his bag impatiently until he finally found his white plastic bottle.

'What's that?' Yusuf asked.

'They're my beauty pills – to prevent my skin from being ruined by cigarette smoke!' he said loud enough for Oskar and me to hear.

'Give me some,' Yusuf begged.

'These are not for you,' Paris said firmly, 'unless you want to grow a pair of tits.'

'*Inoe, ninoe … Ieris naat B wanten tinits.* Yuck! I don't want tits,' Yusuf replied.

Paris opened the top, poured three tablets into his hand and then swallowed them without water. After a thoughtful pause, he took another four tablets and swallowed those too.

Yusuf made a face. 'Isn't that too much?'

'Don't worry,' Paris scoffed. 'At most, they'll just make my *tinits* grow faster,' he replied.

Even though the toll road was relatively quiet, because big trucks were not allowed on the road on Sundays, it seemed to take forever – maybe because I was so hungry but also because

284

there was little to distract our attention. Secretly, I hoped for an overturned truck or something to break the monotony, but nothing happened. All was safe and peaceful, until Paris suddenly screamed, 'It's going to rain! It's going to rain!'

We all turned in his direction to see him staring at the wide-open fields beside the road.

I looked at the sky, where a bright sun dazzled my eyes.

'It's going to rain. It's getting so dark. The sky is almost purple. Close your windows!' he screamed.

'What are you talking about?' Yusuf asked. 'It's not going to rain.'

'Yes, it is. I can see it. Look at the rainstorm over there. It's like a cyclone!'

I wrinkled my forehead.'What are you going on about?' I asked.

'Just joking, just joking,' he said hurriedly and then began to laugh loudly. 'Fooled you, didn't I? I fooled you all, didn't I?!' he said, repeating himself and laughing uproariously again.

I looked at Oskar and gave him a nudge, hoping that he might put some sense into Paris.

'Hey, what's going on?' Oskar asked Paris.

'I'm happy! I'm so happy I could die! I want to dance. Please, please, turn up the radio. I want to dance!'

Oskar, instead, turned off the radio but Paris rose and put his feet on the seat and then tried to stand, his head hitting the ceiling of the car.

Yusuf pulled on his arm, trying to get him to sit back down.

Paris shook his head back and forth, then laughed and screamed, 'Lalalalalala … hahaha …' Suddenly, he stopped, as if instantly depleted of energy, and dropped to the seat.

Blood drained from his face, and he looked pale and ill. 'What kind of pills were those?' Oskar whispered to me.

'Birth control pills,' I told him.

'Are they supposed to make you high?'

'I don't think so,' I said, shaking my head. I then unsnapped my seat belt in order to move more freely and turned my body around to see what was happening in the back seat. Paris, with his back to Yusuf, had leaned over and was resting his forehead against the rear window as Yusuf massaged his shoulders. At least he was calmer now.

'My body hurts,' Paris sighed wearily. 'I can't move my neck. It's like someone is strangling me,' he moaned.

Yusuf spoke in a worried voice: 'What is wrong with you? You must have taken too many pills.'

'No! There's no such thing as too many! Don't you understand? And take your hands off me. I don't want you touching me. Fucking drag queen!'

All of us were shocked into silence.

'He's possessed,' Yusuf mumbled and moved away from Paris to the corner on his side of the back seat.

Paris suddenly started pulling on the door latch as if to open it. Unsuccessful, he then began to smash the door with his arm. Luckily, Oskar had turned on the childproof door lock.

'Stop the car! Let me out of here!' Paris screamed in Oskar's ear. 'Stop the car, Oskar!'

Oskar pulled over to the side of the road.

'Unlock the door!' Paris screamed. 'Open it now!'

Oskar slowed and steered the car to the side of the toll road. The road was quiet, and the open fields were empty. I didn't know what to do. Influenced by Yusuf, I thought Paris might really be possessed. As if this were the case, Paris again shrieked and leaned over Oskar to hit the unlock button. Just as quickly, he threw open the rear door, jumped outside, and ran out and into the middle of the toll road in his high heels. I leapt from the car to try to catch him.

'Run me down!' he screamed, with his arms high in the air and the hair of his wig whipped around his face by the wind.

Rushing out to the middle of the road, I grabbed him managed to drag him back to the roadside, though he fought me like a madman every step of the way. He scratched me and bit me and then beat me with his fists. The devil was truly in him.

I held my arms around him as tightly as I could to prevent him from moving. Oskar, who had also gotten out of the car, yelled for me to sit Paris down on the ground so that he could be more easily brought under control.

I did as he said but kept my arms around Paris to stop his flailing.

'You're the santri,' Oskar said. 'What are we supposed to do?'

'I don't know. Just because I'm a santri doesn't mean I know what to do in a case of possession!'

I looked at Yusuf who was standing frozen in fear not far from us. I pleaded to him with my eyes, but he just shook his head.

'Aren't you suppose to read a prayer, the *Yasin* or something,' Oskar suggested, seeing Paris writhing around.

Yusuf came closer. Maybe he was going to read the *Yasin*, I thought, but then he said, 'But Paris is Christian, isn't he?'

That's right, I suddenly realized. Paris was Christian. What did Christians do when a person was possessed? Damn, damn, damn, I swore. But then Paris suddenly stopped moving and curled up in surrender in my embrace. He stared up at me. He didn't seem to be able to see me but the hollow, haunted look in his eyes is something I will never forget.

'He's hot, very hot,' I said. Now that Paris was no longer fighting us, we carried him back to the car and placed him in the centre of the back seat. Yusuf and I then got in on the opposite sides to prevent him from being close to a door.

I tried to remove his wig, thinking it would help to cool him down, but he stopped my hand's movement with his own to keep the wig in place. He then righted himself slowly and leaned against me. He asked me to hug him.

The journey from that point on was very tense. Yusuf kept moving his lips, reciting prayers from *Al Fatihah* and the *Al Ikhlas*, thinking that they might pacify the devil that had taken possession of Paris's body (even though, as he himself had pointed out, Paris was Christian).

Oskar kept his foot pressed down on the gas pedal. Every time we passed another car, my heart jumped in my throat. Once again, I worried that we might die.

When we reached the rest area where we had planned to eat, I tried to lift Paris in order to carry him from the car but, surprisingly, he forced himself to stand.

'I don't want to make a fuss for you. Thank you,' he said as he walked with Oskar and me on either side of him, our arms behind his back.

For a second, Paris seemed normal but then he started to shiver. His body trembled and heaved like a volcano ready to explode. Unable to stand any longer, he collapsed on the asphalt beside a row of parked cars. People slowed their step as they walked by and looked at us. I dropped down to the pavement and positioned Paris's body so that his head was lying on my thigh.

'Help!' Oskar screamed. I was startled: it was the first time I had ever heard Oskar ask for help.

The hairs on the nape of my neck stood on end. A wave of

apprehension rushed through my body. With Paris's head nestled weakly on my thigh, I stroked his hair. His eyes were open wide as he stared at the blue sky above.

I looked around me. People had begun to gather. A few of them approached.

'What's wrong?' a man asked.

The crowd grew larger as people emerged from the rest area's food court to see what was happening.

'We need help,' Oskar cried weakly, in frustration.

'He's possessed,' I heard Yusuf explain to someone when Paris's body suddenly stiffened, and he began to shiver again.

'Take him to the mushola,' suggested an older man, who appeared out of the crowd dressed in faded mosque apparel: white shirt, sarong, and a peci on his head.

With some difficulty Oskar and I carried Paris through the parking area, past several fast-food restaurants, to the small prayer room near the public bathrooms. At the mushola a few people were resting and woke with surprise when Oskar and I placed Paris on one of the carpets there.

The old man who had suggested that we bring Paris to the mushola approached and recited a text into Paris's ear. He took Paris's right hand and pressed his thumb into the base of Paris's palm by his thumb and then in the crooks of Paris's other fingers, one by one. Paris did not react; he kept staring up at the ceiling of the mushola.

The man saw the question in my eyes. 'This is no possession,' he said definitively.

'But he's Christian. Maybe they have different devils,' Yusuf put in.

'No, it's not possession,' the man said again.

I was confused, but finally a rational thought came to mind:

'A doctor! We need to find a doctor!' I yelled in panic.

'There's no doctor here,' I heard a voice say. 'What's wrong with your friend?'

'I don't know. Maybe an O.D.,' I said without thinking. With that comment, the mood of the crowd instantly changed, and I could almost smell their antipathy. I heard their 'oh-ohs' and the clicking of their tongues, as they whispered to one another, 'O.D., O.D.' They assumed that Paris was a drug addict.

Paris's body stiffened again in my embrace. In the midst of all the commotion, I heard a woman whisper loudly, 'Is that a woman or a man? Looks like a banci to me.' As worried as I was about Paris, I wanted to get up and punch the woman in the face. Oskar ran around the rest area looking for help, accosting strangers to find someone with medical skills, but was completely unsuccessful. There wasn't even a proper first-aid kit in the place.

'You need to take your friend to a hospital,' the man beside me suggested softly.

I quickly rose and carried Paris to the car, and ordered Yusuf to find Oskar, who was still looking for help. When they returned to the car we sped out of the parking lot, leaving that accursed rest stop behind us. It would take us an hour and a half to reach 'civilization', a town big enough to have a proper hospital. I could see tears streaming down Oskar's face in the rear-view mirror.

Paris, in my embrace, opened his eyes and whispered softly, 'I'm going to go away. You take care of my business when I'm gone.'

With the car going 140 kilometres per hour, there was a long, silent gap before Paris began to shiver again. Suddenly he stiffened, and a white foam dripped from the side of his mouth.

Yusuf sobbed, and I whispered to Paris, 'Hold on, hold on. We'll be there soon.'

A Beginning at the End

It wasn't birth control pills that killed Paris. It was the drugs that Iwenk peddled: ecstasy laced with who knows what. That's what I concluded when the doctor informed us that Paris had, indeed, died of an overdose, and after I'd gone through his bag and found the illegal drugs inside the white bottle in his bag. I reconstructed in my mind the events in that changing room that night: When the police came into Starlight to break up the melee that night, Iwenk, hearing the commotion outside and not knowing what was happening, must have poured his stash of pills into the white bottle in Paris's bag on the sofa in the changing room when Paris left the room to go to the bathroom. Iwenk knew that if the police found the drugs on him, he would be arrested. Paris, he figured, had enough money to bribe his way out of the situation.

Dumb fucking luck.

At the end of July, not long after Paris died, on the day I received my certificate of graduation from school, I ran into Iwenk on the way home from school. I accosted him and ordered him to follow me to a quiet place where we could talk. I thought of beating him until he was unconscious or bashing his head on the road and then dragging him along the asphalt, as Oskar had once done. But he greeted me indifferently, as if innocent and not knowing what had happened. Trying not to let my emotions get the best of me, I told him what had happened. I explained the scenario as I had figured it to be. I knew that my guess was correct when I saw horror and fright bloom in his eyes. Even so, he said nothing, could not move, was still as a stone. I was trembling with anger from head to toe, but my anger was ineffectual and fell like a leaf falling from a tree. Iwenk could not have foreseen the consequences of what he had done. He didn't know that Paris was taking birth control pills; he assumed that Paris was lying when he said the pills in his bottle were 'beauty pills'. He didn't know that Paris would down a handful of them.

Iwenk fell to his knees and held my calves, bowing his head as he cried.

I could do nothing. I left him without saying another word. He hadn't meant to kill Paris, or to hurt me or Oskar or Yusuf. They say that vengeance will not bring back the dead. That's true. But Paris would live forever in my life.

After graduation, I stayed at the pesantren for another week, but with nothing to do except recite prayers and stare at Arabic script, which I still had yet to master, the days seemed far too long.

So it was that I decided to leave, to move out of the pesantren. I abandoned dear Yusuf, who, since Paris's death, was little more than a walking corpse, never saying a word to me or anyone else. I simply couldn't live there any longer.

At the week's end, my parents came to get me. My mother's eyes were pools of tears. When she asked why I never came home, I couldn't reply. But that day I did go home with them, never to return to the pesantren. I said goodbye only to Ali. I wanted to tell him that I had tried my best to take care of his brother, but the words wouldn't come out of my mouth. He, too, said nothing, just nodded and gave me a hug as I took my leave.

I would miss that place, the pesantren with its woven bamboo walls, which was the beginning of true life for me.

I stayed at my parents' house, sleeping on the sofa in the front room and eating without complaint the food they gave me. Then one day a visitor came, a bank manager who gave me several savings passbooks that Paris had owned. The man said they were mine, that I was Paris's rightful heir. He had brought with him a notarized document, signed by Paris, proving this to be the case. I didn't know what to say.

For a time I let the money lie untouched. But then I remembered Paris's last words to me: 'Take care of my business when I'm gone.' I also recalled him once telling me that he intended to leave Indonesia and to live in Thailand or the United States, where he could become the woman that was inside him, and live that way. A month later, after I had begun to emerge from my grief, I went from one salon to the next to collect the money owed to Paris. Whether by conscious design or not, Paris had planned my future, taking me to the salons he supplied and introducing me to their owners, silently indicating that he was in fact grooming me to take over his business. Now I knew why Paris had studied the queens' speech and made sure that I learned it as well. As I came to discover, the cross-dressing hairdressers would sometimes try to deceive me by speaking in code to colleagues, thinking that I could not understand them. I always smiled when I remembered what Paris had told me: 'Mastery of a language allows you to control the situation.' How very right he was.

Thereafter I continued to manage Paris's business, and never set foot in Starlight again. My career as an angel was over. Eventually, I left home for good and started my own business, one that was honest and above-board: a seafood restaurant just like one where we had once eaten, which I named, in memory of my friend, 'Seafood à la Paris'. The business proved to be a success, and became my main source of income, with the salon supply business a secondary source.

Here, my story ends.

Oskar never contacted me. I didn't contact him either. In a sense, I guess, we were even: I had once saved him and he had once saved me.

Oskar once told me that I was his best friend, that Paris was my best friend, and that Yusuf was our best mutual friend. But if it is in the stars, and if our wings which were ripped apart that fateful night can somehow be healed, maybe one day we will be able to fly to a nest we can share together. Perhaps the moment will come when, one day, we'll find ourselves together at Seafood à la Paris. Who knows? Maybe ...

Afterword

In *Not a Virgin*, Nuril Basri accurately captures a segment of today's youth culture in communities on the outskirts of metropolitan Jakarta. It is a detailed ethnography set amidst brawls between rival schools as well as recreational drug use and trade typical of modern male youth culture.

But it is also set in a Muslim society, including a *pesantren* (Islamic boarding school) and hard-line vigilante groups. Modernity is seamlessly blended with the study of traditional martial arts and the search for magical invincibility. The boarding school is close enough to the major highway that links the community with Jakarta, and thus is linked to the outside world. This is seen in one of the characters, Oskar, seeking safety when wounded in a brawl, and later on learning martial arts and 'buying' invincibility from one of the teachers at the school.

In fact, throughout the novel there are hybrid blends of various aspects of such phenomena. The author is a keen observer of such hybridity and infuses the novel with it. Thus here the *pesantren* not only serves as a place to learn about religion but also for its students to carry out other activities. It is not a world unto its own: public-school student brawls affect the lives of its boarders; cellphones and use of the internet disrupt religious studies. Being situated in a secular outside world means that the students connect with other young people and engage in non-religious activities. It is an honest portrayal of young men in today's Indonesian society. What renders the story even more special is the fairly explicit descriptions of male sexuality, which in many ways reflects the hybrid and blended setting.

Ricky, the main character, is a cisgender young man who meets Iwenk, another cisgender teenager he meets when taking refuge from a brawl in a salon run by transgender women. Ricky learns from Iwenk that being kept by a transgender woman of means does not compromise their masculinity or heterosexuality. Iwenk has been doing so, in addition to selling drugs. Ricky, in need of money to care for Oskar, who is badly wounded in a brawl, eventually decides to be the kept boy of the effeminate Paris, who hails from a wealthy family. As much as Ricky is ready to be Paris' toyboy, it turns out that he does not want sex with Ricky, just companionship. We are then told that Paris really wants to be a woman and takes contraceptive pills to transition. This is a nice blend of masculinity and its transgression, in gender expression and identity.

We find another approach to gender expression and sexuality in Yusuf, with whom Ricky is forced to share a room with. He also transgresses his masculinity in more than one way. He is flamboyant, receives money from gay men who have sex with him, and who he flirts with.

While Oskar, with Ricky's help, learns martial arts from a master in the *pesantren*, to earn the money to pay for the invincibility he wants to survive brawls (a masculine activity), he poses nude for a female photographer. Together with Ricky he joins a male beauty contest at Starlight, a gay club in Jakarta, and the two of them end up showing off their bodies to the men who come to the club. Does that reduce their masculinity? They don't think so, and Iwenk even admits to having been kept by transgender women. But towards the end they are raped by unscrupulous gay men who first drug them.

Nuril Basri does not forget to include a phenomenon that

takes place frequently in Jakarta clubs: an attack on Starlight by hard-line Islamist vigilantes. So Islam is presented in a complex manner in the *pesantren*, with its goings on there, and in the thuggery and vigilantism of a hard-line group.

In fact, it is this constant complication of religion, youth culture, gender identity and expression, and sexuality, which makes *Not a Virgin* fascinating. To cap it, Nuril Basri makes his characters speak Indonesian transgender and gay slang (*bahasa binan, bahasa gay*). In English translation this puzzles the reader somewhat, but then even transgender and gay Indonesians must decipher new vocabulary as they gather with friends.

Dédé Oetomo

DÉDÉ OETOMO is a Founder and Trustee of the GAYa Nusantara Foundation (www.gayanusantara.or.id) in Surabaya, Indonesia. Currently, he also chairs the Regional Advisory Group of the Asia-Pacific Coalition on Male Sexual Health (www.apcom.org), and is a member of the Advisory Council of the Coalition on Sexual and Bodily Rights in Muslim Societies (www.csbronline. org). He received his PhD in linguistics and Southeast Asian studies at Cornell University in 1984. He is an adjunct lecturer in gender and sexuality at the Faculty of Social and Political Sciences and the Faculty of Humanities at Airlangga University in Surabaya. In 1998 he received the Felipa da Souza Award from the International Gay and Lesbian Human Rights Commission.

Gayspeak, Queens' Speech and Salonese[1]

The cryptic language spoken by the gay and transvestite characters in this novel is sometimes referred to in the book as 'Gayspeak', other times as 'Queens' Speech' and sometimes, too, as 'Salonese'. In Indonesian, the common term for this language or dialect is 'bahasa gay', gay language. The language is also known as 'bahasa banci', banci being a somewhat derogatory term (unless they are the ones using the term) for male-to-female cross-dressers and drag queens, which is why I also refer to it as 'Queens' Speech'. Finally, because one of the main settings in this novel is a salon run by cross-dressing hairdressers who speak this language, and because Ricky, the initially naïve protagonist of the novel, is confused as to what to call the language, I chose for him to refer to this argot as 'Salonese'.

Although Indonesia has considerable linguistic diversity, with hundreds of different distinct languages, Indonesian Gayspeak (or whatever we want to call it) is very much based on Indonesian, the country's official national language, and serves as a symbol of and tool for solidarity, which unites gay men and other people who speak it. The language represents a creative usurpation and transformation of the more formal and dominant Indonesian language. It is a conscious and often humorous language game.

---

1 I could not have written this article without the assistance of American scholar, Tom Boelstroff. Much of the information about Indonesian Gayspeak is based on his research. See, among others, http://www.bahasakita.com/bahasa-gay-is-bahasa-gaul.

CREATIVE DERIVATION IN INDONESIAN GAYSPEAK

Competence in Indonesian Gayspeak requires intonation, pragmatics – how context contributes to meaning – and ideology about the language itself, but what gay men and others who appropriate this language find most salient is the vocabulary. However, the Gayspeak lexicon is more than just a collection of words; it is a set of patterned derivational processes that together constitute a language game. True fluency in this language is demonstrated not just by knowing the vocabulary but also by understanding the processes that underlie it, and thus being able to coin new words and terms oneself.

In Indonesian, there are a number of ways to create 'gay' terms and with them a 'gay language' or Gayspeak. Some of the most common methods include:

• Infixing, inserting the infix '-in-' between the consonant and vowel of every syllable. Thus banci becomes binancini and lelaki becomes linakini. Often the resulting word is then shortened to two syllables. Thus binancini, for instance, becomes binan.

• Lexical replacement, in which one word is replaced by another, for instance the Indonesian pronouns aku (first-person singular pronoun) and kamu (second person) are replaced by the corresponding Dutch pronouns ike and jij.

• Neologism, in which a term is replaced by a form that shares the same first syllable or sound but does not have a prior meaning of its own. For example, cakep (good-looking) becomes cuco, and jahat (bad, evil) becomes jahara.

• Semantic shift, a fancy term for slang, whereby a word is given a new meaning. For example, goreng (to fry) refers to anal sex and kucing (cat) refers to a sex worker.

• Suffixation and vowel shift, which is usually used to transform a standard term, in general a noun or adjective. In Indonesian Gayspeak, the most common suffixes are '-ong' and '-es'. Thus, banci (transvestite, drag queen) becomes bencong; berapa (how much) becomes brepong; lelaki (man or male) becomes lekong or lekes; and sakit (sick but also 'queer') becomes sekong or sekes.

• Syllabic substitution, in which one common word replaces another with which it shares a syllable (typically the first syllable). For instance, tidak (no, not) is replaced by tinta (ink).

GAYSPEAK IN ENGLISH

English has no shortage of 'gay' words and terms; indeed there are several dictionaries of them.[2] Yet in translating this book, it would have been inadequate simply to insert Gayspeak words. The processes that Indonesian Gayspeakers employ in the use of their language display the creativity of the characters and constitute an important aspect of the book's humour. In translating this novel, therefore, it was necessary to create an English equivalent of Indonesian Gayspeak. There were challenges, caused primarily by the more complex verb structure of English and the English language's non-phonetic and highly irregular spelling. (In Indonesian, the same verb form can be used for every purpose; tense and mood are indicated in other ways. Moreover, Indonesian spelling is very consistent and phonetic. Unlike English, one does not have to learn how a word is pronounced; it is immediately obvious from the spelling.)

In creating an English Gayspeak for the characters in this novel, most of the tactics mentioned above were adapted and sometimes modified, along with other tactics. Yet before they could be employed it was necessary to phoneticize the spelling of

---

2 For example, see: Rodgers, Bruce: *The Queen's Vernacular; a Gay Lexicon*, first published by Straight Arrow Books (San Francisco, 1972), later republished under the new title *Gay Talk* (New York: Paragon Books, 1979). Also see Baker, Paul: *Fantabulosa: A Dictionary of Polari and Gay Slang* (London: Bloomsbury Academic, 2004).

all Gayspeak words and phrases. Generally speaking, Gayspeak is a spoken, not a written language, and because of the many playful tactics that speakers employ in the use of this tongue, its written form must be phonetic, not distorted by customary English spelling—where, for instance, the word that sounds like 'tho' is written 'though,' and 'thought' is pronounced 'thawt'. Use of the International Phonetic Alphabet was one option for producing a highly accurate and 'narrow' representation of Gayspeak, but the IPA system of phonetic notation would be unfamiliar to most readers. (Plus, with all its odd and unfamiliar symbols, it would have seemed out of place when coming from the mouths of drag queens!) Therefore, it was necessary to make use of a more approximate, 'broader' system of notation. I chose to use Truespel, a phonetic writing system developed in the late 1980s by computer specialists in reaction to the user-unfriendliness of IPA phonetics in computer applications.

Even with the use of Truespel, readers are likely to find it difficult to make sense of Gayspeak in this novel, at least at first, but that is the intention of those who speak the language: Gayspeakers use the language so that non-speakers remain ignorant of what they are saying. However, Truespel uses no special symbols and is thus easily learned. Take the following sentences as examples.

Customary Orthographic Rendition	Truespel
Are you dating him?	Aar yue daeteeng him?
No way! He's just my friend.	Noe wae! Hes just mie frend.
I just finished, darling. It was a busy day at the salon.	Ie just finishd, daarleeng. It wuz u bizee dae at thu sullaan.
If you lay your hand on me, I'll call the police.	If yue lae yer hand aan mee, Il kaul thu pullees.

The trick when reading Gayspeak passages is to keep in mind that they should be spoken and are to be pronounced as written. The other trick is to study the tactics and learn the derivational processes employed in the creation of Gayspeak. In the following list, the Truespel word is indicated by quotation marks; the word's customary orthographic rendition is enclosed in brackets.

• Infixing: By adding an '-in-' the word 'laet' [late] becomes 'linaet'; the word 'heer' [heer] becomes 'hineer'; and 'no' [same spelling] becomes 'nino.'

• Lexical replacement: Drag queens in the English-speaking world often adopt female names for themselves. In this novel, this is shown in their use of pronouns where 'Ie' [I] becomes 'Ieris' [Iris], 'he' becomes 'Helga,' and 'yue' [you] becomes 'Yoelandu' [Yolanda].

• Phonetic similarity: 'I don't know' becomes 'I.N.O.'; 'busy' becomes 'B.C.'

• Prefixation: By adding an 'in-' before a word that starts with a vowel: 'u' [a] becomes 'ina' and 'out' [same spelling] becomes 'inout.'

• Semantic shift: 'nugit' [nugget], deriving from 'chicken nugget,' refers to a young man. Meanwhile, a 'paeshint' [patient], someone who is sick (which in Indonesian would be 'sakit,' a derogatory word for homosexuality) is 'queer.'

• Shortening: 'Friend' becomes 'F', 'the' becomes 'D,' etc.

• Simplified verb structure: 'B' serves as 'to be' and can be used for all tenses. Similarly, the suffix '-en' on a verb—'tauken,' from 'tauk' [to talk]; 'breengen,' from 'breeng' [to bring]; and 'waeten,' from 'waet' [to wait]—permits the word to be used in all its tenses.

• Slang: Examples of existing slang include 'looker' for 'good-looking man' and 'B.J.' for 'blow job'. Examples of new slang include: 'in D paamz' [in the palms] means to be dating (from 'date palms'); to be 'straight' or 'normal' is to be 'aan paar' (from 'on par').

The reader of this novel might not be able to guess the meaning of all Gayspeak words and phrases that appear here, but, again, that's the intention. Gayspeak is a game, the fun of which comes from trying to figure it out. The careful reader will probably find some inconsistencies which, in fact, are not intentional but lapses on the part of the translator. Yet their presence too is a reflection of how Indonesian Gayspeak is always evolving, with speakers making up new words on the spot and sometimes incorrectly applying a derivational rule. But as with formal Indonesian, Gayspeakers and listeners are a forgiving lot, and they readily overlook grammatical errors if the gist of what is spoken is clear. I hope the reader will be as forgiving with me.

John H. McGlynn

JOHN H. McGLYNN, a graduate of the University of Michigan, Ann Arbor (1981), lives in Jakarta, where, in 1987, he and four Indonesian writers established the Lontar Foundation, the only organization in the world devoted to the publication of Indonesian literature in translation. Through Lontar, McGlynn has ushered into print more than two hundred books of and about Indonesian literature and culture. As the translator of scores of books and other publications under both his own name and his penname, Willem Samuels, he has garnered much international praise for his work.

Books by Indonesian authors

FICTION
Cigarette Girl by Ratih Kumala
Harvesting the Storm by John Waromi
Not a Virgin by Nuril Basri

NONFICTION
Jakarta Undercover by Moammar Emka
Jakarta Undercover II by Moammar Emka

Books set in Indonesia

FICTION
Island of Demons by Nigel Barley
Island Secrets by Alwin Blum
Mataram by Tony Reid
Olivia & Sophia by Rosie Milne
Shaman of Bali by John Greet
Snow over Surabaya by Nigel Barley
Twilight in Kuta by David Nesbit

NONFICTION
Bali Raw by Malcolm Scott
Bali Undercover by Malcolm Scott
Bandit Saints of Java by George Quinn
In the Footsteps of Stamford Raffles by Nigel Barley
Raffles and the British Invasion of Java by Tim Hannigan
Toraja by Nigel Barley
You'll Die in Singapore by Charles McCormac